Painting

Mercy

Painting Mercy

A Sequel to Orla's Canvas

by

Mary Sharnick

www.penmorepress.com

Painting Mercy by Mary Donnarumma Sharnick

ISBN-13: 978-1-946409-58-4(Paperback)
ISBN 978-1-946409-59-1(e-book)

BISAC Subject Headings:
DRA001000DRAMA / American / General
FIC045000 / FICTION / Family Life
FIC011000 / FICTION / Gay

Editing: Chris Wozney
Cover Illustration by Christine Horner

Address all correspondence to:

Penmore Press LLC
920 N Javelina Pl
Tucson AZ 85748

DEDICATION

For Allison Feldman and Thomas Brayton IV

....not mild, not temperate,
God's love for the world. Vast
flood of mercy
flung on resistance.
                    —*Denise Levertov*

ACKNOWLEDGMENTS

With continued and sincere gratitude to Michael James, Midori Snyder, Chris Wozney, Lauren McElroy, Christine Horner, and Danielle Boschert of Penmore Press.

To Kristen Baclawski, generous friend and technical advisor—there would be no books without you.

In New Orleans, thanks to:John Ngo and your grandchildren for inviting us into your home, extending your gracious hospitality, and sharing your story. Anita Graveson at Hotel Monteleone, for treating us as if we were your personal and only guests. Glen Hobgood, driver-become-friend. You showed us the way. Captain Wade of Pearl River Eco-Tours, for introducing us to the bayou with friendliness and expertise. Lisa and Violetta at Forever New Orleans for embracing Orla.

Stellar mentors Rachel Basch and Louis Bayard. You inspire.

Allison Feldman and Thomas Brayton IV. Joseph Antoci, M. D., Ryan Aghamohammadi, Samantha Austin, Samantha Crone, Sarah Feldman, Caelen Gadwah-Meaden, Michael Nejaime, Olivia Pettinicchi, Alex Pozin. Kathleen Green and

Kennedy Morris. All the rest who have shared the classroom with me. You have transformed school days into a joyful life. Thank you.

Mary Ellen Fabry, Louis Cohen, Justin Cohen, Ronald Fabry, Joe and Leslie Hadam. Kyle and Pam Kahuda, Barbara Ruggiero, David Whitehouse, Joan Ruggiero, Phil and Barbara Benevento, Ruth and Frank Steponaitis, Elaine Muldowney and Robert Morgan, the Sloan family, Rena and Jim Shove, Theresa Fratamico, Raeleen Mautner, the Minkler family, Maria and Don Michaud, Joan Keyes Lownds, Kevin Lownds, Tracey O'Shaughnessy, Lucia DeFilippis Dressel, Stephen Hassler, Sue Cossette, Jeff Wacker and Julia Metcalf, Marion and Robert Bradley, Nancy Bradley, Louise Bradley, Paula and Carmine Paolino and family, Robyn and Robert Moran, Kelly and Sam Hahn, Steve Parlato, Janet Parlato, Chantel and Orlando Acevedo, Tim Watt and Amity Gaige, Bob, Liz, and Cole Cutrofello, Gerard and Mary Chiusano and family, Ricky Manalo, CSP, James Benn, Carol Snyder, Francine Knight, Jeanne Archambault, Pam Hull, Patricia and John Philip, Suzanne Noel and Jim Wigren, Sharon and Dan Wilson. Thomas McDade, Dan and Joyce D'Alessio, Ivy Bennett, Cathy Buxton Holmquist, Lila Lee Coddington, Diana Smith, Judith Kellogg Rowley, Tom Santopietro, Sam and Linda Lazinger, Pam and Howard Burros, Carla and Ken Burgess, Michelle and Dennis Lapadula, Nancy O'Brien, John Lindberg and Heather Widener Lindberg. Barbara at the Beacon Falls Post Office. Colleagues past and present.

Donnarumma and Sharnick cousins on both sides of the pond. Fran and Maureen, Teresa and Ed, Michael and Ellen, siblings and siblings-in-law extraordinaire. Nieces and nephews—I love you and yours! Cashen Matthew South, what a mercy you are.

Parents Louise and Carmen Donnarumma, Veronica and Robert Sharnick.

Wayne Sharnick—

"As we enter our home, the way we enter love
Returning from elsewhere to call out
Each other's names, pulling the door closed behind us."
                                        —*Sophie Cabot Black*

BOOK ONE—REUNION

And now you'll be telling stories
of my coming back
and they won't be false,
and they won't be true
but they'll be real.
                    —Mary Oliver

PAINTING MERCY

Chapter One
Leaving Manhattan

Leaving the City is never easy, at least not for me. But leaving I am, at least for the summer. And by train, too. Almost two days of rail travel already logged now, the Tuesday before Memorial Day, 1975. Mind you, my parents offered to pay for a flight. Quick, efficient it would have been. Thank you, I told them, but I want to journey slowly, to let go the incessant hustle, slough off the insistent grit of the metropolis. I need to savor the distance between, feel the miles lengthen and chug from Penn Station to Chicago, then rock cradle-like on the storied *Crescent* heading south, tracking ever-deeper south, disembarking finally, sleepily, in New Orleans just working up to its summer steam. A meandering rather than a sprint. Time to consider what I've been up to and what I'll do next.

You see, Manhattan's pounding pulse, its cacophony and song, clash and communion, trash and bounty, all of it, have held me in thrall since I first visited during the summer of

1962. It was then, soon after my eleventh birthday, that Tante Yvette Dubois, my daddy's maternal aunt, became a fairy godmother of sorts, transforming me from a small-town girl from misspelled St. Suplice, Louisiana, to a "promising young artist of America." I was one of a dozen child painters whose work was selected for display at the Metropolitan Museum of Art, where Tante Yvette at age seventy-seven still manages student programs and docent tours.

Tante Yvette had taken an interest in my art when she saw it featured at our church fair in St. Suplice during her annual visit to my grandmother, her sister Belle Dubois Castleberry. Evidently others at the Met, not biased by blood, detected some promise in my paintings as well. Painting is what I do, who I am. Tante Yvette knew that right away.

But make no mistake, she's no pushover. Once I decided to study at New York University and eventually make Manhattan my official residence, she told me, "Do not think yourself special, Orla. There are thousands of other painters like you who want both a life devoted to art, and a lucrative life at that. You mustn't slack off. And you must put yourself in the company of those you wish to emulate. And, I beg of you, do not mistake the dress of the day as fashion. Good God."

Trim as an oar and pointed as an arrow, Tante Yvette has taken me to dinner and often to task every Monday promptly at seven for the past six years. Her apartment, all ice blues and grays, exudes the same coolness she has cultivated in herself. Although she frequently alludes to John, though never by his last name, whose white-only shirts and magenta silk smoking jacket line the closet in her den, I have never met her paramour. One black-and-white photo of him in profile (think Clark Gable) sits silver-framed beside the Waterford clock in her bedroom; his mahogany leather slippers are tucked under the nightstand that matches hers on the other side of the queen-sized bed. When I asked if I would meet him, she said, "He has family, so it's not feasible."

Like so many other adults who peopled my formative years, Tante Yvette is a study in contradictions. Demanding hand-written thank-you notes, impeccable table manners, and polite dinner conversation, she has consistently broken a number of taboos. Considered the personification of integrity by virtually all who know her, she has managed at the same time to keep a married lover for almost seventeen years, apparently without condemnation or retribution. While she can recite verbatim Roman Catholic prayers in Latin, I've known her to attend church services only for weddings, funerals, baptisms, Easter, and Christmas Eve. Perhaps because she lives away from family, perhaps because she is French by birth, perhaps because she cares not a whit about what others think of her private life, or more likely simply because she apprehends the world as a venue in which to exercise her own agency, she has invented an existence simultaneously open and mysterious. She's drawn me into it. Sometimes, I think, with a plan.

For example, you'd think she would want to avoid Contessa Beatrice D'Annunzio who, during World War II, had an affair with and a daughter by my grandfather, Dr.

Peter Clemson Castleberry. I believe that Grandmother Castleberry's accidental discovery about the affair and Gabriella, its attractive, illegitimate result, led to Grandmother's fatal heart attack. I was with Grandmother when she read the telling note. Nonetheless, it was Tante Yvette who wrote the Contessa about Grandmother's death and brought me to visit her at her villa in Fiesole right after I graduated high school.

"Not every young artist has such an excellent connection so near Florence. The Contessa will help you. You resemble your grandfather." I still blanch at Tante Yvette's brutal practicality. "And you must spend at least four full days at the Uffizi," she had declared. "Keep a notebook and pen at hand. You will reflect on your initial reactions to some of the pieces long after we return to the U. S."

Tante Yvette even arranged for a rental after I left university housing. My landlords, Charley Thompson and Evan Childs, together thirty years ("no matter who says we mustn't be," they duetted the moment they opened their door to me), have become surrogate uncles to me. I love them. They own a wallpaper shop, *Paper*, right below their apartment. Tante Yvette's been decorating her own place with their silks and sea grass for two decades. Charley is the front man, always impeccably dressed in starched collars and vivid bow ties. Graying hair and a mustache to match. Evan directs the installation crew of three, swooping into rooms in denim overalls and a black wool beret, no matter the season. Tante Yvette invites the two of them to gallery openings.

Now that I'm leaving, they've let my tiny one-bedroom with a small bath and a hot plate to a doctoral candidate from Copenhagen who is researching the architecture of the Morgan Library.

"You can return, Orla Gwen, whenever you like," Charley told me after a fierce hug. "Yes," chimed in Evan, "we'll toss out anybody for you. Even the scholarly Hans Kvelt."

I'm traveling light. Just a week's worth of New York clothes (black hot pants, poppy floral mini-dress, fishnet pantyhose, and the Valentino ankle-strap wedges that cost a month's rent). Sketch pad, of course, a brand new hardcover of Graham Greene's *The End of the Affair*, and my boyfriend Diego's address in Argentina, where he is visiting his family before he resumes sculpting at the Art Students' League come September. Perhaps I'll write him a good-bye. Soften it with an enclosed watercolor of the two of us reclined. Or maybe I'll end up craving his return and wonder if he will have an urge to return to me also. Neither possibility troubles me at the moment. I admit I have loved experiencing him, the man with the beautiful name—*Diego Juan Ignacio Godoy*—rather than loving him, himself. I have enjoyed his towering above me, the tangled brown pasture of his hair, the clearing of his throat before he spins a baritone tale about the pampas and his grandmother's disturbing witchcraft. We are more touch than talk; I, agile and willing, he, assuming and sure, with hands that do not disappoint. My flesh pressed to his, stroked and molded to damp shining every time. I have enjoyed him enormously, the way one enjoys a fine wine, a skillfully cooked meal, cool cotton on

7

hot skin. A sin? Experience? Nature unfolding? My questions are themselves answers.

Maybe in a few weeks I'll decide to send for my other belongings, or perhaps I will look forward to reclaiming them in New York. Charley and Evan are allowing me to store my things in the antique armoire that commands the marble foyer outside their apartment.

Initially a metaphorical foster child come to paint among established artists, I realized I had been adopted by the City completely the first time I gave my home address as 3251B Bleecker Street, Greenwich Village, instead of the Castleberry Place, St. Suplice, Louisiana. What surprised me was that, until I said the words, I had been unaware of Manhattan's familial embrace. Sure, Tante Yvette was a phone call and a subway ride away on the Upper West Side. True, Charley and Evan fancied me family. ("We'll keep an eye on that Diego. He must treat you as you deserve, not as he thinks you deserve, honey.") But little about the place sounded, resembled, or felt like the small southern town of my birth and childhood. While the City honked and throbbed, screeched and hummed with taxis, buses, subways, trucks, and messenger bikes, St. Suplice trilled birdsong and the steady thrum of insects interrupted by faraway train whistles and the occasional utility truck. Men decked out in hunting or fishing gear tipped their camouflage caps at little children and old folks with canes who inevitably paused from their respective play or trudging to look up and wave. Thirty or so sedans, well used wood-sided station wagons, and various service vehicles driven by longtime locals went about the daily business of village life in the hamlet just twenty miles north of New Orleans. On a day that sparked sustained neighborly conversation, the ambulance or fire engine would have been called to action, likely to resuscitate one of the elderly ladies taken ill in the nursing home over on Hester's Ridge, or to salvage an earth science experiment gone bad in the worn-out elementary school lab. And Mamma told me last time we talked—Sunday evening, as a matter of fact— that Denny Cowles, back two years from Vietnam, with plenty of scars inside and out to show from his deployment there, had practically raised the dead late Saturday night when he drove his pickup truck through town on a drunken spree.

Flinging empty Budweiser cans at roadside mailboxes, he ended up at St. Marguerite's, the Catholic church, where he climbed up and into the steeple and yanked on the bell pull for most of half an hour. Mamma said he kept yelling "I wish the fucking gooks had killed me!" Soon as he could get there, volunteer fire chief Tom Millette hosed Denny into submission, like the police used to do to Negroes looking for their civil rights when I was a child. By the time the sheriff and old Father Carriere's young assistant, Father Higgins, dragged Denny inside the choir loft, then down the narrow stairs to the vestibule of the church, a good portion of the town's men were waiting outside, a few toting their guns. Mr. Skerritt wanted Sheriff Metcalf to arrest Denny, my daddy told me after Mamma handed him the phone. "But Bob turned him over to me," said Daddy. "Had to jab him with a strong sedative and haul him back here to keep tabs on him."

Evidently, Denny was reacting to word that his long-imprisoned father was about to be set free, paroled from the state facility that found caring for his half-paralyzed body since 1962 more troubling than his having murdered Mrs. Sharp and her infant girl Belle when he set fire to their shack in The Hollow. The moment his release was finalized, the authorities would contact the sheriff, who'd get in touch with my daddy, given that Mr. Cowles would surely need medical assistance while getting out of jail and being taken home. "And I'll go with Bob to retrieve him," Daddy told Mamma and me.

Part of the reason Mr. Cowles was being paroled, I learned through Daddy (who heard it from our friend Attorney Charbonneau, Mr. Cowles' lawyer) was that Mr. Cowles told the parole board he had simply acted unwisely on behalf of his family. He couldn't read, he told them, and his illiteracy had cost him his job to Mr. Sharp, "a nigger who could read the signs on the new interstate." He hadn't known Mrs. Sharp and the newborn were in the house. He only wanted to keep his job.

How burning down the Sharp place would've done that, I couldn't imagine. Maybe Mr. Cowles thought it would drive Mr. Sharp from town. Daddy said, and Sheriff Metcalf concurred, "The state is just plumb tired of having to attend to Jimmy's medical needs."

Denny, who throughout his childhood had protected his mother and sister from the chronically abusive Mr. Cowles, no doubt couldn't stomach the thought of living with his father again. And worse, Daddy said that when Denny woke from his drug-induced stupor Sunday morning, "He told me, 'I've become my father, Doctor Prout, and then some. The government dressed me in a uniform and ordered me to torture innocent people the way my lowdown daddy tortured us.'" He cried then, Denny did, according to Daddy. "'And I did, Lord help me, I did. I am one first-class torturer. Got medals to prove it. Only ones I'll never hurt are my mamma and my sister Katie. They been in their own war all these years.'"

Though my daddy, Prout Castleberry, M. D., has no official title designating him St. Suplice's doctor-in-residence, he acquired the position by default when he returned from Boston after his mother died, back when I was eleven. You might say the town admitted him to practice about the same time he admitted to me that he was my biological father. That was when my name changed nearly overnight from "Orla Gwen Gleason" to "Orla Gwen Castleberry". If it hadn't been for my painting and how Grandmother Castleberry acted right in the end, I don't think I'd have been able to tolerate that summer. I might've been ringing the church bell, too.

At any rate, Denny's sister Katie was the ostensible reason for my return. Mamma said, as soon as I dropped my bags in my bedroom, I should immediately come over to *Easels and Lace*, my gallery and her dress shop adjoining the house, for a final fitting on my maid-of-honor dress. Katie, Mrs. Cowles, and Katie's mother-in-law to be, Elodie Clayborne, would be there, too. Come Saturday morning, Katie would marry Keith Clayborne, older son of the Garden

District Claybornes. Keith's mamma and daddy own the largest tile and flooring business in the state, according to Katie, who had been Granny Clayborne's private nurse before the octogenarian died of an aneurysm. The Claybornes had a spacious weekend camp out by Slidell, "a green-shuttered, shrimp-colored rectangle on stilts," Katie said. That's where she first met Keith one evening when she and Granny sat staring out over the glittering water. Granny Clayborne told her grandson, and none too softly, "Here's the girl for you." "And I guess I was," Katie said, every time somebody told the story.

Last October, Katie had flown up to New York to a nursing conference, and over dinner at Manetta's asked me to stand up for her. It's not as if we were as close as sisters, or even first cousins, but we were neighbors who had lived nearly every moment of childhood together. Katie had let me punch her shoulders black and blue after I learned my mamma had lied to me and married one man, Sean Gleason, when she loved another. I hid Katie from her daddy in my bedroom whenever Mr. Cowles ranted through the neighborhood brandishing his leather belt and going on about how Katie hadn't set the table right or had switched on a light before dark. I was glad that while her daddy was locked away in prison her mamma had sent her to nursing school, "so you won't have to depend on a man for your subsistence." Mrs. Cowles had been cooking at the hospital down at Convent since Katie and Denny were school-aged. "Those nuns gave me a full scholarship, can you believe it?"

Katie told me many times over. "Even when I had to repeat chemistry."

I got to know Katie's Keith just last New Year's Eve, when she brought him to Sam's Fish Shack to meet me and Tad Charbonneau, the attorney's son, now a lawyer himself. Tad has been my best friend for as long as I can remember. You might say he's my anchor and confidant, trustworthy as a priest in a confessional. For New Year's Tad had come up from New Orleans, where he was starting out as an immigration lawyer at Ciampi and Vester, the law firm he had joined after graduating Tulane Law and passing the bar. Both he and Keith are big fans of the *Jazz*, and they hit it off immediately, discussing the team as well as Keith's enjoyable if less-than-illustrious college basketball career at Furman ("I aided the team consistently with my virtually permanent presence on the bench," he'd said). That had left Katie and me to gossip about Mrs. Clayborne's initial reaction to her son's fiancée, whom she described to all in range of her voice as "a girl who for some reason wants a career even though she won't have to work."

Now the aroma of frying fish wafts through the train as a porter walks in from the adjacent dining car, saying the next and final stop will be New Orleans. The smell brings me back to Sam's place and New Year's Eve again, and I giggle, recalling the orgy of food Tad and I had enjoyed.

Just before ten that night, if memory serves, Sam had hollered to the four of us from the kitchen, "I'm too old to stay awake 'til midnight. Here's the key. The outdoor lights are off. Stay as long as you like. Got plenty of just-fried catfish and gumbo on the burner if you want it."

Katie and Keith left with him, Keith winking at Tad as he closed the door behind them. But Tad and I stayed on, making short work of the fish and spooning soup into our mouths until we had scraped the pot clean. For a little while we watched Guy Lombardo and Times Square on Sam's tiny black-and-white TV above the bar. Together we did the dishes and cleaned up the place with a broom and sponges that had outlasted their looks. Then Tad walked me home just the way he always had, starting from when we went to band practice after supper on Thursdays in elementary school. His arm around my shoulder, mine around his waist, we counted down the old year with the second hand on his Grandfather Charbonneau's pocket watch and, together, hollered a cheer to welcome in the new. Tad bowed his head to kiss the top of mine and, feeling the comfort of his gentle touch, I'd wondered whom Diego might be kissing in New York and whether I was in fact dating the wrong man. I stood on tiptoe and grazed Tad's chin with my lips. "Look," he pointed. I turned and saw. Somewhere over Hester's Ridge a spray of fireworks crackled and sparked, emblazoning the midnight sky. A long "Eeeeeeee" sounded as the electric sizzles met their watery end in the Chartres River.

Now it was the flashing station lights and the train's piercing whistle that roused me.

The *Crescent* eased itself into New Orleans' Union Passenger Terminal, where Daddy had told me someone would meet me. I expected to see Earl Sharp, who owned St.

Suplice's only car service. I gathered my things, made my way down the aisle even before the train had come to a full stop, and was first to hop off the exit's bottom step. I scanned the long expanse of track looking for Earl. But instead I spotted a lanky figure holding a briefcase in one hand and hiding his face behind a printed sign that read CASTLEBERRY with the other.

"Tad!" I exclaimed.

And I knew without a doubt the real reason I had returned.

Chapter Two
Fitting and Proper

Katie looked beautiful, even with Mamma kneeling on the round plinth below her to hem the wedding dress just at her knees.

"Wow!" I said, and rushed over, stooping low on the white-planked floor myself to kiss Mamma on the cheek, since her mouth was full of pins.

"Isn't she lovely?" asked Mrs. Cowles, who was dressed in her own lemon-meringue lace confection, standing by the easel that held my largest blue hydrangea painting. The boat neckline Mamma had designed for her broadened Mrs. Cowles' narrow shoulders and the tea-length full skirt accentuated her small waist, a waist that, had I been painting it, would have resembled a twelve-year-old girl's. Mrs. Cowles was becoming one of those rare older women who, no matter their age, always retain a girlish figure. Only the thin lines around her mouth and eyes hinted at her fifth decade and, even more telling, her chronic suffering.

"I must admit," said a coiffed blonde, broad-shouldered woman sitting in the fern-patterned wing chair (had to be Elodie Clayborne), "you and your mother look great. Just great."

I had never seen the Cowles women so radiant. They'd had their hair cut and styled—"a practice run," said Katie. Mrs. Cowles' do, flattering to her salt-and-pepper hair, was a page-boy just to her chin, while Katie's consisted of a long mass of auburn waves lifted up with pearl combs on either side so that her hair grazed her shoulders.

Mamma stood up and, all of a sudden swaying, grabbed both Katie's hands. She shook her head so vigorously that her signature chignon came undone.

In the instant, Katie changed from bride to nurse.

"You okay, Mrs. Castleberry?"

"A bit dizzy, can't think why."

Mamma wriggled her shoulders, then twisted her hair into place once more. She stood up straight and seemed to be herself again.

"Probably not drinking enough water," she said.

I hurried over to the sink in the galley kitchen on the east side of the salon and poured Mamma a tall glass.

"Here," I said, and she drank the whole thing in two quick swallows.

"Thanks, Orla," she said, and I took the empty glass back to the sink.

She returned to her professional self, straightening up and standing tall.

"I'm fine. Really," she said, and her voice told me it was true.

Katie became a bride again.

"Look at what your mother created," she said, spinning around full circle. "I told her I wanted a short dress, with a shape like my uniform, you know, a shirtwaist, because that's what I'm comfortable in. And, besides, our little reception is going to take place at the Clayborne cottage. I don't need any train to trip over."

I stared at the dress. Fitted at the waist and trimmed with a thin satin waistband, it had a cap-sleeved bodice with a sweetheart neckline and a slightly flared skirt, all made from cotton lace lined with a barely blush fabric.

"It's downright sexy, Mamma!" I pretended to gasp.

"But still good for church," Katie said, pointing up at the little scalloped sleeves.

"My boy will love it, I'm sure," said the woman in the chair. "And that's what counts."

Mamma folded her arms across her chest and smiled at me.

"Oh, how rude of me!" said Katie, hopping off the platform and walking over to Mrs. Clayborne. "Elodie Clayborne, Orla Gwen Castleberry, my maid of honor."

Mrs. Clayborne stood.

"Keith has told me all about you, Orla, and at last we meet. I've been enjoying your paintings." She gestured around the perimeter of Mamma's salon. Mamma had at least eight canvases of my floral paintings displayed on

18

wooden easels. On the walls she had grouped miniatures by subject; those more politically inspired were relegated to the sewing rooms. "Perhaps you'll let me purchase one for my sitting room."

"Gladly," I said. "Happy to meet you, as well." I shook Mrs. Clayborne's manicured hand.

Mrs. Clayborne was as stout as Mrs. Cowles was string bean thin. Her skin was breathtakingly taut and clear. It seemed never to have met the sun or found cause to wrinkle. When she smiled at me, only the dimple in her left cheek interrupted the broad expanse of smooth flesh. She was what my late grandmother, Belle LeFleur Castleberry, would have called "an elegant woman of a certain age." Formidable, too, I wondered? But, it appeared, not someone whom Katie couldn't handle. They seemed easy together. Not stiff at all.

"Will you be wearing a lace dress, too?" I asked her.

Mrs. Clayborne took a seat on one of the two sand-colored linen couches Mamma had arranged facing one another in front of the platform. She was dressed in a fitted turquoise suit that made me want to paint a bird's nest with tiny speckled eggs. She crossed her stockinged legs at the ankle and rested her smooth hands on her lap.

"No, just a peach linen sheath for me, made by my longtime seamstress Anita at home. But, look," and she leaned over the glass coffee table between the couches to take the lid off a square box with the *Easels and Lace* sticker on it. "Your mother made me this, and I simply love it."

Her smile was genuine and revealed teeth as precisely maintained as everything else on her person.

It was a corsage of silk mallow flowers, just like the one on Katie's waistband. Bits of lace enfolded the petals. Its center bled a bit with magenta and orange.

"I'm going to pin it to my dress instead of a live corsage. That way all three of us will have something in common." And she gave a little nod to Mrs. Cowles.

"Yes," Mrs. Cowles smiled at Mrs. Clayborne, not moving from her place by the easel. "Your mother has made me a wristband of mallow flowers, as well. That way I won't worry myself silly over pinning it." She waved her hands, in apparent relief.

Mrs. Cowles was unused to formal wear, that's for certain. Seems my whole life I've seen her in only two outfits, her cook's uniform and a shirtwaist dress with little pink rosebuds that she wore to Mass. Rubber-soled work shoes or plain beige pumps and white cotton gloves on religious holidays. And maybe a white cardigan over the dress during the cooler months.

Mamma winked and grinned at me. I guessed the shared silk mallow flowers were her creative attempt at making some potentially trying relationships less so. This wedding had all the elements of grand opera, what with Denny's post-traumatic stress, Mr. Cowles' being a convicted felon, and the Clayborne family joining forces with a clan that typically *was* the help rather than those who *hired* them.

"Now, your turn, Orla," Mamma said. "And while you get ready, we'll prepare to celebrate."

While Mamma walked over to the half-refrigerator, pulled out a bottle of champagne, popped it open, and poured each of us a glass in my late grandmother's wedding flutes, I went into the dressing room to don my outfit.

"To wedded bliss," Mamma said as I sashayed back into the main salon.

"Yes," said Mrs. Clayborne. "May you find what others seek."

And though she held the crystal flute delicately, Mrs. Clayborne surprised me when she downed the champagne so quickly that Mamma was still raising her own flute to her lips.

Katie raised her glass to me.

"I'll wait to toast you," I said, "if you don't mind. Spilling is my specialty."

"Nice," said Katie, and I curtseyed.

Mamma put her flute down onto the coffee table. While I stepped up onto the plinth, she got down on her knees again. She had just determined my shift with an organza flounce was suitably hemmed, when someone knocked loudly three times on the double doors.

"Hmm," Mamma said, "I'm not expecting anyone else until three o'clock."

"I'll see who's there," said Katie, who was already heading toward the knocking.

Before Katie got to the doors, Mamma draped the mango-colored shawl as she wanted it over my shoulders—"For church," she said—and my daddy's voice boomed from outside, "May we men safely enter?"

Mamma laughed and nodded at Katie.

Followed by Sheriff Metcalf right behind them, my overtly jovial daddy pushed Mr. Cowles in a wheelchair. After thirteen years in prison, Katie's daddy looked really old, though he couldn't have been more than forty-five. His formerly red hair had gone yellow and his chin hung down onto the collar of his plaid shirt. He was dressed just like old Father Carriere when he took off his priest's garb for a picnic. Seeing Mr. Cowles this way a body might never believe how strong he used to be and the pain he had caused his wife and children with his brutish hands.

"Oh!" Katie put her hands to her mouth. She was shaking so hard the petals of her mallow flowers fluttered.

"You're home," said Mrs. Cowles, the way a person might declare, "It's raining" when she expected sun. Her face betraying nothing, she walked to her husband. When she stood before him, looking down at him in the wheelchair, he raised his pale hands to her, not as if he were about to strike her, but palms up and open, hoping, it appeared, that she'd take them into hers.

"My," she said, as she did. "Thirteen years." Her steady voice filled the room. "And I saw you only ten times." Still, not a quiver.

Instead, it was Mrs. Clayborne who took in a quick breath and dabbed her eyes with her pocket kerchief.

The Cowles family had owned no car for the longest time after Mr. Cowles had smashed up their Buick sedan trying to escape from the police. The only time his wife got to the prison was if my daddy or Attorney Charbonneau had medical or legal business to attend to. And for more than a decade Mrs. Cowles had had to take the bus that ran but twice a day to and from Convent for every shift she worked. Then Denny came home when the United States decided to pull out of Vietnam in 1973. He bought himself a used pickup truck after he had earned enough cash painting for Mr. Carroll, his father's loyal though disappointed best friend. The truck got dented some during Denny's routine drunken escapades, but it ran. Now he drove his mamma to and from work, boldly ignoring the schedules Mr. Carroll set for him, but eventually getting his painting jobs done. And even those who otherwise had no use for Denny noted that he always got out from the driver's seat and walked around to the passenger side to open the door for his mamma, putting out his hand for her as if she were an aristocratic lady.

"Long time," Mr. Cowles said, his voice sounding like sandpaper.

"Yes," answered his wife, and she let go his hands. He folded them on his lap so they rested on a seat belt contraption that must have kept him from falling out of the wheelchair

I went over to Katie and put my arm around her shoulders.

"Come on," I whispered. "We'll do this."

Together we walked to her soon-to-be mother-in-law, who was re-situating her kerchief in her jacket's breast pocket.

"Mrs. Clayborne," I said, not letting go of Katie, "may we introduce you to Mr. Cowles?"

The three of us walked over to the wheelchair that Mrs. Cowles now stood behind.

"Mr. Cowles," she said, not icy, but just about. She offered her hand.

He shook it with barely a grip.

"Ma'am," he said, his voice rusty from apparent disuse.

Mamma poured him, Sheriff Metcalf, and Daddy what was left of the champagne.

"Wish I could, Minerva," Sheriff Metcalf said to Mamma, "but I'm on duty."

I took the glass meant for him and gave it to Katie.

"Drink up," I whispered. "It'll help."

Daddy went and sat down across from Mrs. Clayborne, who had again arranged herself on one of the couches. He acted as if nothing unusual were going on.

"We went by your place," he said, looking to Katie, who still stood with me, and then to her mamma, who had taken hold of the wheelchair handles, "and Denny was just leaving from his lunch hour to get back to painting the former Crowther place."

"Son of a gun didn't even say hello," muttered Mr. Cowles. "Just as disrespectful as he was before the army."

No one responded to Mr. Cowles, and Daddy just went on. "We didn't want to re-arrange anything without your say-so, Mrs. Cowles. So when Denny told us we might find you all here, we decided to come by."

Daddy paused a moment, taking in all of us gussied-up ladies in a telling glance.

"And I must say I, for one, am glad we did. You all look marvelous."

Katie took her cue from him.

"Well, Doctor Prout, if we look good, it's all your wife's doing."

Daddy looked to Mamma.

"Now isn't she something?" he said, getting up, walking to Mamma, and wrapping his arms around her. "She even makes my white physician coats look elegant with her fancy needlework identifying me."

Elodie Clayborne smiled.

He went over to Katie and gave her a good strong hug.

"I promise," he said, "I won't spill the beans about these dresses to your groom, Katie."

She smiled at Daddy, the kind of smile a body can't pretend.

"Thank you, Doctor Prout." Then, she added, more quietly, "For everything."

Then we all lost our voices. Two cars passed by. All three overhead fans whirred. The faucet dripped in the galley. And it seemed as if my brain was ticking out loud, steadily as a grandfather clock. I couldn't stand it. So I started talking.

"Mamma, are you making a mallow-flower boutonniere for Mr. Cowles?"

"A what?" Mr. Cowles said. His voice sounded gravelly, but at least it wasn't a growl.

Sheriff Metcalf, who stood by the doors the whole time, as if his charge could have escaped, chimed in. "You know,

Jimmy, those sissy flowers men are obliged to wear when their beautiful daughters get married."

The sheriff shifted balance in his pointy boots and pushed his ever-present cowboy hat back on his head.

Katie giggled, while Mrs. Clayborne raised a neatly tweezed eyebrow.

I wouldn't have believed it if I hadn't heard it myself. Mr. Cowles laughed a regular-sounding laugh. Not a snarl, not a sneer. Just a laugh followed by a half-smile.

"Why, of course," Mamma said. "I've made one for the groom, his best man and brother Dagin, and both fathers."

Whether she had or not, I hadn't thought to ask. But I knew she would now.

Katie walked away from me, bent down, placed her hands on the wheelchair's arms, and kissed her father's forehead.

"You turned out beautiful," he said.

"Thank you, Daddy," Katie whispered.

Sheriff Metcalf looked at Daddy and pointed to his watch.

"Well," said my daddy, "we won't get in the way of you ladies any more. If it's alright with you, Mrs. Cowles, we'll head back to your place. I've got the medical equipment folks coming this afternoon to install the appliances you all will find helpful."

Mrs. Cowles turned the wheelchair over to my daddy again.

"I'll be there right away," she said. "See you at home, Jimmy."

"Bridget," he answered.

"And don't worry about lunch, Mrs. Cowles. Bob and I have seen to it. Take your time."

Then they were gone, my daddy wheeling Mr. Cowles down the ramp while Sheriff Metcalf took the steps. Daddy made Mr. Cowles practice twice using his upper body to move from the wheelchair into the police cruiser. We all stared.

Soon as the sheriff's car pulled into the street, Katie burst into tears. She cried and cried. Wailed, really. And just like that, she taught me how her life's sorrow sounded. Nobody tried to stop her. We couldn't have, anyway. Instead, Mamma got Grandmother Castleberry's monogrammed napkin from the champagne bottle to keep her from sniveling onto her dress. Then Mrs. Cowles, Elodie Clayborne, my mamma and I encircled Katie, our arms all intertwined, our heads together touching hers in a huddle. We held her tight so she wouldn't fall apart. Without speaking a word, we laced ourselves together. Really, there was nothing better could have happened, nothing else we should have done. We all just held on as if we were one live helping creature until Katie started breathing regular again. Then, slowly, one by one, we let go when Katie nodded that it was okay.

Mrs. Cowles was first out of her dress and back into her cook's uniform for the evening shift at the hospital. Next Katie put on her denim bell-bottoms and button-down chemise. She would go home, I knew, and make sure her daddy was as comfortable as she could make him. I changed back into the floral cotton maxi-dress I'd worn on the train, determined to be available should Katie need me later. Mrs. Clayborne phoned the car service to say she was ready to return home to the Garden District in New Orleans. And Mamma, in the same black linen shift she wore every time she dressed a bride, took care to smooth and hang each of the three wedding dresses with gestures sure and tender enough for a newborn.

But what about Denny? What would he do when Daddy and Sheriff Metcalf weren't there? When he was alone with his father? He kept guns and knives. Knew how to use them. Might even be justified. I shuddered to think and hoped Daddy would return soon. Maybe he and Sheriff Metcalf had figured something out. Maybe Mr. Cowles had changed, if a person can change. At least he was physically compromised. All I know is it felt like a big pause, a wide hollow space between knowing what once was and what was yet to be. Leaving the others for a moment, I stepped outside the fan-cooled salon to think. The early afternoon heat, with its promise of a hot, humid summer, fell upon me like a damp woolen blanket. My shoulders sagged. I wondered if each of the Cowleses felt this way most all the time.

Chapter Three
Domesticity

On Thursday, Mamma and Daddy were hosting the New Orleans Medical Society over at The Links. They had arranged for the physicians and their wives (the only female doctor being unmarried dermatologist Giulia Graveson, who Mamma was trying to fix up with local landscape designer Joey Carroll) to get out of the city and enjoy the pool and some golf during the day, then have dinner and a quasi-meeting later. It still felt a bit uncomfortable that Mamma and I were now bona fide members at The Links. She used to be the Castleberry maid 'til she officially married Daddy Prout, going on ten years come August. Before she became Mrs. Castleberry, she had to use the help's entrance, the help's cafeteria, and the help's bathrooms. Now the help can no longer refer to her by her given name and, man or woman, the club's staff members wouldn't think of letting her open a door by herself. I hardly go there, though the lobster bisque has been known to seduce me every now and again. Old Mrs. Allaire, one of the club's board members, who used to call me "the Castleberry maid's child" now fawns over me as "handsome Doctor Prout's artist daughter." The truth is, I'm both. Always was, always will be. Two for the price of one. That's me.

I had invited Tad over for supper. We were accustomed to dining later during the warmer months, when it was cooler on the veranda. So it was already seven o'clock when I found myself chopping parsley for the potato salad. I had mixed the potatoes with celery, onions, Hellmann's, and chopped hard-boiled eggs, just after my early-morning swim over at the Haldecott's dock, which jutted nicely into the deepest part of the Chartres River. The river was running fast this morning, and I'd felt refreshed and energized by its current. Beau Haldecott had joined me. He had been one of the "big boys" when I was a child, some five years older than I. His nanna was my grandmother's great friend and nemesis. Nanna Haldecott couldn't stomach the thought that Grandmother Castleberry had thrown over bigotry during her final years, making a practice of including the Negro minister, Reverend Makepeace, and his family at her annual Easter Egg Hunt. After Nanna Haldecott's death and their inheritance of the property, Beau's folks continued to invite me to use their dock facilities anytime. And, truth be told, I much preferred swimming a leisurely walk from our home, among friends or alone, to conforming to the social requirements of The Links. Beau said that he had a lunch appointment with Tad over there come noon, where they would likely run into the bevy of doctors. Though I was curious about the reason for their meeting, I didn't ask Beau the particulars and he didn't offer any. Respecting attorney-client privilege and all that.

La Bohème filled the house with palpable emotion. I kept Grandmother Castleberry's well-used record player on the credenza in the front foyer so that whenever I was alone I could turn the volume way up and listen to the music in every room, both upstairs and down, and even outdoors in the garden where I often painted. Grandmother Castleberry had taught me to appreciate opera. Anytime I place a needle on an opera recording, I can start painting. I change the opera depending on my subject. There's nothing like *O soave fanciulla,* the duet between Mimi and Rodolfo in *La Bohème,* for feeling big feelings that find themselves emanating from my brush. Not that I was painting now. Nonetheless, the duet felt like the right one to play.

I put the potato salad in the refrigerator and went into the pantry to get the serving pieces so I could set a nice table on the veranda. I'd use the Contessa's linens with the lilies on them. *"I gigli,"* she called them, forever speaking to me in Italian the same way Grandmother Castleberry and Tante Yvette had in French. Evidently all three women believed I needed civilizing. Hearing the duet for the third time this evening (for I never tire of it, but crave it, actually, the way one craves water when thirsty), I suddenly thought of my landlords. I knew that, come morning, I'd try to do them justice on canvas.

Then, right behind me, louder than the opera, "Your *sommelier, mademoiselle."* I leapt.

"Jesus, Tad," I said, "you scared me."

"Well, you're blasting that music so loudly, what else could I do? Pining away over—what's his name?—Diego?" Tad leered. "Will I be meeting him this summer?"

"Jealous?" I asked him, and stuck out my tongue.

We might have been eleven and twelve again.

"Only if you consider him more important than me."

"Hmm," I said, "I'll have to think about that. And, no, you won't be meeting him this summer. He's in Argentina."

"Good riddance to him," Tad laughed and put two bottles of chianti down on the counter.

Then, "My apologies for surprising you, dearest Orla." He bowed. That gesture, become a standard of his as soon as he got taller than me, sometime during middle school, always made me want to forgive any real or imagined flaws I counted as his.

Nonetheless, I punched his arm and he grimaced in mock pain.

"The summer Grandmother Castleberry died and Mr. Cowles murdered Mrs. Sharp and the baby, every morning when you came by our little house off Main Street, you clomped up the four porch steps in those laced-up utility boots. They were as telling as an aristocrat's calling card. Guess I still expect to hear them."

"Please," Tad said, raising his hands dramatically, "I am now a person of grace and bearing." And he bowed again.

I walked around him to check the string beans on the stove and kept talking.

"'Here he comes, Orla,' Mamma said every single day. 'Marching on to some historical battle or another.'"

I believe she cares for Tad nearly as much as I do. I can't even remember life before him.

"Ah, yes," Tad said, rubbing his hand on his chin, "the boots made me think myself a tough and valiant soldier. That was the summer we discovered Old Doctor Castleberry's World War II secrets. That was a tough summer for lots of folks around here, when I think back." He studied the label on one of the wine bottles. "Including you."

"Yes," I said, and felt my neck and cheeks flush hot and red. "It was the summer of secrets, alright."

I looked down at my sandaled toes, freshly painted pearly white, and wondered why I'd had never noticed, until Mamma and I helped dress Mrs. Castleberry's corpse, they were shaped exactly like hers. How the second toe on each of our feet was longer than each big toe. How my grandmother's left big toe and mine both had the exact mahogany brown birthmark right below the cuticle. How we each tapped our toes incessantly in our open sandals. How it had taken her death to reveal my true paternity. How Mamma and Grandmother both, rival conspirators, had shrouded their secrets—their lies, really—for the unwavering and imperfect love of their children, me and Prout Castleberry.

"Hello," Tad said, reaching under my chin to lift it. "Are you here? I didn't mean to send you into a reverie."

But instead of raising my eyes to his, I found myself looking at his feet instead.

"Wow, no wonder I didn't hear you." I tried to collect myself. "Where did you get those beauties?"

Tad followed my eyes down past his white rugby shirt and madras bermudas to a pair of tan leather driving shoes I had seen before only on Italians while vacationing on the Amalfi Coast with the Contessa. They looked as soft as ballet slippers.

"A gift from a satisfied client," he said, and drew my hand down to stroke the leather. The hairs on his legs were the color of honey. "You like them?"

"Yes," I said, upright again. "What did you do for that client?"

He paused a moment. "Made him some money. Kept him out of a prolonged negotiation, that's all."

"Hmmm. Must be nice."

"Yes," he said. "It is. Very nice." He sounded serious, solemn, even, as if he were remembering something downright holy.

He went over to the refrigerator and pulled out the pitcher of lemon water Mamma always kept at the ready.

"He collects art. I'll introduce you to him when you come down to see my new place. After the first of July, I've been meaning to tell you, I'll no longer be commuting from my parents' home here. We'll go to Maspero's in the Quarter."

St. Suplice without Tad. Ugh. I'd need to find reasons to be in the city.

I pretended not to mind.

"Oh, good. I like it there. Does he have a girlfriend or a wife?"

"Want some?" he asked, lifting the water pitcher.

"No, thanks," I said. He put the pitcher down and reached up onto the open shelf above the sink for a glass.

"No, neither."

He looked at his feet again then, and put the water glass on the counter. Dropping to one knee, he licked his right forefinger with his tongue, then wiped a gray smudge off the top of his left shoe.

I laughed. Always the perfectionist.

"What's his name?" I asked.

He stood again.

"Full of questions this evening, aren't you, my friend?" He looked down at me the way a teacher who's growing impatient might. "His name is Luke. Luke Segreti."

"Ha, 'secrets' in Italian."

"Yes, 'secrets.'"

He poured himself a glass of water and downed it quickly.

"The Contessa would be proud. *Brava*, Orla."

I searched for a corkscrew in the drawer below the liquor cabinet.

Tad poured himself another glass of water.

"Oh, did Beau Haldecott tell you we swam together this morning?"

"Yes," Tad said, sipping the water. "Seems he's looking to expand his boat-building business. He wants to bring in a Frenchman from Marseilles to design a sleek model or two for some clients with cash down at Grand Isle."

"Oh," I said. "So you'll take care of the visa?"

Tad finished off the water. "Yes, that and other red tape."

35

He looked to the counter.

"Hey, what do you say we start on the wine?"

He took the corkscrew in hand.

"If memory serves, you said we'd grill steak, so I thought a chianti would do nicely."

"Good," I said, "thanks. Would you mind taking care of the citronella candles, too?"

By the time he had spaced the potted candles along the veranda rail, I had lit the grill outside the kitchen and set the table. Tad had seen to the overhead fans that hung from the veranda's sky-blue ceiling and was plumping the cushions on the lounge chairs. When he was done, he retrieved two globed glasses from the breakfront in the dining room and set them on the small, wrought-iron table between the lounges. I brought him the first bottle of wine. He poured.

"To another summer together, more or less," he said, and we raised our glasses. "Though work I must."

"Yes," I said. The melodious voices had gone silent and the needle scratched the spinning record.

I put down my glass and went into the foyer, lifted the needle, placed it on its holder, and turned off the record player.

"I'm just going to put the steaks on. Be right back."

When I returned, grilling fork in hand, Tad lay full length, eyes closed, on one of the lounge chairs. Hearing me return, he opened his eyes and raised himself on his elbows. I handed him a glass and he reached for it. Both of us settling into our respective lounges, we drank, gazing out and down onto the road. No one was about now, everyone either done leaving home for the day or out somewhere 'til past dark. The daytime sounds were all but silenced, and the nighttime ones had yet to announce themselves. An occasional warbler flitted from one branch to another on the ancient sycamore between the house and the barn-garage. One small lizard zipped from under one camellia shrub and under a second along the walkway from veranda to street. I felt peaceful and content. The fans above us whirred, their effect soothing and soporific. Only the knowledge that the steaks had to be turned kept me from dozing. I reached for the long grilling fork.

"Let me," Tad said.

"Okay," I said. "Thanks."

"What else do we need?" he asked, before going in.

"Just the potato salad in the refrigerator and the green beans covered on the stove," I answered. "I'll be right there."

"Don't get up," he said. "Just relax, Orla. I am at your service."

We hardly spoke at table, just enjoyed the food and the quiet. Drank nearly both bottles of wine. Our silence was a comfortable, familiar one, as natural as the seasons. But when we had emptied our plates and Tad was saying, "Absolutely delicious, Or–" we heard the crunch of tires on the gravel drive.

I stood up to look.

"It's Earl Sharp."

Tad strode down the front steps and met Earl halfway between the veranda and his gray Cadillac sedan with livery plates. After Mr. Cowles murdered Earl's family, a group of anonymous donors in town had presented him with a check sufficient for him to buy a car and open his own one-vehicle business rather than drive for anyone else. Since Earl had been honorably discharged from the army, where he'd served as personal valet to General Avery Brouillotte, a man unknown to me but evidently considered grand by a few WW II and Korean War veterans in St. Suplice, Earl's business thrived. Even Nanna Haldecott had deigned to put herself in his care when she traveled up to Tennessee every summer to visit her only daughter. According to her grandson Beau, she pronounced him a "a 'good nigger,' often to his face." Beau had cringed when he told me, "That's the highest accolade she's ever bestowed upon one of Earl's race."

"Hi, Earl," I met both him and Tad at the top of the stairs. "Won't you join us for dessert? I made a peach cobbler."

Earl was still dressed in his chauffeur uniform—black suit, starched white long-sleeved shirt, black-and-gray striped tie, and shined black wingtips. He carried his cap. Although he was just thirty-eight, his hair was pure white, having turned so within months of his family's dreadful fate. After my painting of the horror was returned from the Met's exhibit of "promising young artists" in the winter of 1963, he asked Mamma if he could see it ("Miss Yvette done told me 'bout it"). One early evening before we had moved into the Castleberry mansion, Mamma and I put it on an easel in our little sitting room, then went outside onto the small porch so Earl could be alone with it. Hearing the sounds that came from inside him made me hide my head on Mamma's chest while she held me on the porch settee. "I shouldn't have painted it," I whimpered. "I shouldn't have." Mamma just rocked me. When Earl came back out, he said, "Please stand up, Miss Orla Gwen. If it's alright with your mamma, I want to put my arms around you." Mamma nodded okay and looked at me to see if I'd let him. I nodded yes at him and stood up. Then he embraced me. "This is the only way it might stop, Miss Orla. The only way. If a white child like you can paint the ugly like you did, maybe we all got a chance." He made to leave. "No, wait," I said, and ran into the sitting room. I took the painting off the easel, came back out, and gave it to him. "Here," I told him. "It's yours. You should have it." He took it from me, smiled a sad smile, then held the canvas to his chest. He breathed deep, one long breath, and walked away.

"Orla," he said now, "Orla, you alright? What you have on your mind?"

Tad looked at me, then winked at Earl. "Well, we did just polish off two bottles of wine," he said.

Earl chuckled. "Little wine is good, your doctor daddy tells me, Miss Orla. Little." And he laughed again at his own joke.

"Won't you sit down, Earl?" I said, and Tad pulled a third chair to the table.

"Don't mind if I do," Earl answered, and pulled a notecard-sized sealed ecru envelope out of his breast pocket.

"I'll put on some coffee," I said, assuming the envelope was for Tad.

"No, this is no lawyer letter. This letter is for you, Miss Orla," Earl said.

Tad said, "Leave the dessert and coffee to me," and went into the house, so that Earl and I remained alone on the veranda.

"Who is it from?" I asked.

Without waiting for Earl's answer, I hopped up and went into the foyer, opened the desk drawer where Grandmother Castleberry kept all her stationery needs, and found her monogrammed brass letter opener.

Earl spoke louder, craning his neck toward the foyer. "That lady goin' to be Katie Cowles' mother-in-law. Mrs. Clayborne. I drove her back to the Garden District after the dress fittings yesterday."

"Oh," I said, and wondered if Elodie Clayborne had connected the dots, as it were.

Inside the envelope was a rose-scented note that read in smooth, inked script,

> *Dear Orla,*
>
> *Please consider the enclosed check my payment for the blue hydrangea painting that graces your mother's salon. The painting will be just perfect in my sitting room. My husband will send someone to pick it up after the weekend's festivities.*
>
> > *Sincerely,*
> > *Elodie Clayborne*

I unfolded the check. It was made out to me for two hundred dollars.

"My," I said. That was the most any of my paintings had sold for. "Thank you for delivering this to me, Earl."

"My pleasure, Miss Orla," Earl said.

Tad came back out with cups and saucers.

"The coffee is percolating."

I stood up. "I'll take care of the rest."

Earl went on, not appearing to notice my intent to go inside.

"It was the oddest ride," he said, almost as if he were talking to himself. So I stopped to listen. "That woman went on about the terrible thing that Mr. Cowles had done years ago. She asked me if I knew anything about it. 'Yes, ma'am,' I told her. 'I most certainly do.'"

"Oh, Earl, I'm so sorry you had to hear all that."

Earl looked up at me from his seat. He was quiet for so long I heard the grandfather clock tick for nearly a minute before chiming eight-thirty in the foyer.

"Miss Orla, to be honest, hearing is the least of it. The very least."

I felt like a fool.

"Of course," I said. "I'm so sorry, I should have understood that."

Earl shook his head.

"No harm intended," Earl said.

I went inside.

Then and there I knew I'd paint two portraits of Earl. The first the way I recalled him right after his wife had given birth. Amazed. Glowing. Electric. *New Father,* its title would be. The second, the way he was now. White-haired. Burdened. Resigned. *Earl Ever After*.

By the time I had whipped the cream and returned with the peach cobbler and coffee, Earl and Tad were discussing baseball scores and their estimations of various beers. It was tending toward dusk. A breeze rustled the palm branches. Chicory infused the coffee. The cobbler dripped juice and crunched with sugar at the same time. It almost felt like old times on the Castleberry porch after Grandmother Castleberry had declared that everyone and anyone would finally be welcomed, no exceptions whatsoever. Tad, Earl, and I could have appeared a human still life to any passerby. *Folks on a Veranda in the Deep South.* But I had learned long ago that only a real painting can render folks still forever. I had been back only a couple of days and was already hearing stories I'd never have suspected *could* happen, let alone *did* happen. Certainly there'd be more to come. I couldn't predict what they'd be or when they'd occur. So I decided to simply sip the coffee, enjoy the peach cobbler, and revel in the pleasant company of two good men. I already had three paintings in mind and hadn't even stood up for Katie yet. Summer was definitely shaping up.

Chapter Four

In the Castleberry Garden

Friday morning, just before nine, Mamma went over to the salon to meet with Joyce and Elvira, two seamstresses from Reverend Makepeace's church who had been working with her since she opened up shop. They sewed at home most days, at least until the bulk of their work was ready for Mamma's approval and finishing touches. They were finalizing Mamma's new line of fall clutches, legal-envelope-sized evening purses. The under fabric of each bag was silk damask in autumn colors—cranberry, forest green, cinnamon, golden apple. Then lace long-dipped in black tea was sewn over the silk. The purse clasps were available in gold, silver, or pewter tones. When Mamma had brought three samples to The Links in March, orders had filled up so fast she wasn't sure she'd have enough bags ready before October. I told her I would like cinnamon with pewter, please.

Daddy was making his daily house calls, first among them to Mr. Cowles. He always started at seven-thirty. The only reason I knew he had already been there was because he stopped back here to pick up another patient's medical records he had forgotten in his study.

"So I got there, Orla, and saw a standard-issue army tent set up right in front of the house. I wondered if some relatives' children were here for the wedding and the family couldn't house them all in that tiny bungalow."

"Were they?" I had just poured myself some coffee and was still in my pajamas. I had missed the chicory flavor in New York.

"No, but it was the darndest thing."

I waited.

"As soon as I turned off the engine, Denny emerged from the tent in his jungle camouflage, rifle in hand. 'Doctor Prout,' he said, 'everything's fine so far. I just told my mamma and Katie don't expect me to live inside no more. But I'll keep 'em safe.' Then he went back into the tent."

"Lord," I said. "I hope this wedding becomes a memory before anything bad happens."

"Me, too," Daddy said, got the papers he needed, and was gone again.

I heard him mutter on the way to his car, "The poor guy thinks he's a damn sentry."

In truth, Denny had been playing sentry the better part of his life. It's just that Daddy hadn't been around to see it when Denny was just a little boy. One time right outside the schoolyard, I saw Denny jump in front of Katie to take his father's slap that was meant for her.

Though I am embarrassed to admit it, I half wanted to stroll down to the Cowles' place myself just to see Denny's most recent iteration of his feelings. Instead, I finished breakfast, showered, got into a sundress, grabbed my old straw picture hat, and set up my easel and paints in the garden.

I had almost six hours until the wedding rehearsal and the catered supper the Cowleses were hosting in the church hall afterwards. It was time to paint.

Charley and Evan would be the first canvas to accomplish. I selected *Aida* to play, for two reasons: one, its Triumphal March is a masterpiece of staging, just like their events (theirs, of course, on a significantly smaller scale); and two, the I-would-die-for-you devotion Radames demonstrates to Aida parallels the attentiveness they exhibit toward one another.

During the winter months especially, Charley and Evan frequently invite me downstairs on weeknights after dinner, around nine o'clock. I'll hear a paper whoosh under my apartment door just after I get home from the studio, soon after dark. The invitations read as politely worded commands:

"Be prompt, dear. We will serve hot toddies," or *"The film begins exactly at nine. Sherry and chocolates will be served."*

And my favorite: *"Dress as if you are a Hitchcock ingénue. Forget it is the 1970s."*

I would arrive feeling uncomfortable, worried I would not know how to play my parts in their dramatic inventions. But after many visits, from December through spring break, I found myself joining the scenes easily. One night, three needlepoint footstools would be placed before the twin club chairs and the tufted leather wing chair ("Your chair, Orla") centered between them. Another night, afghans might be draped, and fur-lined slippers ("Merry Christmas, honey. These are for you.") would keep the chill away because they had run out of firewood for the fireplace against the north wall of the apartment. Charley and Evan made their homey stage feel like mine, too. And, this morning, as the Triumphal March's notes swelled throughout the house and garden, I tried to capture on canvas the intensity of both men's care for each other. By necessity, even in a city as cosmopolitan as New York, they needed to be sure of one another, to hunker down in their own well-appointed vault, as it were, to build a safe place to call their own. After all, Stonewall was only a few years behind them. And, truth be told, had they been just two homosexuals I'd noticed swishing their way down the street rather than Tante Yvette's (and now my) friends, I have to admit, rather ruefully, that *fags* would have been the initial derogation that would have popped to my mind.

I decided to paint them reaching over me, as if I were a visiting niece or cousin. Evan would be handing Charley an unopened gift, a thin, long box wrapped in shiny green that might hold a fine pen or a hand-painted bow tie. Just their fingers would touch. And their eyes would be locked across me, aware of my presence but focusing only on one another.

46

I painted for the entire opera. Didn't even hear Mamma behind me.

"Hey, you," she said, and handed me a glass of lemonade.

"Hi, Mamma," I said.

She took in what I had painted so far.

"Ah, Charley and Evan," she said.

"Yes."

I was far from finished, just trying to evoke the jewel-box quality of the apartment's sitting room and the middle-aged settledness of their relationship.

"Deep colors," she said. "Like winter."

"Then I'm succeeding," I answered. "What time is it?"

"Almost two," she said.

"Yikes, I've got to get ready."

Mamma held the painting by its edges while I moved the easel into the conservatory where it would stay until I got back to work once the wedding festivities ended.

"Ready for this?" Mamma asked, at the bottom of the stairs.

"What, tonight?" I answered. "Sure, why?"

She sighed.

"Your father called me from his office about ten minutes ago. Said Stan Charbonneau asked him to stop by the Cowles' place. It appears that Denny is marching back and forth in front of a tent with his rifle. Bridget and Katie are at their wits' end. They don't want Jimmy to see Denny's antics, nor do they want to rile up Denny." Mamma fanned herself with her hand. "Prout says Denny saluted Sheriff Metcalf's

47

deputy when he drove by. Assured him all was well and the enemy was within.”

“Mamma,” I said, ready to go upstairs, “if this weren’t the truth, it would be funny.”

Mamma let loose her chignon, then twisted it up again. She swayed like she had the day before.

“You okay?” I asked.

“Prout says it might be the change of life coming on.”

I raised my eyebrows. I couldn’t imagine Mamma old.

“Really? But you’re only forty-three.”

“God bless you for the ‘only’,” she laughed, and ran her palm across her damp forehead.

I took her by her free arm. She let me.

“I’m okay,” she said in a moment, and I let go. “And with a personal physician to boot.”

I nodded.

“Back to Denny,” I said, waiting.

She seemed herself again.

“Unfortunately, it is the truth, Orla,” she said, “and a truth that’s not going to give way to a happier one. Short of prescribing debilitating drugs to render Denny numb and dazed, it’s nothing your daddy’s bag of medical potions can cure, either.”

Mamma sighed again, then turned practical.

“Well, all you and I can do is get beautiful and try to make sure Katie and her mamma have a nice time. The Claybornes, too.”

We started upstairs.

"Oh, Mamma, did you know Elodie Clayborne bought the big hydrangea painting?"

Mamma paused a moment, then spoke.

"She told me she wanted to. So she did. Good, Orla. Good. Congratulations."

And she smiled before heading into the master bedroom humming *Here Comes the Bride*.

Actually, none of us should have been surprised by Denny's response to his father's return. He was already an altered person when he returned from Vietnam. I suppose anyone would have been. Before that, and despite his father's nasty ways, all the way through high school he had been nice enough to make friends and get plenty of dates. All of us kids took in movies as often as we could. I remember a gang of us going to see *Planet of the Apes* and *2001: A Space Odyssey*. Denny was among us. And I'll bet Denny's daddy probably still doesn't know about Beau Haldecott's having driven us— Denny, Tad and me—to New Orleans to see *The Graduate*. (It's a noteworthy irony that Mr. Cowles was always on the lookout to oppose any program or film he believed would compromise his children's innocence.) Denny attended both junior and senior proms with Lizzy Crowther. They were an item for quite some time; I remember Lizzy telling me Denny was "a great kisser." Lizzy took up with Randy Fortner from Metairie only after her family moved there to be close to her chronically ailing Aunt Zita Crowther, her daddy's sister. And Denny certainly took first place as the old ladies' favorite boy. His mamma had taught him fine manners. He always tipped his baseball cap whenever he passed a porch or a veranda with a sitting-still lady on it. "Mornin', Mizz Louisa," he'd drawl, taking his time with his words. Or, if the season had just changed, "Won't be long before Christmas now, will it, Mizz Dockery?" He didn't appear to care when Johnny Carroll teased him, calling him a "kiss ass." But since he'd come back from soldiering, he was prone to both long silences and tirades of foul language and violent rage. Father Carriere did what he could, asking Denny to stop by the rectory once a week to gas up the parish car and see to it that it was clean and running properly. "He's a good man, Carriere is," Daddy said more than a few times. "He told me he hoped I didn't mind, but he had told Denny it was 'Doc Castleberry's orders' that he ask for Denny's help." Whether Denny knew Father Carriere's story was a ruse or not, I don't know. But everyone in town was well aware that every Thursday evening between seven and ten, Denny Cowles could be found at St. Marguerite's. Never at Sunday Mass, though. "Not anymore," he told Daddy one time. "It'd be like the devil himself showing up."

I stepped into the shower, knowing I had to be quick. I had laid out my clothes and sandals earlier, had set up the curling iron, too. Tante Yvette always kept me supplied with *Arpège* atomizers, so I made sure not to use any flowery soap or shampoo. The water rained over me in used-to-be Grandmother Castleberry's bathroom. *Love and war, love and war,* repeated in my brain the whole time. The facts of both surely can complicate a body's life, and not just in an opera. Charley and Evan have been loving each other as certain as day for a long, long time. And after all that time they're still breaking the law and having people call them names and worse, even in Manhattan. I never once heard Mrs. Cowles say an unkind word about her despicable husband. Forgave him his trespasses every time, even when her arms were bruised and she had tears in her eyes. How she was able to go about her business in town after he set Mrs. Sharp and the baby on fire, I cannot imagine. But Mamma told me, and I see what she means now, "All of us, including the Negroes who live by Earl in The Hollow, admire her. They know she is carrying a heavy burden, an endless burden. Despite her white color that protects her some, no doubt about it, she is just a bit like them, burdened all the time. But burdened or not, she still stands up and walks. And without slouching, either. All these many years, she saw to it that her children were fed and educated and loved. She went to work and didn't miss a day. And she expected Katie and Denny to do the same. To try to be good. Anyone has to respect that." True enough. And now there's Katie, hoping for nothing more than a joyful wedding day and a safe, secure life as a married woman. But she's got two wars crashing her nuptials. The paternal one she's been soldiering in her entire life, and the second one that has taken her brother a permanent prisoner. *Love and war. Love and war.* All's <u>not</u> fair, as the cliché suggests. Or at least it oughtn't to be.

Chapter Five
Road Trip

The rehearsal and fish supper both went off without a hitch once Daddy went along with Denny, keeping him at home and telling him to guard the house with his own daddy inside. Attorney Charbonneau had convinced Mr. Carroll to sit through the evening with his troublesome friend and Mr. Cowles' equally disconcerting son.

"Jimmy's harmless but for his words now, but we don't want any of our women alone around Denny and his weapons, that's for sure," Mr. Charbonneau told Daddy when he stopped by. "And anyway, Jimmy will enjoy seeing C," as the men referred to Mr. Carroll. "Denny won't cross his boss, either. At least I don't think so."

Once Father Carriere had put all of us through our paces at the rehearsal, Friday evening through Saturday afternoon passed in a blur of preparations and festivities tinged, at least for the Cowles family and those of us close to them, by the threat of upset and, at the same time, a deep and sustained sadness.

Katie had Denny's promise that he would escort their mother to her place just before the bridal procession. Determined that she "do the right thing," she had also asked Mr. Carroll to push her daddy's wheelchair down the aisle with her so she could be "given away properly." Denny and his daddy would sit at either end of the first pew (Mr. Cowles' wheelchair on the aisle right next to his wife), far enough away from each other, everyone hoped, to stay at relative peace. Father Carriere had asked Tad to act as a master of ceremonies on the altar. "People always get flummoxed at weddings and funerals," the priest had said to us all at the rehearsal. "So Tad Charbonneau will keep all of us, myself included, on the program." Those of us regulars at St. Marguerite's had laughed. Well into his eighth decade now, Father Carriere occasionally forgot the Apostle's Creed or the Prayers of the Faithful. No one minded either his forgetting or his remembered forgetfulness, though. We just liked him. He treats us with a kindliness devoid of ego or pointed accusation. "Remember," he told me when I confessed to destroying Mamma's most prized possession after I realized she had lied to me about my paternity, "forgiveness is always possible. For all of us. For you, for your mother, for me." I wondered if he would feel the same about my affair with Diego or my friendship with Charley and Evan. But I hadn't been to confession since my confirmation in ninth grade and I didn't have any plans or inclination to confess right now.

The tension in the church during the actual ceremony was as palpable as the humidity that had men mopping their brows with their handkerchiefs and some of the women, especially Mrs. Clayborne, fanning themselves with the parchment programs Tad had placed in the pews the night before. Despite the clear delight the bride and groom took in each other (Katie blushing and giggling during the vows, Keith caressing her arm when she shed a few tears after being pronounced "Mrs. Keith Clayborne"), a pall hung over the congregation. There was no ignoring the hard facts about Mr. Cowles and Denny. Their troubles and consternations imbued the atmosphere, despite its hopeful nature, with the kind of gloom one associates with an impending thunderstorm. Fortunately, lightning did not strike, and neither father nor son interrupted the proceedings.

Only after those of us in the wedding party and guests made our way out of St. Marguerite's at three o'clock on Saturday did Mrs. Cowles collapse, though only briefly and likely in relief. She bawled to me and Mamma just after waving off Keith and Katie, who were speeding ahead to the Slidell weekend home in a red Mustang. There the reception at the Clayborne cottage, and an after-party pontoon for those who wanted a sunset on the bayou, awaited us. The couple themselves had reserved the bridal suite at the Monteleone in the French Quarter for a week, planning to take a more extended and exotic honeymoon in Santorini come winter.

"Thank God, Minerva, Orla," Mrs. Cowles said, and wiped her eyes with her kerchief. "Thank God." Then, recovering herself, she took a deep breath and smiled.

Mamma and Daddy were transporting Mr. and Mrs. Cowles in Daddy's car in case Mr. Cowles needed a ride back early. Katie told me that Mr. Clayborne had seen to it that one of those elevator chairs had been installed on the outdoor stairs that led up to the cottage so her daddy would have no trouble getting up and down. Tad was driving me and Denny in his Volvo. Best man Dagin was manning the *Clayborne Tile and Stone* Jeep that held "reinforcements" of liquor, "In case we down what's already at the cottage," he told me. The senior Mr. and Mrs. Clayborne were shepherding the rest of the wedding guests into a chartered van. Once Mrs. Clayborne stepped into the van, Mr. Clayborne, red-cheeked and perspiring in his blazer and too-tight collar, paused, waved me over and said, "I've got champagne icing in a cooler here. Would you like a bottle for the ride?"

"Thanks, but I'll just spill it on the dress Mamma made me and she'll be spitting mad. How about I catch up with you at the cottage?"

"As you wish," he said. And he looked me up and down, pausing too long at my chest.

"You fill out that dress just fine." He grinned, looking pleased with his words. "See you in a bit, young lady." And he touched my cheek.

I turned away. Mr. Clayborne's palm was sweaty. And his hand looked like a raw pork chop.

Denny insisted I sit up front while Tad drove.

"I like to spread out," he said, and leaned against the car door behind Tad while extending his legs all the way over the back seat to the passenger side.

At least Denny wasn't in his battle gear. His mother had prevailed upon him to dress up for her. She'd managed to get him into a blue blazer, a pair of khaki slacks, and boat shoes like the rest of the wedding party. He even wore the mallow-flower boutonniere that Mamma had indeed made for all the male members of the wedding party, in quite a rush, I might add.

"Hey now, Tad," Denny said, sounding like his old self, "you planning on being a priest, or what? Up on that altar telling us when to stand, when to sit, and all."

Tad laughed as we left St. Suplice proper and headed for the highway toward Slidell.

"No, that life's not for me, Denny. Just helping out Father Carriere. He's showing his age and waging a valiant fight against it."

Denny sneezed.

"God bless you," I said automatically.

"Ha!" Denny said, and sneezed again. "Some God if He does that. More likely He'll damn me."

Tad broke in.

"So, Denny, speaking of priests, I understand you take care of Father's car."

"Yeah. Sometimes we watch a little ball on TV when I finish. Maybe have a beer. Carriere's okay. He can't remember anything."

Denny took the handkerchief Katie had folded into his breast pocket and blew his nose.

"But, the way I see it, remembering is highly overrated."

Tad laughed.

"Maybe so."

"Watch out Father doesn't try to recruit you, Denny," I said. "Old folks love a soldier. Imagine, you'd be a soldier *and* a priest."

Tad chimed in.

"Like Archbishop Hannan. 'Phil,' the managing partner Vester calls him. They served in WWII together. Hannan was a chaplain. Parachuted lots of times. I met him on the golf course when the firm hosted a Catholic Charities fundraiser for the Vietnamese orphans who recently came over via one of the airlifts."

I slipped my feet out of my heels.

"Gook babies," Denny said. He rolled down the window and spat. He rolled the window up, then wiped his mouth on his arm. "Be the same as niggers here, you watch," he said.

My toes felt as if they had been released from prison.

"Gook niggers the real niggers will hate like the whites hate them. Ha!"

I stretched my toes, extending them as if they were my arms.

"'Of course that was a different war," I said. "A so-called *good war*. Not like the one you went to, that's for sure."

Denny drummed his fingers on Tad's headrest.

"Got that right. Folks hate soldiers now. Fuck, we hate ourselves."

Denny sneezed four times in quick succession.

"Must be allergic to weddings."

I chuckled.

Denny blew his nose again.

"No chance of me being a priest. No chance of me going to church anymore, either. Today was strictly for my mamma and Katie. Mamma!"

He yelled the word like a battle cry and raised his fist.

Then he sat himself up a bit and leaned toward Tad. He nudged my shoulder and winked at me.

"So,Tad, if you're not going to become a man of the cloth, are you planning on getting hitched to Orla, then?"

I felt myself getting very hot, though the air conditioner was on full blast.

Tad laughed again and started humming "Going to the Chapel." I joined in. But he didn't answer Denny's question.

Denny didn't let up.

"Seems like you two never been apart since even before we were allowed to walk to the schoolyard by ourselves."

I piped up, "I'll have you know we've hardly seen each other these past six years, what with my being in Manhattan and Tad down here, first at Loyola, then Tulane Law."

"Still," said Denny. "Seems like a foregone conclusion. Everyone in town thinks so. Mamma said just last night nothing would surprise her less."

The names scrolled through my mind—*Orla Gwen Gleason Castleberry Charbonneau.*

Tad said nothing, sped up, and changed lanes so we were passing the other vehicles on the highway. Silver sports car, laundry truck, black limo with darkened windows. Felt like I was on the subway on a long stretch of track.

"The last time we saw each other in person had to have been last winter," I said. "Right, Tad? Right after New Year's Eve when you met Keith."

I heard myself babbling. Tad didn't answer me. Just fiddled with the radio full of static. Didn't matter where he moved the dial. "Shit," he murmured, turned off the dial and slapped it like some disobedient pet. Then he stared straight ahead. After he had passed at least a dozen more vehicles, he asked, "What about you, Denny?"

He sounded as if he were redirecting a witness. "What are you planning? Any ladies in your future?"

Denny snapped his fingers, pulled a pack of Camels out of his breast pocket and lit up.

"Smoke?" he asked the both of us.

"No, thanks," I said.

"Maybe later," Tad told him.

"Me? I'm planning to... I'm planning to... Shit, I can't even plan what I'll say next. Tell you one thing you probably missed in law school, Tad, getting the inside of your head fucked up."

I saw the first sign for Slidell. It was thirty miles away.

"What!" Tad said, passing a meat truck with a partly worn sign that should've read *Fine Cuts of Pork and Beef* but read *Fi Cuts f ork an Beef* instead. "You mean to say you've never watched *The Paper Chase?*" He sounded jovial.

"Don't believe I have," Denny said. His voice had gone cold. "The war must have kept me from it."

"Sorry, buddy," Tad said. "I meant no offense."

I found myself gnawing the inside of my bottom lip.

"No offense taken," Denny said, dropping his sarcastic tone.

He drummed on the headrest some more.

"You know," Denny continued, exhaling puffs of smoke with studied care instead, "your whole childhood your mamma tells you violence is wrong, and your whole childhood your father smacks you, your mamma, and your sister around. Your father commits murder, for God's sake." He scrunched the partly smoked cigarette into the ashtray on the right door and lit a second. "Then you go to boot camp and get rewarded for smacking the imaginary enemy around. By the time you get to the jungle and the real enemy, you can't even tell who he and sometimes she is. All them gooks look the same whether North or South, Cong or not, so you don't care who you smack around as long as you come out of the jungle alive. As long as you come back to the world alive. You become a first-class smacker. You become a murderer, too."

He changed positions, and sat erect mid-seat, with one leg to the left of the middle hump, the other to the right. He got very agitated. His face twitched.

"I did bad things, Tad, very bad things."

He jabbed my left shoulder with the index finger on his free hand.

"Orla, you would hate me if you knew what I've done. You cannot imagine the things I have done. Worse than my daddy. Much, much worse. Very bad things."

I kept quiet, hoping Denny would calm down.

Tad was driving too fast. I could hardly read an entire sign before we whizzed by it. I gripped the edges of my seat. He saw me from the corner of his right eye. I let go for a moment, but when he swerved around a garbage truck he just about hit, I grabbed the edges of my seat again. My teeth were clenched.

"But here's the thing, Orla," Denny continued, apparently oblivious to the car's pace, "I got three medals, three fuckin' medals for doing them!"

Then Denny put his head in his hands between the front seats.

"Medals Mamma put in a picture frame and hung right between Christ on the Cross and a portrait of 'John F. Kennedy, First Catholic President,' the damn thing reads, in the dining room."

He tried to clear his throat, but it wouldn't come clear all the way.

"So when you ask what I'm planning, Tad, I guess what I mean to say is, all I'm planning is to off myself. The only thing stopping me is my mamma. She is the only good in the world, as far as I can tell. She is the one and only lady in my life." He coughed. "Fucking prostitutes don't help, no matter what I ask them to do. Beer don't help. Joints and pills don't do nothin' but make me mellow for a while. But a while ain't enough. A while ain't forever."

A sign told me Slidell was ten miles away.

Tad raised his torso in his seat and slowed the car down to the legal limit. He spoke slowly and deliberately, as seriously as I've ever heard him, turning his head to take a quick look at Denny. He even took his right hand off the steering wheel and gripped Denny's left arm.

"Denny, we certainly hope you don't do that. No one wants you to die. No one, you hear."

A horn sounded twice behind us, and then its driver passed, giving Tad the finger.

Denny rolled down the left window and returned the gesture. "Fuck off!" he yelled. "Fucking fag!"

Tad gripped the steering wheel.

"Certainly not," I echoed Tad. "And we don't hate you. I could never hate you, Denny."

Denny groaned. Tad stretched and rotated his neck and re-focused on his driving.

"I'll go to hell," Denny went on, "that's one thing I'm sure of. That's where I belong. Being alive since I came back to the world feels like being on transport almost all the time, the plane shaking and vibrating, me and the others waiting for the order to jump. Just before they push you out of the plane in your parachute, you know you're gonna be pushed into hell. But you wait in the shaking plane until you're shaking yourself, both from the plane and from your leaking guts, shitting in your pants like a goddam baby or a very sick person, very sick. Then somebody you gotta salute, yells, 'Jump!' and you jump. You do what he says and you jump."

Denny snapped his fingers again and again, as if he were keeping time to a beat the two of us couldn't hear.

"That's why I didn't take communion from Father Carriere," he said. "How can I take communion?"

He sounded like a prayer. Then he snapped and snapped his fingers and got sarcastic again.

"Taking communion would be like lyin' under oath, Counselor."

He stopped a moment, chuckled, and got calmer. Then quietly, friendly-like at first, he said, "Hey now, Counselor, I noticed you didn't take communion, either. Former altar boy like me, you didn't take communion, either."

Tad's grip on the steering wheel tightened so much his hands turned white.

"What bad things you been doin'?" Denny asked, his voice teasing. But then, harsher, as if he were his daddy before prison. "What bad things you done while I was in the jungle, you smart, golfing-with-the-aristocracy, looking-like-a-priest, never-been-to-Nam lawyer?"

I looked to Tad. His mouth was set shut and he didn't respond. He rotated his head, his neck moving back and

63

forth, left and right, like some puppet whose strings were being pulled by an invisible hand.

Denny stopped snapping, fell back onto the seat, and muttered, "Now there's a story I'd like to hear. Maybe sometime you'll tell me that story."

Tad's nostrils twitched. What did Denny know that I didn't?

In a short time, he snored.

Tad and I kept silent the rest of the ride, both of us staring straight ahead. "Forgive us our trespasses" was the mantra in my mind. However heinous or harmless those trespasses might be.

Slidell.

We pulled off the highway onto the local road. Suburban subdivisions appeared, then disappeared just as quickly, replaced by weekend and camp houses lined up on stilts close to the water. Tall reeds replaced metal road barriers. Signs alerted drivers and pedestrians to alligators. Elegant blue herons flew and swooped above. And, just as Katie had described, a large, shrimp-colored home with green shutters awaited us.

"*Welcome,*" a painted wooden sign read. "*Clayborne Cottage.*"

Chapter Six
Photographs

Tad turned into the long drive, directed by Dagin, who had already changed into shorts, flip-flops and a Hawaiian shirt vividly orange and yellow. He held an open can of beer. His shaggy hair had curled in the humidity, and he smiled what I had come to recognize as the signature Clayborne smile, passed on from smarmy father to both his charming sons. Dagin's was more pleasing to me than Keith's due to its imperfection, a slight space between his two otherwise dazzling front teeth.

"Ready to party?" he asked, as we rolled down the windows. "Huh, Orla, you ready?"

He ran a hand through his curls.

"Sure," I began. "I'm ready."

Then Denny woke with a start.

"Hey there, Dagin, I need a john pronto."

"Right upstairs," Dagin grinned. "I'll show you."

Dagin's nickname was "Scholar," Keith had explained, based on his younger brother's ability to calculate to the exact fraction the lowest grades he could earn and still not be expelled from Duke.

"He rarely carries a book," Keith had told us over some beers the other evening. "Instead, he walks about the campus with a flashy red portable turntable and the latest singles. He said doing that is almost as good as walking a dog to get the girls interested."

I watched while Scholar and Denny sprinted ahead. I didn't feel like moving yet.

My daddy's car was parked up close to the stairway and we saw the elevator chair rise with Mr. Cowles in it. Two fellows up top, couldn't tell who they were, got him out and into the cottage. Denny hurried up the stairs behind them while Dagin folded the wheelchair and carried it up and in.

Tad and I both took our time getting out of the car.

"Let's not go up there yet," I said.

I was tired out from the conversation in the car.

"Okay," Tad replied. "That's a capital idea."

Instead we walked from the driveway onto a long expanse of grass where a few benches had been placed in an apparently random fashion. One benefitted now from the shade offered by a cluster of tall palms. We both sat, knowing without saying so that we needed some time to recover an upbeat mood befitting the occasion. At the end of the dock, past the stairway-cum-elevator chair and house, a cobalt-blue pontoon barge was moored. A canvas cover shaded its deck. The barge looked as if it could carry about twenty people. But no one was on it or even by it yet. I looked forward to the evening cruise. Perhaps by then the irregular pulsing of the day would have subsided.

"Jesus," Tad said. He rubbed his chin. "Denny is really messed up."

"You said it," I answered.

Tad rubbed his chin.

"Jesus."

I twisted my hair.

"I hope He's listening."

Tad loosened his tie and unbuttoned the top two buttons on his shirt. I rested my heels on the bench, glad to feel the damp grass under my bare feet instead.

"Do you think he will?" asked Tad.

"What, off himself?" I countered.

"Yes."

I wiggled my toes in the grass.

"Their house is full of guns and knives. Denny hunts."

Tad looked toward the road as a truck entered the driveway.

"Don't know. Maybe his love for his mamma will keep him alive. He does love her. And she him."

The delivery truck calling itself *The Finest Food in the Bayou* pulled in near us. Two men in khaki shorts, shirts, and pin-striped aprons with caps to match got out, opened up the double doors in back, and pulled out covered aluminum trays of food. Smelled like jambalaya and fried shrimp. Maybe some greens in pork fat, too.

"Afternoon," the taller man said.

"Afternoon," we called back.

They walked on toward the cottage. I crossed my legs Buddha-style on the bench.

"You know, Tad, I saw something he did."

Tad pulled at his shirt collar while I dropped my heels onto the grass.

"What who did?"

"Denny."

He looked at me, puzzled.

"Where? In Nam?"

I took a deep breath and stared at my painted nails.

"Yes."

I wanted to bite them the way a body wants to scratch an itch.

"How?"

I twisted my hair again instead.

"Remember when Denny was discharged a couple of years ago? His was among the last of the units to leave Vietnam, sometime in March of '73."

"Yes," Tad said, reaching down and ripping up blades of grass. He dropped them on the ground one at a time.

"Well, you were being an intern somewhere or other, if I recall, and I had come down during spring break."

"Yes, I remember," Tad said. "I was interning in Tampa."

The delivery men returned to unload four more trays. I waited until they were almost at the stairs to continue.

"Anyway, one evening, we had just finished supper. Mamma was drawing a bath upstairs and Daddy and I were about to watch *All in the Family*. I remember because we both like the show and Daddy groaned when the doorbell rang. I'm sure he thought he was being fetched by Earl Sharp for an emergency in The Hollow."

"Okay," Tad said. "So what does that have to do with Denny?"

"Hey, you two," hollered a voice from the deck above and ahead of us. It was Keith. "We've got champagne waiting on you up here."

"Coming!" Tad answered, and we both stood up. I put my heels back on.

Walking as slowly as we dared toward the house, I went on.

"I answered the door. It was Mrs. Cowles and she was crying. She carried a large manila envelope in her hands."

"'Come in, Bridget, come in,' Daddy said, and he took her by the arm and brought her into his study. 'What can I do for you?'"

"And?" Tad said.

The delivery men waved as they passed.

"Enjoy the party," the shorter of the two said.

Tad and I waved.

"Well, of course I had to give them privacy, and I swear it wasn't until the last round of commercials had ended that she and my daddy came out of his study and he called for

Mamma to come on down and make a pot of coffee for them."

We had reached the open-slatted stairway leading up into Clayborne Cottage.

"As soon as Mamma, Daddy, and Mrs. Cowles were conversing in the kitchen, I tiptoed into Daddy's study and saw what looked like a puzzle with its pieces just about all in their proper places, but not glued together yet. Only it wasn't a puzzle, it was a black-and-white photograph, the kind you would see in a newspaper, that had been torn apart and rearranged."

We were halfway up the stairs, Tad ahead of me. Inside Dagin was singing "Happy Birthday" to someone and there was clapping after.

"What did you see?"

I stopped climbing. Paused. And almost didn't tell. Because once I told I'd never be able to un-tell, just the same as I can't un-remember what I saw.

But I started telling anyway. I looked right up at Tad and I told.

"In the photo, one American soldier was holding the arms of a Viet Cong soldier, it must have been, behind his back. Denny, wearing boots much bigger and thicker than the ones you used to wear as a kid, had just kicked the held soldier in his face. Denny's foot was still up in the air, stopped there permanently by the camera. Both Denny and the soldier holding the man, whose mouth was bleeding, whose mouth was already more open and bigger than any mouth should be, were laughing. And printed in ink at the bottom of the photograph were the words '*Tag. You're It.*'"

"Jesus," Tad said. It seemed as if that was the only word left in his vocabulary. "Jesus."

Tad reached the top step, me one below. We took a breath each, gathered ourselves, and nodded to each other. Only then did Tad knock on the door. He took my hand in his to escort me in first.

"Here you are, beautiful," said Mr. Clayborne, champagne glass in hand, and pushed the door open. He kissed me wet on the mouth. Took all I had to get past his sliminess and not ruin Katie's party.

Denny appeared, getting in Mr. Clayborne's way, and I admit at first I was glad to see him. Then he started up again.

"Hey now, you two. You were proposing out there, weren't you, Tad?" Denny said. He raised his eyebrows and motioned to Keith, whose smile had appeared to be affixed with glue since this morning.

Tad looked at me the way he used to whenever Lizzy Crowther whined that he wasn't playing fair, that he pitched the baseball too hard at her. I looked back up at him, hoping my gaze told him not to worry.

"No one's proposing anything except a toast to Katie and Keith," I said, as Mrs. Clayborne handed us both filled flutes of champagne.

"To Katie and Keith," she said, and we drank.

The crowd was but a small one. The elder Mr. and Mrs. Clayborne were both only children, and Mrs. Cowles' sister

Bernadette lived all the way over in Iowa with her husband and six children. Mrs. Cowles had told Mamma that it was just too expensive a proposition for them to come all this way for Katie's wedding. Mr. Cowles, on the other hand, had two brothers closer by. One, Martin, ran a fishing operation down on Grand Isle in the Gulf. The other, Ennis, was a fire ranger in the Florida Keys. Neither of them wanted anything to do with Mr. Cowles, "Though Ennis told me he prays against his brother's damnation every day," Mrs. Cowles told Mamma. According to Katie, her mamma phoned both brothers every Christmas Eve and on their birthdays, and called her own sister once a month. Katie had received a card with a generous check from both her uncles, and her Aunt Bernadette had sent her a handmade patchwork quilt, each patch with Louisiana flowers she had sewed by hand. I know because I helped her arrange the cards and gifts in the Cowleses' dining room the morning of the wedding. Mr. Clayborne's secretary and her husband, Carla and Russell Huber, I learned, were standing next to the two men I hadn't recognized when they'd helped get Mr. Cowles inside. Both were golfing buddies of Mr. Clayborne, Blake Carteret and Carson Field. Their wives, Mr. Carteret told me, "had taken off on a trip to Paris, ladies only. And,"—at that, he slapped Mr. Field on the back—"we're glad they did. We're free men for two weeks, if you know what I mean."

I smiled as friendly-like as I could, then made my way to Mrs. Clayborne. I wanted to thank her for buying my painting. Just as I got close to her, though, Denny slid in front of me.

"Hey now," Denny said to her, "why don't we get a family portrait or two, Mrs. Clayborne? You know, for posterity."

Mrs. Clayborne put down her champagne flute and smoothed her dress. She motioned across the room to Katie's mamma, who stood behind her husband's wheelchair.

"Yes," said Mrs. Clayborne, "let's do that. Your family first, Denny. Your family, now that you're all back together again."

"Jesus," Tad whispered to me. "She really has no idea."

"None," I whispered back.

Cameras flashed and Denny covered his eyes.

Chapter Seven
Master Suite

As soon as most everyone had arrived at the cottage, around five, the guests had fallen into predictable groups, with most of the ladies preferring the fan-cooled screened porch just off the dining room, while Mr. Clayborne and his male guests braved the sun deck outside the kitchen. Both areas were of a piece floorwise, separated only by a decorative lattice divider. From where I lay I could see Daddy's safari hat peeking just above the rail. And I heard Sheriff Metcalf's voice going on again about the time he bagged three turkeys in one afternoon of shooting. Mrs. Clayborne's well-modulated narration meanwhile carried clear through the early evening air as she regaled her audience with tales of her own wedding day, punctuated by a hailstorm just as she and her husband were emerging from the church. "I should have understood it as an omen," she said, to much laughter. Bride and groom, Dagin, Denny, Tad, and I had changed into shorts and bathing suits and set up umbrella chairs, beach towels, and other hot-weather accoutrements along the length of dock leading to the pontoon and the river. Scholar Dagin ensured that our own personal cooler never emptied. The day's events, the hot sun, and the satiety of food and drink had rendered us virtually motionless. We were plumb tired out. Keith's supine position and almost-immediate snoring offered indisputable proof. And had nature not required me to do so, I would not have bothered to rouse myself from my lounge chair to walk upstairs,

Mrs. Clayborne yoo-hooed down from her perch as soon as I stood up. I had come to really like her, and not just because she had bought my hydrangeas. She looked out for her guests. She made folks feel comfortable. In short, she was just plain nice. And nice was what Katie deserved. I hoped they would come to enjoy one another.

"Follow the long hall and make your first left into the master suite. You'll find everything you need."

"Thanks." I waved my straw hat to her.

Once inside, my eyes adjusting to the dark and my body to the instant cool of the cottage, I made my way as Mrs. Clayborne had directed. The door to the master suite was closed, like all the others along the tunnel-like corridor. Each one, I noticed, had a charming, hand-painted sign affixed to a shell hook with a bit of thin twisted metal. The one in front of me read *Arthur and Elodie Clayborne.* I couldn't help but stroll along the corridor to look at the others: *Granny Clayborne, Keith and Katie Clayborne* (I touched the paint to see if it was dry)*, Dagin "Scholar" Clayborne,* and at the

75

farthest end of the hallway, *Clayborne Special Guests*. That's where Mr. and Mrs. Huber were staying, Katie had told me. I walked back to the master suite, lifted a conch-shaped doorknob from its latch, and went in.

"Oh," I said.

The suite could have been from a photo shoot in *Architectural Digest* or *Coastal Properties*. I felt as if I were weightless, floating inside an aquarium. The walls were a glossy midnight blue, the sun kept at bay behind plantation shutters which, like the ceiling trim, were shiny white. The had-to-be-a king-sized bed was piled with patterned pillows in a linen swirl of sea life. The floor, large marble squares of wavy blues that seemed to ebb and flow even as my feet padded across them, made me want to stay. To lie down, close my eyes, and disappear.

The door to the bathroom was closed, too. Again, a conch-handle beckoned me to open it. I pushed the door and blue transformed to white. Alabaster marble with thin streams of navy and turquoise run through it—floor, shower, and walls. The towels, turquoise all, were plentiful and fluffy. And shells, shells everywhere—holding soaps, tubes of lotion, washcloths tied with turquoise ribbons. If I didn't know better, I'd have sworn Triton himself held court here.

I had just about forgotten my purpose until nature reminded me that I needed to attend to practical matters. After I did and right as I was ready to return to the dock and the evening cruise, I heard footsteps outside the bathroom door.

"Be right out, Katie," I called. No one answered. Maybe it was one of the other ladies, instead.

I neatened up the sink area, meaning to leave everything as I had found it. Then I adjusted my cut-offs, halter, and hair, and opened the door.

"Hello, beautiful."

It was Mr. Clayborne. He was naked. My eyes shot up to the ceiling sky of painted constellations. I dared not look down. Stared at the full moon.

"Excuse me," I said, talking to the moon, and tried to walk around him, but he grabbed both my arms and held on tight. I felt him excited against me. He was hurting me, squeezing my arms too tight.

"Let go," I said.

He smiled broadly so I could see his chiclet teeth. He tightened his grip. I couldn't let him see me becoming afraid.

"So help me, I'll scream."

"Now just calm down, beautiful."

I struggled to escape his hands, but they wouldn't budge. He had become a vise.

"Let me go."

I tried to sound like a dog trainer.

He laughed.

"The door is locked from the outside, the air-conditioner is on so no one can hear you, and you've got me all to yourself. You're one lucky girl. So let's you and me just have a nice time."

He rubbed himself against me and I squeezed my legs together tight. My stomach churned and my eyes filled with water. Then I pretended I was in New York. Alone and on the street in the City.

"You bastard," I said.

He laughed. His arms were too strong.

"I knew you were a spunky one. Good. I like the spunky ones best." And he dug his fingers into my skin.

That's when I spit in his eyes, bit his nose hard, and kneed his bulging crotch. He lost his grip and I ran, slamming the bedroom door behind me.

"Bitch!" I heard him holler after. "Not like Katie!"

I swore he said that. I'd swear it in a court of law.

Chapter Eight
Bayou Blues

Daddy was just closing the car door after settling Mr. Cowles in, and Katie and Keith came over to say good-bye to her parents and mine. Dagin was with them, smiling his toothy smile and smelling of sunscreen and beer. Mrs. Clayborne, as gracious as ever, handed Mrs. Cowles and Mamma beautifully wrapped boxes of chocolate seashells through the car windows. Thankfully, there was no sign of her husband. I made sure not to take my sunglasses off or to say anything. I couldn't yet be sure of my voice.

"Here you are, Orla," Mamma said. "Have fun. See you at home when you get there."

I nodded and blew her a kiss.

"I know Arthur will be kicking himself he wasn't here to see you off," Mrs. Clayborne said.

My stomach rolled at the sound of the bastard's name.

Daddy said, "Now, don't you worry a bit about it. Just tell him we enjoyed ourselves."

His too-robust tone told me he was eager to get going.

"Good time," Mr. Cowles said, his voice as hoarse as ever. "Katie."

"Daddy," Katie said.

"Married now."

"Yes. But I'll see you all soon."

"She will," said Mrs. Clayborne. "Katie is surely a family girl. And now she's got two."

I stared at Mrs. Clayborne through my dark glasses.

Was she plain stupid? Or maybe she had decided to pretend. Maybe it was better that way. I don't know.

Dagin looked at his mother. "He lit out of here like a bat outta hell. In the Jeep. Didn't stop when I waved at him. Just held the horn and screeched out onto the road." He looked down the driveway.

Mrs. Clayborne frowned.

"Did he say anything to you, Keith?" she asked.

"No, ma'am," Keith replied.

For an instant, he lost his smile.

"He...," Katie was about to say something, then didn't.

She looked over at me, but couldn't see my eyes the other side of my dark glasses. In any case, I did not return her gaze, turning it instead to my parents and the Cowleses.

"What, dear?" her mother-in-law asked.

Mrs. Clayborne smiled brightly at her new daughter-in-law.

80

Katie shifted her weight and dug the toes of her right foot into the grass the way a lovely colt angles a hoof.

"Oh, nothing," Katie replied.

Then Katie's lips closed tight, making a straight red line over her teeth.

She took Keith's hand while Dagin turned and headed back to the dock.

"Well, tell him thank you for us," said Mrs. Cowles. "Thank him for a lovely reception."

And with a wave of his safari hat, Daddy got into the car and took to the wheel.

Where Arthur Clayborne went to, I don't know. What I did know was that if he stepped onto the party pontoon tonight, I would never set foot on the vessel. The alligators could have him as far as I was concerned. Their teeth in his flesh would be fine by me.

As it turned out, most of the guests must have felt comfortable just where they were because, as dusk gathered and Captain Horatio Wade arrived to start the pontoon boat's engine, only Katie, Keith, Dagin, Tad, always-hatted Sheriff with Norinne Metcalf, and I boarded. Denny dragged his beat-up, army-issue knapsack along the dock, and Dagin carried his turntable case and a stack of singles with him. He had put the records in a tall plastic case with a zipper.

"Here, Orla," he said, and handed me a carton of Camels and a leather envelope designed to hold six cigars.

"Planning a smoky trip?" I asked.

He smiled his special smile.

"Keep the mosquitoes away."

Sheriff Metcalf handed a long cotton shawl to his wife.

"How it will be possible to feel cold this evening, I don't know," he said to the group of us. "But if it is, Norinne will."

"Oh, shush, Bob," she said. "I must be plain cold-blooded."

"Certainly not," Tad said. "Not the way you heat up the tennis court, anyway. Why, you were on fire at The Links the other day."

Norinne didn't respond, but her grin told us she was pleased that Tad had noticed. Then she spoke directly to him.

"Bob and I haven't had a night out since the baby in February, and I've been back to tennis only for a week."

"And I've hardly had a wife until today," teased the sheriff, planting a big kiss on Norinne's mouth while he took her head between his hands.

It was hard to forget Mr. Clayborne's hands on me.

"Who's watching Alice?" Katie asked.

"My mother," Norinne said, then added, "She's going to stay the night," and then, as if she instead of Katie were the bride, "Bob has taken us a room at that lovely bed and breakfast near Convent. You know, *La Petite Réserve,* with the lily-pad pond in front."

Katie clapped her hands.

"So you're a romantic, Sheriff Metcalf," she said.

Bob shifted back and forth a bit, looking like an embarrassed teenager. He had put his gun back into his belt holster, though, since leaving the cottage, and he fingered its jet-black handle.

"No, not exactly. At least that's what Norinne says."

Norinne did not dispute him, only shrugged her shoulders.

"How about desperate?" he leered at his wife. "Let's just say I'm desperate." And he took his hand off the gun, rubbing Norinne's shoulder instead.

We all laughed.

Norinne was pretty in the way folks think of girls next door. Nice skin, no makeup, and hair with just enough red to suggest vitality and spirit. When he wore his cowboy hat, Sheriff Metcalf looked like the Marlboro man. Only thing missing was the horse. I actually heard Lizzy Crowther once say she hoped she'd get pulled over by him.

"A desperate desperado," Denny said a couple of times, though not to anyone in particular.

The air was heavy, sultry.

"Ready?" asked Captain Wade.

He stepped into the boat, unleashed the rope wound around the bollard, and pushed off into the canal, heading toward Pearl River.

"We'll cruise to Honey Island Swamp," he said, "then into the bayou. Go from day to night there, so you lovebirds can smooch without the rest of us looking on." He chuckled. "Make yourselves comfortable." He took a pair of wire-rimmed, circular glasses out of his safari jacket pocket and put them on. They slipped a bit down his nose, made him look like a retired professor or what John Lennon might look like when he got old. "As you can see, I've bolted vinyl banquettes along both sides of the pontoon. And, just in back of my pilot's perch, a couple of two-seaters for any lovebirds."

Keith made a playful rush to one of the couches. "I call this one," he said.

The captain pushed his glasses up, but they slid down again. "Of course, as you see, they're facing the stern. You won't want to be looking at me."

Norinne went over and dropped her shawl on the second loveseat.

I actually found the captain interesting to look at. He defied the stereotype my New York friends imagined a swamper to be. Then again, I hadn't ever spent any time with folks who lived full-time in the swamps and bayous. I expect they had to enjoy some risk. They never knew what might come slithering up the toilet or plop onto the roof. The stilts that held their houses up couldn't withstand much flooding. Unless they set up birdhouses, also on stilts, for purple martins, mosquitoes would envelop their dwellings in swirling black clouds. And going outside in the dark surely required carrying a pole or a gun. You had to know you wouldn't be the only creature interested in opening the aluminum garbage containers. Human nature wasn't the nature in charge out here.

"So let me know if I can do anything for you," Captain Wade continued. "There's sweet tea for the pure, and a case of beer and a dozen bottles of champagne for the less so in the coolers here, courtesy of the groom's brother. Marshmallows and hot dog treats for the alligators, too, if you're of a mind to tease them up."

"Hey, there, Dagin," Denny said, "right brotherly of you to bring along provisions. Well played, Scholar."

At that, Denny took center deck and strummed an invisible guitar. He sang:

> "*All night,*
> *She wants the young American,*
> *Young American, young American,*
> *She wants the young American.*
> *All right,*
> *She wants the young American.*"

"Mr. Bowie, I believe," said Captain Wade.

Tad looked surprised.

"Don't be so startled, sir. I'm not as ancient as I look," the captain said.

Tad bowed. "My apologies, Captain. An impolitic assumption on my part."

Captain Wade chuckled again. "The truth is, I have a granddaughter who lives with me and keeps me up to date. Bowie's good, but I really go for Anka."

"Ugh," Tad groaned. Then, "Sorry. I seem to have left my manners at home."

Now the captain smiled.

"You are of a mind with my granddaughter, I see. Perhaps you should meet her."

Tad said, "Thank you. Very kind of you."

Non-committal and polite. But no bow this time. "I think I'll imbibe instead of offend," he said, drawing a laugh from the captain, and made for the coolers.

Denny motioned to the turntable and records.

"Go ahead," Dagin said. "You're in charge of the music. Captain here has got the electricity." To the rest of us, "Drink up."

He offered the captain a drink, sweeping the cooler with his right arm.

"Only upon our return. So save me a couple, will you?"

Dagin saluted and put two cans aside.

"He don't love you like I love you," Tony Orlando sang, and Sheriff Metcalf took his wife's hand and danced around the loveseats. Keith grabbed Katie, and Dagin, me, and we swayed by the stern. *"...trying to tear us apart."* Dagin held me lightly, spun me around gently, smiling at me at every turn. He made me want to dance with him. He was his mother's son, thank God.

"Dancin' Orla," he said. "Pretty, dancin' Orla." Crooked-smooth smile. Soft fingers. Not like his daddy. No, not one bit.

Tad watched and smiled. Dagin saw and offered to let him cut in.

"Thank you, Scholar," he said. "I'm enjoying the view of you two."

My breasts tingled a bit at Tad's words, and I let Dagin spin me some more.

Denny helped himself to a Miller while Tad opted for the champagne, popping the cork and pouring for Norinne, Katie, and me.

Denny downed the canful in three gulps, got another, and plopped onto the couch on the starboard side of the pontoon. He again strummed his invisible guitar. When the music stopped, Dagin said, "Thanks, Orla," then lay down on the deck beside Denny, his legs bent, his hands behind his head.

We listened to Grand Funk Railroad's "Bad Time" and Lobo's "Don't Tell Me Goodnight". Bob and Norinne had taken the couch directly facing the stern and held hands, looking out onto the water. Right behind them sat Katie and Keith, slouched down and stretched out with their heads back onto the white vinyl. Both were barefoot now, and Katie's hair had long lost its combs. Keith stroked it and she closed her eyes. Tad sat upright on the banquette opposite Denny, conversing with Captain Wade. "The only time I lived out of the bayou was when I was serving the country in Korea," the captain was saying. "And I couldn't wait to get back here." I knelt at the other end of the boat, holding onto the rail, watching the inky water, feeling at loose ends.

It had been quite a wedding day. Brides and wives and other women wronged. Good and charming and horrible men. When Alice Cooper's "Only Women Bleed" sounded through the warm breeze-swirling dusk, I stood up. Listened to the lyrics. I had gotten away. I still had choices. But I was afraid for Katie. It seemed as if she had bargained with the devil and traded one hell for another. Or maybe she had found a purgatory and thought it good enough. Maybe she had settled for purgatory, thinking it was her best or maybe even only bet.

The sky was magnificent. Orange fused with maize, then violet and pink. Silver, gray, pearl opalescence. Birds overhead crisscrossed, taking flight before night came, their sounds trumpets among the shifting colors.

"Okay, we're entering the bayou now," said Captain Wade.

His voice drew our attention, made us straighten up and watch. No one spoke. We seemed visitors to a foreign place, anxious to lay eyes on the not-yet-explored, the still unknown. The pontoon boat was our passport, Captain Wade our guide.

He steered the boat into a narrow, canal-like pass. The swamp's running water went still. Its black ink turned brown. Open sky with warm breezes disappeared and the air hung ceiling-like in an enclosure of humid heat. We were outdoors, yet felt within.

"Whoa," Denny said. He found and clutched his knapsack. "Only thing missing are the gooks."

As if a switch had been flipped inside him, Denny became electrified. His body twitched. His nose moved up and down, up and down. Thumb and middle fingers snapped on both hands. His sandaled right foot tapped the deck.

"Gooks," he said again.

Then, as if the same switch had been flipped off, he went limp and fell back onto the banquette.

The boat, meanwhile, skimmed further into the bayou, then slowed, and slowed some more. Captain Wade cut its engine and we came to a standstill.

"I'll have one of those cigarettes now," the captain said, and Tad went over with the pack he had opened already.

Dark was coming on. Ancient trees rose, rooted beneath the muddy brown. Columns primeval, they loomed tall and silent. Spanish moss dropped swaying lace curtains onto the dense, still air. Ropes wound round, matching greywhiteblackloden branches. Snakes or curling vines, who could tell? Feral pigs snorted behind thick, thick elephant ears, serrated reeds, and groves of mallow flowers. Rutting were they, feeding on kill, shaking their bristly hair against insects that bit or burrowed or stung? I did not know their vocal clues. The bayou spoke a language new to me. Turtles the size of sleds—"Even the alligators don't bother them," Captain Wade told us.—sat in plain sight. Like monuments to revered national heroes, they rested on tree limbs brought horizontal by lightning strikes or rot. Lily pads in profusion seemed but gardens until first the eyes, then the snouts emerged from among them. The alligators waited, glided, not needing to seek prey, but only to pounce upon it as it appeared, oblivious until too late. Innocent until seized.

Earlier, in daylight at Clayborne Cottage, I had encountered predatory nature. I had thought myself safe. And now night was coming. I breathed slow and deep, stared into the water, looked for hints. If I were lucky, I'd hear the growl-purr or the splash of a tail in time. I'd see swirling pools before a slithering water moccasin lunged and bit. I'd feel the tickle of gorgeous web before the spider loosed its poison. But even if I saw and heard and felt nothing, I had to admit to myself there'd be no escaping nature, predatory or otherwise, on this or any other journey. Nature, I could see without a doubt, was stronger than I.

Chapter Nine
The Party's Over

Darkness fell. A black curtain dropped, unfurled but once and completely. Crickets' incessant staccato played background music for melodic hoots of owl. A mist rose that moistened and frizzled my hair. Flying creatures I could not see flapped and whizzed above and close to my face. A scream that sounded like a child's made me afraid. I stayed by the rail but dared not hold it anymore, sure that something would grab me from the other side.

"Hey, now," Denny said, and I jumped. He stood right behind me. "Everybody but us is asleep. Drunk or asleep. Or both." He chuckled. "It don't matter none."

He had a flashlight and shone it upward at the canvas covering so a soft light bathed the inside of the boat. The only other light emanated from six candle-lit lanterns hung from the poles that held the canvas awning in place.

I turned to look. Captain Wade was snoozing at his post, bent over the wheel. Tad lay face down, his right arm hanging off the banquette, palm resting on an empty cigarette pack. Two empty champagne bottles lay sideways beside his shoes. Katie was in Keith's lap, her arms wrapped around his neck and his around her waist. Sure enough, Norinne had pulled her shawl around her shoulders and had arranged herself so that her legs rested on her husband's lap. Bob's cowboy hat rested on his forehead, its brim covering his eyes. Dagin moaned and woke from his position on the floor for a moment. "Hey, man, douse the light, will you?" Then he turned on his side and covered his head with his arm.

Denny went over and got his knapsack. He brought it to the rail. Shining the flashlight into it, he pulled out a bottle that read Bayer Aspirin.

"Want some?" he asked, and shook a handful of pills out of the bottle. Maybe there actually were a few aspirin in there. But not many.

"No, thanks," I said. "I've had enough stimulation for today."

"Suit yourself," he said, and selected three pills to swallow.

I hoped they wouldn't rile him up too much.

We both sat down cross-legged on the deck. The noise of the bayou was tremendous. A full orchestra of life. Only I couldn't see the conductor. That was the thing. The music and its conductor were beyond me. That made me excited.

Excited and afraid. The boat was really so small. We were all so small. I wished Denny were a boy again.

"Hey now," he said, and he rifled through his backpack again.

"What are you looking for?"

He put his face close to mine so that our noses touched.

"Vision, Orla. I'm looking for vision. Insight. Immmmmmmmmm."

He was making a humming sound, but from his throat, not his lips. A sound as sustained as those in the bayou. Guttural. Deep. He seemed unaware of it.

"Hey now, here it is," and he pulled out one serious pair of goggles. "Immmmmmmmm. Immmmmmmmm."

"Stay still, now, and I'll share my vision with you. Compliments of the United States military. Immmmmmmmm. Immmmmmmmm."

The night-vision goggles were held in place by a leather contraption that looked like what gets put on a man in an electric chair. I adjusted the headpiece on my hair and fit the goggles to my eyes.

Denny stopped humming to stand up. He pulled me up with him, pointed me toward the bayou, and said, "Now look."

He hummed again so that I was hearing two kinds of music, his and the bayou's. And now I saw the music, too.

"It's like a movie reel," I whispered.

"Immmmmmmmmm, Immmmmmmmmmmmm."

Against a grainy black background, flickering white figures moved, some far off among the elephant leaves and low shrubs. Something fast scurried up a tree. Lots of small insects flew in front of the lenses.

"Immmmmmmmmmmmmmmmmm. Now, wait a minute. When I tell you, look down."

I lifted the goggles so I could squint at Denny to see what he was going to do. He had gone over to one of the coolers and picked up three bags of marshmallows and the plastic container filled with hot dogs. He brought them back to the rail and flung the hot dogs into the water.

"Immmmmmmmmmmm. Immmmmmmmmmm."

I pulled the goggles back into place. It took only a moment.

"Oh, oh, my God, Denny."

Gliding white figures calmly, sedately even, came to the bobbing, white-now hot dogs, opened large mouths, and devoured them. When there weren't any more, the pearly alligators swam close to the boat, banged up against it and pushed at it. Their mouths opened and closed on my movie-screen goggles, and they growl-purred, growl-purred.

"Ah," Denny said.

"What the hell..." Tad was awake. "Who's banging?"

"Hey there, Tad," Denny said. "It's only the alligators."

"Jesus," Tad groaned. He nodded off again.

I tried to get the contraption off my head, thinking to give it to Tad. When I finally unloosed it from my hair, I got Denny's flashlight out of his knapsack again and turned it on.

I aimed it up at the canvas awning. Through the canvas I saw the shadowy S-curves of snakes and shivered.

"Can't a guy get some sleep?" Dagin said.

The two couples rustled about, but didn't wake.

In the commotion, Captain Wade cleared his throat and said, "I must have dozed off."

He stood up, straightened himself out, then sat down again in his captain's perch.

I decided to wake Tad, even though he'd likely get annoyed at me.

Shaking him by the shoulders, I asked, "Want to see?"

"If you insist," he said, shaking himself awake and upright.

He stood up and, before donning the goggles, turned toward Denny's deep-throated hum.

"Immmmmmmmmmm. Immmmmmmmmmmmmmmm."

"Jesus!" Tad cried, and ran to the pontoon's rail.

I turned around fast. Denny stood teetering barefoot on the rail, holding onto a canvas roof pole with one hand while emptying a full package of marshmallows into the bayou with the other. The marshmallows dropped like oversized confetti.

"Give me your hand, Denny," Tad said. "Now."

Denny sneered.

"God-damn fancy lawyer, think you can boss me like a sergeant. Asshole."

Tad stood his ground and went for Denny's arm. But quick, with a bark, Denny kicked him in the stomach and Tad lost his grip.

"Army, man, army taught me to make short work of assholes like you."

"Jesus," Tad said, folding into himself. He backed away.

I came and stood by Tad, who was straightening up. He spoke again in a firm voice.

"I don't want to boss you, Denny. I just want you to come down."

I looked up at Denny, right into his wide-open eyes.

"Yes, Denny, like we said in the car. We don't want to lose you."

Denny laughed the laugh of a horror film villain and dropped the plastic marshmallow bag. It floated down into the water. Then he gave Tad the finger with his free hand.

"Come down, Denny." I sounded like a school marm. "Come down right now. What would your mamma say?"

"Immmmmmmmmmmmmmm. Immmmmmmmmmmmm."

Everybody was up now.

"Denny!" hollered Katie. "Don't be stupid."

Bob Metcalf ran to the other side of Tad. They nodded to one another to grab Denny by the waist. Tad kept talking all the while they moved closer.

"Denny," he said, "remember how this morning you said you'd like to hear my story, why I didn't take communion either?"

Denny turned his head toward Tad.

"Yeah, man," he said, "I remember. Immmmmmmmmm. Immmmmmmmmmm."

Tad and the sheriff were inches from Denny's waist.

"Well, you come on down and I'll tell you. I swear, Denny, I will tell you."

Denny cocked his head, listened.

"You been bad, too, then? But not as bad as me. Nobody as bad as me. Immmmmmmm. Immmmmmmmmmmm."

Dagin was on his feet now, and he chimed in, too.

"Hey, Denny, we got more beer here. I need you, man. We've got to finish up all this liquor. We have a bet going, remember?"

Denny saw that Bob and Tad intended to grab him and, quicker than they could, he pulled a paring knife out of his trunks with his free hand. He sliced himself across his chest. Didn't even flinch.

"Whoa, boy," Bob Metcalf said, backing away himself. "Calm down."

"Touch me and I'll slit my throat," Denny said. "Think I'm just one of your country boys, Sheriff? I've been to the war. The big fucking war. I'm not scared of dying no more. Living's what scares me now. So lay off."

He made another pass with the knife, this time vertically, so a thin cross of blood moistened his chest.

"Okay, okay," the sheriff said. "But, like Orla said, think of your mother."

That's when Katie got spitting mad. She wouldn't let Keith keep her with him like he wanted to. She threw off his arms around her and marched up to the rail.

"You can't scare me, Denny." She grabbed her brother's arm that held onto the pole. "Now don't you even think about leaving," she said. "What about Mamma? How could you leave Mamma, Denny!"

He looked back and down for a moment. He held the knife aloft like a sword he didn't want anywhere near his sister. Then he talked softly, kindly even, to her.

"You take care of her now, Katie. You can take care of her. You got a good man to help you. You got Keith." He looked to his brother-in-law. "Thank you, Keith. I can go now. I gotta go."

He let go the pole and stretched out both his arms as if to dive. Katie grabbed him by the waist, but he flung himself forward and she lurched after him.

"No!" she screamed. She held on. I don't know how, but she did. Tad and Bob Metcalf grabbed her in turn, pulling her back so she wouldn't go over the rail with her brother. Katie's grip slipped from Denny's waist to his legs, upside down now, so that his bathing trunks encircled his calves. Dagin and I joined the conga line of would-be saviors, each of us trying to pull Denny back and up. Straining to release him from something stronger than the lot of us, we held on while Bob Metcalf let go the human line to shoot and shoot and shoot his gun over the rail into the now-roiling water.

Everything exploded, howled, screeched, buzzed, screamed, and I couldn't tell what was Denny, what was the gun, what was us, and what was nature meeting an intruder.

Then, finally, whatever had been pulling Denny fell away. I can't tell you how many bullets it took. But it or they finally fell away.

Captain Wade must have started the engine, because the pontoon vibrated. A radio crackled, too, and the boat lit up like a carnival booth. We were lifting Denny up. Everyone but the captain was lifting him up. It was hard. But we had to. He had to know we wanted him more than the 'gators did. And we finally got him. I don't know how we managed. All I know is we got him up. We put our arms under his shoulders and dragged him down onto the deck. Then we were moving, moving, moving. I shined the flashlight on his face first. He still had eyes. They stared up, but didn't blink. Katie knelt over him in the ooze, touching him everywhere, crooning, "Denny, Denny, Denny." She went to hold his wrist for a pulse. But his left hand was gone. Quick, she tried the other side. But there was no arm below his elbow.

"He'll bleed to death," Katie said. "He's bleeding to death."

Her voice keened.

Norinne grabbed her shawl and Katie tied it as tight as she could above Denny's left wrist while Sheriff Metcalf made a tourniquet of the shirt Tad threw him.

We were speeding on water, back on the Pearl River again.

"I radioed," Captain Wade hollered above our voices. "Ambulance will meet us at the public dock in Slidell. It's the closest to the hospital."

Dagin was vomiting off the stern and Norinne went over and rubbed his back. The rest of us were kneeling around Denny, kneeling in Denny's blood that wouldn't stop streaming over the deck.

"Jesus," Tad said.

"Yes," I agreed.

What else was there to say?

Chapter Ten
Obituary

We buried Denny, appropriately, I think, on Memorial Day. Tad and his father, Mr. Carroll, Keith and Dagin Clayborne, and Sam (who had offered his Fish Shack to the family as a gathering place afterwards) were pallbearers. Young Father Higgins celebrated the Mass. And old Father Carriere wept when the bagpiper played "Amazing Grace" for the recessional. Mrs. Cowles had wanted a bagpiper, she said, because the pipes played the saddest music she knew of. Somehow Stan Charbonneau found one on short notice before a holiday weekend with its parades and all. I couldn't help but think that Denny would have liked his mamma's choice of song. The congregation sang it strong. I know they did it for her. But I have to tell you, I did it for Denny, too. He was suffering personified. And now his sufferings were over. Earl Sharp came to the service with Reverend Makepeace. He wore his army uniform and saluted the casket as it passed.

PAINTING MERCY

"I once was lost, but now I'm found,
Was blind, but now I see."

On Tuesday, everybody went back to their lives—the newlyweds to the Monteleone to be alone, Mrs. Cowles to cook at the hospital in Convent, even though the nuns had offered her time off. "I daren't take it," she told Mamma. "I'd just fall apart, and, besides, my husband's got to eat." Tad to his fancy law firm in the city, Daddy to his morning rounds, and Mamma to her next bride.

As for me, I decided for sure to stay the whole summer. I was plumb worn out. I needed to paint and paint every day. So when Tuesday morning came and I had the house to myself just after nine, I turned the volume up on the final tomb scene in *Aida*. I put aside the Charley and Evan canvas and started on another one, as big as the mural I had done of the Freedom Riders back when I first started painting in the '60s. It would take some time to get it right. On the left, close up, with no background, I'd paint a partial of the American flag, some stars on blue showing, and all the rows of red and white. The flag's edges would be frayed, shredded a bit. And, dripping from the red rows, big drops of blood. Dollops of blood, in fact. They'd be falling on a bayou, with as much of its nature as I could manage in the center of the painting. Lots of shade and darkness. Narrow streams of sunlight piercing through. Mysterious. Primal. At the bottom right corner, on the diagonal, looking toward the flag, with barely a glimmer of light above it, a pair of hands holding binoculars, raising them upward, searching.

BOOK TWO—RENDINGS

Nature goes her own way, and all that seems to us an exception is really according to order.
—Goethe

Chapter Eleven
An Invitation

"Tad!"

I answered the phone on its fifth ring, having run in from the garden and Denny's canvas, almost finished. It was mid-July, and Tad had been living in his new place for two weeks. I'd immediately missed his nightly proximity. Though I lacked no creature comforts in my inherited Castleberry home, I yearned for our duet of companionable conversations, our leisurely perambulations, even our palpable silences. From the day of Denny's funeral through the first of July, Tad and I had lapsed into the assumptions and practices of our childhood togetherness. Nightly, after he had doffed his lawyer's suit and I had traded my brushes for wine glasses, we met for supper on the veranda of my parents' place or at one of the worn picnic tables outside Sam's Fish Shack. We swam off the Haldecott dock under the moon and dotting stars. We strolled around and through our old haunts—the elementary school field, the gazebo by St.

Marguerite's, the abandoned box factory by the train tracks, the cemetery, where we paused and crossed our foreheads at Denny's modest grave. When it rained, we let drop the bamboo shades otherwise cinched tightly under the robin's-egg ceiling of the veranda and shuffled a deck of cards. We breathed the citronella of tinned candles and the eucalyptus of Mamma's handmade wreaths on the double front doors whose long windows had been dressed in muslin against the sun. We talked past dark from matching lounge chairs, our skin damp with evening's sultry wet. I found myself dismissing thoughts of Diego, even when a postcard from him arrived signed "Kisses." Instead I hugged pillows in my solitary bed and woke to pre-dawn fantasies that featured Tad's tennis-toned legs wrapped around mine and his head nestled in the crook between my neck and undraped breasts.

Although I knew that Tad's new and proper place was at the pistachio-painted shotgun house across from the Ursuline convent in the French Quarter, he had long ago imprinted his image in my living memory of Home. His folks had celebrated his twenty-fifth birthday just after the New Year with the down payment on his gem of a place. (And it must have cost them a pretty penny, that practical, straight-line structure of noteworthy historical value. And who better to appreciate an historical house than Tad?). But the natural pleasure I'd felt at his good fortune was interrupted by a selfish rat-a-tat in my head: "He's gone now, gone now. Close by, but gone nonetheless."

But here he was at the moment, the sound of him at least. His voice graced my ear with delight akin to the cool-sweet of ice cream, crisp-feel of linen, surprise-sight of swallows a singular V in flight.

"I'm taking my time getting it right, Orla," he said. "I researched the colors and had the rooms painted. I've gotten the bedroom and front room organized, the latter so it can sleep two guests on pullout sofas. Dad suggested some clever reconfiguring of the kitchen. So now it allows six comfortably for dinner. I hope you'll approve of my arrangement." Pause. "So, I want you to come. You will come, won't you? And you'll advise me about the rest? I've purchased a substantial fish tank for the front room. You know, a full-wall affair, for some light and motion. Some nature."

Smiling. Twisting my hair with my fingers.

"Of course I'll come," I said. Licking my upper lip. "When?"

Pause.

"Hold on. I'm looking to see if I have to go in Saturday morning. Vester, the senior partner, has me working on a number of the Vietnamese orphan custody cases."

Horn jazz in the background. Then a siren coming—there, gone by.

"Good, my calendar is clear at the moment. Can you come Saturday, Orla?

We'll go to Maspero's as I promised."

"And meet what's his name of the gorgeous shoes?" I asked.

Laughter.

"You mean Luke. I'll see if he's available. He's just back from Venice. He was collecting tapestries and some Murano chandeliers for a client up near Tulane."

"Okay, Saturday," I said. "What time?"

I let go my hair and picked up a pencil by the notepad. Twirled it like a baton on parade.

"How about noon? Come here first. Then we can have the whole day."

Pause again.

"Oh, and plan to stay the night if you wish," he said.

Flutter below my waist.

"We can go to Brennan's for brunch on Sunday. I'll ask Katie and Keith to join us."

Try to be calm. Subtle.

"Well, we'll see about Sunday. Mamma has an open house planned for autumn brides. She might need me."

Pause.

"At any rate," I continued, "Earl will have to drive me to you. Manhattan has convinced me to remain license-less, and St. Suplice has yet to boast a subway system."

Chuckle. "Okay, then, whatever you decide."

Pause.

"Good. I'll see you then, Orla. And thanks in advance for your decorating help."

"My pleasure. I'd be insulted if you didn't ask. Good night, Tad."

"Good night, then."

Just about to hang up. Then, quick as a lightning strike, "Oh, one more thing." I hesitated. I held my breath, felt my nipples against my blouse, then went ahead and said it.

"I miss you."

Lovely warm chuckle. Another siren.

"Well," Tad cleared his throat, "Of course I miss you, too."

A second chuckle. "Good night, then."

"Good night."

I lowered the phone into its cradle as if it were an egg that could crack. Tad's voice cocooned me. I wanted its timbre to resonate in my brain until I could hear it again in person. Was Saturday a date? Was he inviting me to his bed? I couldn't tell. He missed me, too. He had asked me to stay. But how? Like a sister bunking on his couch in the front room? Or not? What was he thinking? Could he read my mind?

I had myself to blame for my muddle. I had avoided testing our relationship to see if it could and would evolve into a romantic one. No doubt Tad and I had long enjoyed an intimacy come of our shared history, our mutual regard, and our understanding of each other's chosen passions. No doubt we relished the physicality of tested friendship—the easy hug, the pat on the back, as well as the knowledge of our respective tastes, hopes, quirks. No doubt, too, we'd garnered without even trying the approval and good will of the community that had raised us.

Truth was, I was skittish to discover our future. My affair with Diego suggested the binary view, lover *or* friend, was sorely limiting, even if for the most part pleasant. What I didn't yet know, however, was whether lover *and* friend could co-exist. If Tad even wanted them to, if he'd ever considered an *us* in that fashion.

I wrapped my arms around my chest in an X. The missing number, the answer to an equation yet to solve.

"Surely friendship and romantic love can commingle," I imagined him saying. "Look at John and Abigail Adams." And who knows how many more couples from his historical compendium he would be able to enumerate and explain? Would we have that conversation? Did I dare initiate it? Might the two of us become a "NOTABLE COUPLE IN AMERICAN ART AND LAW" as I admit I'd imagined even before the sun had risen that morning?

I was not unschooled, for God's sake! I would have read Tad's cues if he had provided any. I'd seen Diego's eyebrows turn to question marks that night in the museum. I'd nodded yes, and we stripped in one of the Greek sculpture galleries, hiding from the guard behind a Praxiteles-inspired sculpture of Aphrodite. I knew how a hand clasp awakens trembling, Diego's stone-roughened fingers brushing mine like a hummingbird's flutter. I had studied desire in his espresso eyes. Held its rigid urgency in my eager hands. Cheered my pulsating flesh when it forgot all but itself.

But it was not enough. I wanted it and Tad both. Together. Rings on our fingers. Promises made. Till death do us part. No flower child I, that's for certain, though I'd pretended well enough to get by in New York.

Upstairs, right after Tad's call, I took my leather weekend satchel from the top shelf in my bedroom closet and lay it unzipped by the balcony doors. I opened the delicates drawer of my dresser and lifted out a lilac lace bikini-and-camisole set. Then, from the drawer beneath, white gym shorts and a gray tee-shirt that read "NYU" in purple. I would pack them both. I'd have to discover the appropriate one to wear come Saturday night. It was time to phone Earl Sharp. But not before I retrieved my neglected diaphragm from the armoire in the bathroom, packed it, and checked to see if I had razors and Pond's cold cream for my legs. Come Saturday morning I'd shave all the way up. Under my arms, too. Just in case.

Chapter Twelve

Priests

"They'll be here at seven," Mamma said, exactly one week after Father Carriere got hurt. "Father Higgins has an appointment until six-thirty, and he's got to drive now that Father Carriere has had his keys taken away."

Denny's death had taken a significant toll on Father Carriere. The first Thursday after the funeral, the elderly priest had been puttering around his black Cadillac sedan, which Denny had routinely looked after. Evidently, Father had been washing it in the long drive that led to the rectory's carport. When he reached onto the roof with the king-sized orange sponge Denny had favored, he slipped on the sudsy water that had dripped onto the pavement, fell down, and broke his right wrist trying to break the fall. Father Higgins didn't find him until after ten when Father Carriere failed to appear in the den where the duo met nightly for a nightcap of single-malt Scotch. Daddy had set the wrist and found the old priest otherwise okay. But his forgetfulness and the arthritis that pained his knees, along with his limited ability to manage the altar steps, let alone the stairs to his bedroom, finally guaranteed his removal as pastor of St. Marguerite's. Tonight's supper was to be a private farewell, "as festive as we can make it, Orla," Mamma had said. "Archbishop Hannan is sending him away from us, to the Ursuline orphanage in New Orleans, I'm pretty sure."

I wasn't looking forward to a funereal dinner with two men of the cloth, that's for certain. But Father Higgins surprised me. His shag hairstyle was only the start. He was a Peace Corps alum, having served in Madagascar. "I do a great hissing cockroach imitation," he said, brushing his blondish locks from his eyes, "though I have been told to avoid doing so except during visits to elementary-school science classes." He had driven a cab in Chicago during his college years there. "Great city, if I do say so. Although the '68 Democratic National Convention was no picnic." And he deferred to Father Carriere, even when the older priest repeated a story four times during supper.

We were already partway through our raspberry soufflés when Father Carriere looked up from his confection and said, "Tad Charbonneau called today."

I stopped eating, held Grandmother Castleberry's silver dessert spoon midair instead.

"We've been missing Tad around here," Daddy said. He winked at me and I blushed. "I enjoyed, or more aptly endured, several sets of tennis with him at The Links last month. He taught me some humility, for sure." Daddy smiled at Father Carriere. "Or maybe it was simply humiliation."

Father Carriere smiled.

"He's preparing you for old age, Prout. A tough lesson. A tough lesson indeed."

Daddy nodded in agreement.

"Yes, sir, that seems to be an accurate assessment, and I am sincerely sorry that you are gaining a growing expertise in that arena. I will do my best to mitigate your travails."

He raised his almost-empty wine glass to the priest.

"I know you will, Prout," the old priest said. "At least I've got Archbishop Hannan's promise that you can continue to treat me from afar."

"A pleasure to be at your service, Father," Daddy said. "Plus, when I come down to the city to visit you, we can take a spin at the Carousel Bar in the Monteleone."

Father Higgins piped up.

"Don't forget to invite your protégé, Father."

Father Carriere didn't appear to register Father Higgins' comment. Instead, he put down his spoon and mistook his napkin for the handkerchief in his shirt pocket. No one corrected him.

I tried to be blasé, but was bursting to know what Tad's phone call had been about. Just before I asked, though, Father Higgins saved me the trouble.

"Well, what did Tad have to say, Father Carriere?" he asked, returning the conversation to its original topic.

Father Carriere started to put his napkin in his pocket, then saw the handkerchief there.

"Oh, Minerva, I am so sorry," he said, placing both napkin and handkerchief on the table.

"No worries, Father," Mamma smiled. "Why, just yesterday, I dropped a yellow facecloth into the laundry meant for Prout's white medical jackets. Clorox turned the face cloth into a pattern not meant to be."

The priest smiled back at Mamma.

"Thank you for your kindness, Minerva."

He patted the handkerchief and the napkin until his good hand rested on them, unmoving. I had not noticed the age spots on his hand before.

Then he looked over at Father Higgins, who mouthed, "Tad's phone call."

"Oh, yes, thank you, John. Tad told me he's been assigned to represent a Vietnamese child, a girl, if I remember correctly, who's landed in New Orleans and needs a foster parent or an adoptive family."

The priest paused, unable to find the words to continue.

Father Higgins interjected, pacing his mouthfuls of soufflé between his sentences.

"Is she an orphan, or only here without a parent?" he asked.

He scooped another spoonful of soufflé into his mouth and pushed his hair away from his eyes.

"Oh, right, John, we talked about that earlier. I had forgotten." Father Carriere continued. "I'm not sure if she's an orphan or not. Some of the children are not, I understand."

"Oh, no?" Father Higgins kept the conversation moving in time to his dessert spoon.

"Archbishop Hannan told me that some of the children have Vietnamese mothers who stayed behind in Saigon. Brave women they must be, indeed, to have put their children onto the planes during the airlifts, hoping to eventually get them into the States." The priest paused, looked like he was gathering all his resources to say something important. "Lifting them to life, even if that meant losing them to themselves." He fingered his soufflé dish. "Now that's faith. Remarkable faith." His eyes blinked and blinked. He crossed himself awkwardly.

Mamma patted her mouth with her own monogrammed napkin.

"Can you imagine?" She looked across at me. "Turning your children over to strangers like that?"

Again, Father Carriere furrowed his brow and frowned. I saw now that this was how he looked when searching for words. His frustration was palpable, marked by his drumming on the table.

"Are you talking about the mixed-race children, Father?" Father Higgins asked.

The younger priest nodded in response to Mamma's offer of a second helping of the soufflé.

"Yes, that's it." Father Carriere found his words again. "The children of American GI fathers. Nobody wants them in Vietnam. Half-breeds."

"Where are the children living now?" I asked.

I left my own dessert to walk around the table, pouring second cups of coffee from Grandmother Castleberry's silver service.

"At one of the Ursuline properties," Father Higgins said. "Up in the Garden District. They've converted one of the old convents into a temporary orphanage. That's where Father Carriere will live, too—right, Father?"

"Evidently I'm to act as a surrogate grandfather," the older priest said. "Archbishop Hannan tells me a number of the children haven't seen men other than soldiers for a very long time. He says they're understandably wary of young men." The older priest coughed and drank from his water glass. "They've watched young men butcher their families. They've seen too much."

Mamma smoothed the front of her dress.

"They're lucky to have you, then" she said. "They'll soon love you as if you actually *were* their grandfather."

"I certainly look and feel like one," said Father Carriere.

He stroked his chin, then pulled on his left earlobe.

I put the coffee service on the wheeled dessert cart and returned to my chair.

"What's Tad's job?" I asked. Truth be told, I was not conversing to be hospitable. I was just plain nosy. I wanted to know what Tad would be doing and where I could find him if I wanted to.

Now Father Higgins looked to the older priest for an answer.

Father Carriere was sure this time. "To find the little girl, and the other children, foster families or, in some cases, adoptive families. He'll be working out of his office, I imagine, with visits to the children and their social workers from time to time."

"Oh," I said. "There must be quite a bit of red tape involved."

"No doubt," Daddy said. "I can't imagine their papers are in good condition, if they even exist any longer after all the bombings and the takeover of the American Embassy."

Father Carriere opened his mouth to say something. But, instead, his jaw clamped shut. He lifted and rested his casted right arm on the mahogany table. His face contorted and his eyes twitched with effort, until, in a burst of frustration, he banged the table with his left hand.

"Tad wanted me to tell you something, Orla, but I can't remember what it was."

I got up, went over to pick up the coffee again, and stopped by his chair to pour him a third cup. I returned the pitcher to the tea wagon, then came back to his chair and knelt beside him.

"Don't worry," I said. "I'll be seeing Tad on Saturday. He can tell me then."

The older priest coughed again, covering his mouth with his good hand.

"I'm lucky I remember my own name," he said, and forced a smile.

Mamma came to the rescue.

"You know what I remember, Father?"

Father Carriere looked across the long dining room table and smiled at Mamma.

"What's that, Minerva?" he asked.

"I remember you baptizing Orla. And how when you poured the water on her forehead she screamed loudly enough for even hard-of-hearing Mrs. Fontaine to ask who was torturing a baby inside the church while she strolled by outside with her poodle."

We all laughed but for Daddy, who stood and took five cordial glasses out from the breakfront. Of course, he hadn't been at the christening. He'd let Mamma pretend I was Sean Gleason's baby. He seemed upset now. I looked down at my half-eaten soufflé and frowned. Truth be told, part of me was glad he was upset. He'd left us! Now he poured crème de menthe into his mother's glasses, a green rain of sweet liquor. Mamma stood to take each glass from him to pass around, whispering "Sorry" in his ear as she did. I wondered why she was the one apologizing. Father Higgins stood, as did I to follow his lead, and, raising his glass, said, "To our pastor and friend, who will love the orphans and be loved in return. May they thrive in his goodness just as we have and do here in St. Suplice. And may God have mercy on the lot of us as we enter into futures we can't yet fathom from pasts we have yet to fully understand."

"To Father Carriere," Daddy said, and we all drank.

The older priest bowed his head and wiped his eyes with his napkin.

Little did I know then how prescient Father Higgins' words were. Mercy, indeed.

Chapter Thirteen
Domestic Arrangements

"Orla!"

Tad opened the screen door trimmed in paint that told of pines rather than palms. He reached out his arms and rested his chin atop my head the way he had—you already know but I love telling—since he'd shot up taller than me in eighth grade. I slipped out from under him, my own customary move, and looked up at his welcoming face. A bit of shaving cream lingered below his left ear. I let drop my bag, then reached up and rubbed the white meringue away. He took my hand and kissed it. And, no, I will not stop myself from mentioning again the courtly way he has.

He grinned.

"I knew I'd need you to make me and the place completely presentable."

"It's gorgeous, Tad. Congratulations. I love the pine and pistachio combination outside."

He grinned again.

"Well, her married name may be Charbonneau, but you know how my mother does love her Irish roots. So green the house shall be. Mother calls it *Siobhan's Cottage* after her own mother. It appears Mamma saved her little inheritance from Granny to help me have this place."

"Nice," I said, and patted the green door as if I were patting Granny's arm itself. I didn't know her, though my own mamma had told me that Tad's grandmother had wheeled him in a pram for the three months she visited after his birth. She never came back to the States, having broken her hip soon after her return to Dublin. By the time I was born a year after Tad, Mrs. Charbonneau had begun making yearly visits to her mother. Tad went with her twice. Then, just after he graduated Loyola and before he started studying law at Tulane, he, his mamma, and his daddy traveled to Ireland to bury her. His mamma wore Granny Siobhan's green plaid cape to Midnight Mass every Christmas Eve no matter the temperature.

"Mother is having a little brass plaque made. I'll place it under the porch light, I think."

"Yes, right there." I pointed to the right of the door just under a wrought-iron outdoor sconce.

Tad noted where my forefinger lingered.

"Come, come into my abode," he motioned. "Thanks to both my parents' generosity, not to mention my father's carpentry skills, I think you'll find some order and comfort to the place."

The first room was navy blue, tamed a bit by teak plantation shutters closed against the sun. I stepped onto the vivid Oriental rug his mother had let him take from the guest room in St. Suplice. I especially loved the persimmon diamonds popping from it. The place smelled of fresh paint and eucalyptus. A third scent, too—cool, not floral—that I didn't recognize. Under the street-facing windows, a sleek black leather couch with large coffee-linen pillows tilted by each armrest. An armoire-sized fish tank with water swirling, without fish yet, on the far wall. A whirring white ceiling fan above.

"Wow, Tad, beautiful."

He stood with his back to the screen door.

"Go ahead, have at it." He opened his arms as if he were parting the Red Sea. "Peruse the scene."

I turned to him and smiled.

"You know I will, down to the last detail."

While he lit the three brass floor lamps in the front room, one either side of the couch and the third next to his desk, I walked to the corridor (the shotgun's path, as it were), that ran the left side of the three-room, one-bath house. It was painted a glossy magenta with equally glossy, pristine white trim. A sisal rug the color of sand and bordered in black trim ran the length of it. Black and white photographs of Grand Isle beaches and large sea birds formed two carefully measured lines from the front room to the kitchen. Just as I made to follow the hallway to the kitchen, Tad motioned me back.

"I've made this room my office-cum-guest-room," he said. He pointed to his Grandfather Charbonneau's desk, then at the couch. "It converts to a bed."

He rolled up the curved wood that housed the desktop to expose the work area that held his diagonally arranged leather appointment book, his taupe monogrammed notecards and envelopes, and his ever-present fountain pen and ink pot. A small black-and-white photograph of his mother and father in their wedding garb was framed in brass and rested beside the inkwell. On the other side of the desktop, closer to the appointment book, was a second photo, this one in color, taken recently, of Tad and another, older man, someone I didn't recognize, smoking cigars and dressed in tuxedos. It looked like they were at a lawn party of some sort. There was a green-and-white striped tent behind them and they squinted against the sun, smiling.

"Who's he?" I asked.

Tad came over to the desk, picked up the photograph, and handed it to me.

"That's Luke. You know, 'Luke of the beautiful shoes,' as you call him."

Involuntarily, I looked down. Tad was wearing the fine leather loafers.

"You'll meet him at Maspero's this evening at eight. He's hanging paintings for one of his clients all afternoon."

"I see."

I handed him the photograph and he placed it perfectly where it had been when he picked it up, rearranging it twice so that it balanced exactly with his parents' framed picture.

"He must be impor–," I began, but Tad interrupted, "Look," and pointed above the desk before I could finish my sentence. "See, Orla, you have a gallery here. May it be the first of many others featuring you in this city." He pointed to the photograph of him and Luke. "Luke can help with the introductions. He deals with a number of the galleries in town. Makes them lots of money. Maybe he can make you some money, too."

He grinned.

"Thanks, my friend. If that happens, be assured I will entrust all my financial dealings to you both."

I had to smile. Of course I had spotted my paintings as soon as I walked in, but hadn't wanted to appear proud. Tad was kind to have hung them. I loved him for it.

"This is really sweet of you, Tad," I said, and again he kissed my hand.

There were four of my Civil Rights miniatures grouped together to form a square, left of a larger painting of nearby St. Louis Cathedral. The first, Earl Sharp's burned-down shack still smoldering, the second, a wimpled Ursuline sister in her habit carrying a placard that said, "We're all God's children." The third, Reverend Makepeace's little boy and Tad as I recalled them at Grandmother Castleberry's first integrated Easter-egg hunt, and the last, a self-portrait with me crying down at the shards and ash that had been my paintings after our neighbors-and-Klansmen had set them afire at the 1962 St. Marguerite's Church Fair.

"I'm very touched, Tad," I said, and put an arm around his waist.

"Did I arrange them to your liking?"

"Yes."

"Good."

"Though your guests may be disturbed by their subject matter," I said.

He looked at the paintings and thought for a moment.

"I suppose," he said, removing my arm from his waist and taking my hand in his instead. "If that's the case, then they'll have to avert their eyes and turn instead to the bar masquerading as a trunk here."

We walked to the center of the room and he opened the lid of a refinished trunk which had been reconfigured inside with a built-in wine rack and glasses enough for a party.

"Dad's idea," he winked, and lifted up the lid.

"'Son,' Dad told me"—Here he mimicked his father's *basso profundo*—'our profession often requires spiritual assistance.'"

"Well, heads up to Dad," I said.

"We'll have Bloody Marys with lunch," he said. "I've got shrimp and deviled eggs in the fridge. Blood orange salad, too."

"Sounds luscious."

"Come." He wiggled my hand, and we moved away from the bar-trunk and to the hallway again.

"Okay, now the rest."

The second room, his bedroom, was aubergine, "A color that reminds me of moon-infused summer nights in St. Suplice," he said. There was not even the hint of irony in his voice. He made St. Suplice sound as intriguing as a village in Provence or a villa's vista in Tuscany. Then, conspiratorially, he said, "You know, the kind of nights when we used to sneak out to smoke over in the schoolyard."

I giggled, recalling how Denny threw up after smoking two cigars he had filched from his father. Mr. Cowles was never the wiser, thinking instead that his mutt of a dog, Pilot, had made short work of them. Good thing, too, because he would have beat Denny black-and-blue for sure had he realized otherwise.

A massive mahogany sleigh bed, draped in the same white Portuguese cotton Grandmother Castleberry had always favored for her own bed, commanded the space, even blocking the bottom half of the windows, which were covered completely by soft ivory Roman shades. A line of teak shelving arranged high enough for the easy reach of Tad's raised arms framed three walls, and the same woven straw baskets repeated themselves, each labeled, "shirts," "socks," "shorts," etc., in a calligraphied hand of black ink. Again, a white fan whirred on the ceiling.

"The closet is rather small," Tad said, pulling aside a beige linen curtain and latching it on a filigreed wall nail. "Dad removed the door, which when open made moving around the bed difficult. He put in two poles, one very high,"—and here he pointed—"one lower. Now I can hang my suits and sport coats properly."

I spotted two identical towel robes hanging side by side on hooks that nearly reached the closet's high ceiling. They fell just short of the taller of the horizontal poles. They looked as if they had come from the Monteleone or some other high-end hotel, white and fluffy, with cuffed sleeves. Even Tad would need a step stool to reach them. Sure enough, a folding metal step stool leaned against the closet's double-tiered shoe rack. Was one of the robes meant for me?

Two lengths of shelves, painted in the same white trim as the window frames, had been affixed to the wall either side of the bed. Each held a brass reading lamp with an adjustable neck. On the nearer shelf rested a hardcover edition of Gore Vidal's *Julian* and Tad's pocket watch, on the other a thick candle with the same scent I hadn't recognized in the front room and a folder marked "Clippings" in Tad's script.

"What's that fragrance, Tad?" I asked, pointing to the candle.

"Oh, does it bother you?" he asked. "I can put it away."

"No, no, I like it. I just don't recognize it, and I can usually tell."

He walked around the foot of the bed and up the other side to the shelf, then brought the candle to me. He turned it upside down to read the label underneath.

"Sea grass, orange flower, and fig."

He righted it, then handed it to me.

"Nice," I said, breathing in deeply to remember. "Where did you get it?"

He paused and, if my eyes didn't betray me, he blushed.

"We use them in the restrooms at the firm. One of our regular clients supplies us."

"Oh," I said. "Just wondering.

"I'll get you some if you like."

"Thanks. They'd be great in Mamma's salon. Not sickeningly sweet."

I handed him back the candle and he returned it to its place on the shelf, lining up the file folder parallel to the bed.

"And last, the kitchen," he said. "Are you bored yet?"

"Of course not," I answered. "I want to see everything. You know how nosy I am."

"I do indeed," he snickered. Then he laughed out loud. "Remember when we searched for the stash of girlie magazines in Mr. Crowther's garage?"

I thought hard and shook my head no. Then I recalled Lizzy Crowther's getting hurt when we did.

"Actually, I'd forgotten that," I said.

He stopped under the basket marked "tee shirts."

"You said Lizzy's daddy had told her she was never to go into his tool shed because he was worried she would hurt herself among the saws and hatchets and such. I recall that, Orla."

"So she didn't, not that I know of, anyway, at least not until I corrupted her."

Lizzy had cut her toe on a rickety peach crate full of old newspapers the moment we had walked into the shed.

"So she did get hurt after all."

"Yes, she did," Tad said. "And you spit on her cut toe and rubbed the spit with your finger, mixing it with the little stream of blood. You told her spit was as good as alcohol."

"Did I?"

"Yes, and I admired your creative impulse in the moment."

"Must have been—creative, that is. The funny thing is that Lizzy believed me."

"You spoke with authority, my dear Orla. Authority."

"I guess."

"What made you decide to go in there, anyway?"

Tad moved to the doorway of his bedroom and waited.

"I had heard Mr. Crowther telling Mr. LeBrun the barber that Miss January was a looker when I delivered Girl Scout cookies to the barbershop. Even though Mr. LeBrun stopped cutting Mr. Crowther's hair the moment I showed up and tried to hide the *Playboy* under a pile of newspapers, I saw the cover and the naked model. Besides, I'd seen girlie magazines before. Janitor Booth kept them in the bomb shelter at school. Every time any of us girls was sent to deliver him a note about the toilet overflowing or mice in the lunchroom, he'd be sitting on his broken-down chair turning the magazine this way and that for a better view. Didn't even get flustered when we walked in."

Tad looked at me as if we had just met.

"Why didn't I know that?"

I shrugged my shoulders.

"Teachers never sent boys to deliver messages. Only to pick up the milk crates or drag the trash out after finger painting or wood shop. And, besides, I didn't have enough confidence to talk with you about naked women then."

"You obviously do now."

Here it was. Finally. My cue.

"I do," I said, and sat down on the big bed. I crossed my legs and leaned back on my hands, letting my breasts take center stage. "Enough confidence to *be* a naked woman with you, too."

Tad blushed. This time I was sure of it. But he didn't move over me or hug me or even laugh. He just sat down next to me and folded his hands on his lap. He might have been praying. He was as still as I was disappointed.

Honestly, I would have flung off my clothes in the instant had he been eager for me to. But instead I waited unmoving to see what he would say or do. Finally, staring straight ahead as if something on the wall under the "socks" basket had his complete attention, he said only, "Come to think of it, you're right. I mean about the teachers sending only girls on messages. A cultural phenomenon, I suppose."

It was as if he were talking to himself, as if he were realizing something for the first time.

"I guess," I said. "But you and Katie Cowles came into the shed with me. You, me, Katie, and Lizzy. And we never got found out."

I put my left hand on his arm. He still didn't move.

"No, we never did," he said. "No one ever knew."

He finally looked at me, smiled a melancholy smile, and took my hand in his. He rubbed the top of my finger nails one by one, the way he might have taught a treasured child to count to five. "We never got found out."

But he didn't say it like he was recalling something happy from childhood. No, he said it as though he were speaking about something else. Something that made him sad.

He stood up suddenly and turned away from the bed.

"You okay?" I asked, and stood up myself.

He rested his chin on my head again. He talked above me so that his chin moved up and down on my skull.

"I'm really glad that you're here. I want you always to come here, Orla. Do you understand me?"

He stroked my hair. His heart kept time against my face. The two of us this close felt like peace to me. Refuge. Home. Where I wanted to be.

"I need you always to visit here, Orla. What I mean is, come wherever I am."

I slipped my head from under his chin and looked up at him. He wasn't proclaiming undying love, but a need that sounded like desperation. He needed my help, I could see that. His eyes were teary and I cocked my head in a silent question.

A garbage truck rumbled by. Police sirens sounded in the distance. And the cathedral bells tolled a somber measure. But Tad, unusually silent, simply put his forefinger to his lips and shook his head no.

"Okay, for now, if you don't want to talk, but you need to tell me what's troubling you." I stroked his arm. He let me. "Promise?"

He didn't answer, but went from straw box to straw box, lining them up evenly on the shelf. Whatever was bothering him was off the table for now. That much I understood. So I went back to Lizzy and our childhood.

"Well, maybe the girlie magazines were how Lizzy got her sexual education," I said. Jesus, I sounded so perky I might have been a Miss America contestant telling the judges I wanted to work for world peace. "Maybe that's why she and Denny had a good long romantic run before the Crowthers had to move and everything turned bad for the Cowleses."

"Could be," Tad said. "It very well could be."

His voice sounded weary, as if it didn't have the strength to locate the right words for what he was feeling.

"Come on," I said, grabbing his hand, becoming the hostess rather than remaining a guest, trying to jolt him into a more upbeat mood. "You promised to show me the kitchen. Besides, I'm getting hungry. Breakfast was hours ago."

I leaned my backside against the foot-end of the sleigh bed so he could precede me out into the corridor. The phone rang, two shrill bursts at a time, and, dropping my hand, he hurried to the kitchen to answer it. I started to follow him, but decided not to. Best give him some privacy. After the fourth double ring, he picked up the receiver. I couldn't hear his words, but only his pleasant, now-normal tone. I walked to the shelf with the folder to once again inhale the thick candle's fragrance. I found it intoxicating and calming, both. More crisp than floral. But even before I reached the head board's panoply of plumped and scalloped matelasse pillows, pillows upon which I still hoped to lay my head beside Tad's, I spied the pair of hotel slippers beneath the shelf where the candle and the folder rested. They were soft, black, and lined in red, each topped with a round medallion, also red, around which scrolled "Pensione Accademia, Venezia," in golden script. And I knew the way I know paint that they belonged to Luke.

My heart already pounding, I lifted the cover of the folder that I knew must be a Pandora's box. Inside were neatly stapled newspaper clippings dated June 25, 1973, that read, *"Yesterday's UpStairs Lounge Inferno," "Arson Cause of UpStairs Lounge Holocaust," "Fire Combusts Homosexual Hangout."* A sticky note had been placed next to a photograph of a man's grotesquely charred body pressed against a window's flame-melted metal bars. In a hand different from Tad's was written "My friend, Rev. Bill Larson."

Tad's voice still carried from the kitchen as if everything were normal, while I fled to the bathroom, slammed the narrow wooden door behind me, knelt, and retched over the toilet. My chest reverberated, as if from a staggering punch that made it hard to breathe. My brain dueled between fury and love. Gone. My future gone, just like that. I had lost him, Tad, the only man I ever thought belonged entirely to me.

Desolate, I turned around and lowered myself onto the bathroom floor. I leaned back against the commode and sighed. My eyes leaked and my legs stretched out in front of me, as bare and as long as the lonely life I foresaw ahead.

Everyone I have ever loved and loved me back has lied to me. Mamma, Daddy Prout, Grandmother Castleberry, and now Tad. Liars all. Loving and lying. Lying and loving. I sighed again. Listened to Tad's voice from the kitchen. I wanted to pummel him. To beg him. To have him tell a truth different from the one I finally understood.

"Good-bye, then," Tad said, the other side of the door, as I forced myself to stand. "We'll see you tonight." Then, after a long pause, "Me, too."

He was talking to Luke. Luke who should have been me.

All of a sudden I was hiccoughing nonstop. I spied a bottle of Listerine on a shelf to my left. I grabbed it, unscrewed its cap, and must have spilled as much of the orangey liquid as I gargled with. Then I decided to drink two caps full. An antiseptic cocktail. It seared my throat. Burned it raw. Like after the surgeon down in Convent had sliced out my tonsils when I was six. When the promise of unlimited ice cream had made the operation sound like a good idea. But there'd be no ice cream now. Only burn.

"Orla," Tad called, in the same glad way as he used to when he clomped up the steps to our little cottage every summer morning. "That was Luke, confirming our dinner plans tonight. I thought we could have those Bloody Marys now. What do you say?"

Words stuck in my stinging throat. I coughed to let him know I was still alive. My fingers moved themselves before the mirror above the bathroom sink in a childhood game. *Here's the church, here's the steeple, open the door, and here are the people.*

Surprise! But how, how could I have missed it? How could I have not known?

Stupid, stupid, stupid. My own blindness. No artist's powers of observation at work here.

"You okay in there?"

Tad was just the other side of the door. I felt his hand press against the wood.

I pretend-coughed again.

"Be right out," I heard my voice squeak. I had become a mouse in a trap.

What to do? What to say? He'd known I would figure it out. He wanted me to. But he couldn't or wouldn't tell me himself. He had simply, carefully, set the stage. Bought my ticket, and this was the show. What did he suppose I would do, applaud?

I looked at myself in the mirror. Alone with my sorry reflection. I'd have to come out sometime. Lord knows why I cared how I looked now, but I pinched my cheeks anyway, shook my head to rearrange my hair, and smoothed the frothy sun dress I'd picked for the way it cupped my breasts. Breasts Tad had been meant to hold and suckle. To caress and cherish. To gaze at in awe while I nursed the exceptional babies we'd make together.

"Ready," I decided to say.

He moved away from the door, his steps taking him to the kitchen once more. The refrigerator door opened and closed. Dishes landed gently on a table top. A chair scraped the floor.

But I wasn't ready. Not for this. Certainly not for this.

Chapter Fourteen
Face to Face

I opened the door and walked to the kitchen doorway as if leading a funeral cortège. In my mind I stood next to Mrs. Kennedy. We walked ahead of the other mourners, she wearing her signature pillbox hat. Only this one was ebony with an attached black mourning veil that covered her face. Her young President was dead. Shot down right next to her. It was rumored he had cheated on her, too, perhaps many times. But he had married *her*. *She* had carried his children. And his would always be her name, even after she had wed and buried Onassis. She and he, the lovely boy-President, etched forever in history. Rescued from time. Transcendent. Idealized.

> *Bold Lover, never, never canst thou kiss,*
> *Though winning near the goal—yet, do not grieve;*
> *She cannot fade, though thou hast not thy bliss,*
> *For ever wilt thou love, and she be fair!"*

Hogwash. Drivel. None of this mimics Keats. Tad's been fucking Luke Segreti God knows how long while I've been the clueless, hardly-bold lover doomed to an epiphany I never saw coming. No poet's timelessness can cosset me. No, siree, even as I seethe, the cathedral bells strike one. One. Like me, not two.

Tad turned away from the sink and stood by one of the six fire-engine-red bistro chairs, motioning for me to take a seat. When he saw my face he stopped short, rushed around the chair, and said, "Orla?"

It was a question.

I froze in place. Neither the ninety-plus degree heat nor the sun streaming through white cottage curtains could warm me.

"When were you planning to tell me?"

My eyes locked on his. My words icicles, pointed, sharp, transparent. I clenched my fists either side of me.

"Why didn't you tell me?"

A scream rose in my throat.

He looked down at me, the expression on his face the very meaning of sorrow. I bit my bottom lip to keep the scream in.

He spoke in a whisper that sounded like choking.

"I was afraid. Orla. Forgive me." He slumped. "I'm still very afraid."

I stepped away from him, drew back my right hand, reached up, and swung. I slapped and slapped his face. I wanted to hurt him. I wanted him to scream my scream. He let me abuse him, tears streaming down his face the whole time. After a while, I stopped hitting. I watched red splotches blossom on his cheeks. He wiped his eyes with his beautiful long fingers. He said, "I'm so sorry I'm not able to be who you want me to be. I'm so very sorry, Orla."

His voice dropped, a sandbag on a flooding levee.

I softened even as I tried not to.

"I'm sorry, too," I said. My voice crackled, its iciness melting in spite of itself. "I'm sorrier than I've ever been."

Hurt. Every part of me hurt.

We stood face to face, his feet on the black-and-white-tiled kitchen floor, mine on the sisal hallway rug. The doorway framed the distance between us, its threshold a canyon of decision.

Tad spoke in a tremulous voice.

"You've every right to hate me. I should have told you years ago. I've been this way since before I could speak it. But the prospect of losing you..." He took a breath to try and compose himself. "...is far worse than always having to hide who I am. Believe me, Orla, it is far worse."

My body swayed and he kept me from falling.

I reached up and across the doorway to rub his cheek with my right hand. He pressed it there and stroked it. His clean-shaven skin was wet.

"I cannot imagine a life without your friendship, Orla. I simply cannot imagine it."

A sob escaped me. The truest sound my body ever made.

There it was, friendship or nothing, not the fairy-tale partnership I had imagined. Body and soul. Hearts and minds.

A silence hung like a pendulum poised to swing. I felt clammy and my mind rushed. Telegraphed itself in a seeming void. Did I want to live without him? Tap tap. Could I include his secret Segreti, too? Tap tap. Who the hell knew? Was the guy a keeper or some fly-by-night Adonis? Tap tap again. Would Segreti want me intruding into the smiling photograph-of-two? Tap. What I did know even as my sandaled feet rocked back and forth on the door's threshold was that ditching Tad meant losing the most loyal witness to my own life story. Meant giving up shared remembrance. Meant saying goodbye to the only person I could always call on come good or come ill. Tap tap tap. It would be difficult, though, to accept the facts abhorrent to me. Tap. I'd have to be generous. Open. Tap tap tap. I didn't know if I could or even wanted to be. Tap. It was one thing playing surrogate niece to two old homos in Manhattan and quite another to accept a stranger who had stolen the one true love of my life. Who keeps his slippers by his bed, for God's sake. It isn't even the sex, if you can believe that. Mechanics, that. Fluids and functions, huff and puff. Hug. Kiss. Embrace. Kaboom! No, it's the domesticity, the dailiness, his caring gestures, stupid jokes. His knowing light cream rather than milk, grilled over fried, chocolate and hazelnut always, without asking. And never sweet wine. It's the certainty that's taken my breath away. I've been as sure of him as dawn and dusk, death and taxes. Breathing. Beauty. I have to say it. God.

I pushed him away from me, took a deep breath and stepped through the doorway, the threshold denting the rubber arches of my sandals. I knew what I had to do. I hated what I was going to do.

"Much as I want to right now, Tad, and, believe me, I do want to, I could never hate you." I spoke loudly, as if testifying to a judge. "It's impossible."

A car horn stuck, tires squealed, and a cat screeched outside.

"Though you're really messing with me right now. You're really hurting me, Tad."

I couldn't go on. My voice broke and I cried unrestrainedly. When snot dripped from my nose, I ran my upturned palm under my nostrils like a child without a handkerchief. Like a child bereft with no recourse but wailing resignation.

Tad knelt to me, watched, listened, waited. When I had been reduced to sniffling, he reached into the left pocket of his bermudas and handed me a handkerchief.

I accepted it as if it were a priceless artifact on loan from a touted museum. I cradled it in my hands, regarded its raised and scrolled navy monogram, its soft cotton comfort, its perfectly folded squareness, its white-laundered purity. In short, its elegant Tad-ness. The very opposite of the qualities its use guaranteed. I would soil it. I shook it out, blew hard into it, stared at the mucous-y detritus that oozed from inside me, then scrunched the handkerchief up and threw it back at him.

"All yours," I said, trying to smirk. But I couldn't. At least not yet.

He held the messy thing, that was only a thing now, aloft in mock dismay. Then, as if it had always been nothing more than a useless piece of cloth, he let it fall to the kitchen floor.

Still kneeling, he wrapped his arms around me. It was I who could rest my chin on top of his head now.

"Thank you, Orla," he said. "Thank you."

He was crying. Not with grief, though, now.

I didn't want to relax into his tanned arms enfolding me. I didn't want to register the way his heart thumped in time with mine against my breasts. I didn't want to breathe the citrus scent I knew would not now linger on my flesh when waking next to him. But I did. I did.

Then, in an instant, propelled by a force much bigger than myself, a force that told me there was no time to waste, I barked.

"Get up," I said. I had become a drill sergeant.

I spoke as if I were Grandmother Castleberry. As if, like her, I had not only decided to accept but to actually create a life that was the very opposite of the one I had anticipated. Imperious. That's what I had to be.

"Get a grip," I told him, as much as I told myself. "Right now."

And we did. At least we tried to.

Framed by the doorway, then, listening to the seconds tockticktock on the kitchen clock hung on the far wall, Tad and I stood up. Together and apart in irrefutable time, we gripped each other's hands, our fingers inextricably entwined.

141

Chapter Fifteen
Re-Education

I jolted awake when a man passed by outside yelling, "Liar! Liar!" My wristwatch read six-thirty. I was lying barefoot on the front-room couch with both of the coffee linen pillows behind me. My dress spread out like a fan over my legs. Tad, head back, stretched out so that his loafers touched the bar-trunk, snored rhythmically. His hands still rested on my bare ankles. He had motioned for me to rest my legs on his lap, and I had wondered then if this was as physically intimate as we would ever be. We'd each downed three stiff Bloody Marys. On top of the coffee table the deviled eggs sat uneaten. They had gone from yellow and white to a swampy green. The shrimp floated in a pool of used-to-be-ice. I had riddled Tad with questions. "Machine-gun Orla" he had called me. Still, he had answered. I'll give him that. And he hadn't flinched at any of my queries. It was my education, my passageway into the hidden life of Tad Charbonneau, the best friend I never even knew.

"When did you know you liked boys?"

"Always. When Denny and the other guys wanted to look up all your little-girl dresses, I wanted to pull their pants down." I felt myself blanch. "Frankly, I think Denny suspected from fourth grade on. In fact, I'm certain he knew. Remember how he gave me a hard time in the car on the way to Katie's wedding reception? I think he was just trying to verify what he had always thought. After all, I never went off with him and the other guys to peek into the LaFrance house. Mrs. LaFrance vacuumed in the nude every Saturday morning, they told me."

I laughed. "Oh, I hadn't heard," I said.

"Yes," Tad said. "The guys—Denny, Bobby McAlister, Jordan Cordair, and Greg Desaulniers—always snuck over there right after whatever season's practice it was. They would crawl behind the hydrangea bushes and peek into the living room windows as soon as they heard the vacuum start. "'Eleven o'clock,' Denny used to say. 'Time to vacuum,' and the boys would crack up laughing. I always told them I had to pick up Mother's books at the library. 'You don't know what you're missing, Tad,' Denny would tell me. Then he'd wiggle his ass and lift up pretend breasts. Little did he know I was enjoying the show in front of me."

Tad rubbed the tops of my feet.

"He needed my friendship then, though. When his father was home, I was the only boy who would dare go into the house. Granted, I stayed in the kitchen, as close to the screen door as I could. But Mr. Cowles left me alone because he knew my father wouldn't tolerate any of his shenanigans."

Here Tad tapped his fingers on my ankles. "Denny wouldn't have stood for my aberration, shall I say—now, that's for certain. It would have disqualified me for Vietnam if law school already hadn't. At least if the military had discovered my secret."

"How did you keep your secret?"

"I've cultivated a scholarly behavior, at least I think I have, instead of an effeminate one. Do you think so?"

"Obviously," I said, and wiggled my toes. "That's how I've always misread you, anyway."

Tad pursed his lips and nodded his head to some unasked question inside his brain, I imagined. "But you know who read me exactly right, who always knew, Orla?

"Who?" I asked. Tad played my ankles like a piano.

"Father Carriere." He shook his head again.

"What makes you think that?" I asked.

"Well," Tad said, shifting his position a bit on the couch, "one afternoon about ten years ago while I was setting up for ten-o'clock Sunday Mass, out of the blue he said, 'We all have burdens that test us, Tad. And I believe you have a heavy one already.' Somehow I knew what he was saying. I know I blushed and was working up a sweat even with the fans whirring. But I didn't say a word in response. In fact I recall simply staring at him. 'I have faith in you, Tad,' he said. 'I believe you can carry your burden. God's grace be upon you.' And he made the sign of the cross on my forehead."

"Jesus," I said. "He really is the best of the grownups, you know? And his mind is being taken away as his punishment."

I stretched my toes. "No good deed goes unpunished, Tad. Rule of Prometheus, I call it. Rule of Prometheus."

"I wonder," Tad said.

"What about your parents? Did they freak out?"

"Mother came right out and asked me after she heard me lie to you on the phone. I said I had to go on a retreat and couldn't make your prom. 'Oscar Wilde was Irish, too,' was what she said, as if she were talking to the air. We had been reading him in English class at Prep. The *Complete Works* was sitting right on the credenza in the front foyer. Then she went outside and took the sheets off the clothesline. She's never breathed a word since." Tad shifted back to his original position on the couch. "The next morning—clearly they had talked about it in their bedroom—Dad got up from the breakfast table and said, 'Be careful, son. Be very careful. In public and in private.' He cleared his throat and said, 'Of course, be assured your mother and I still feel the same about you.' Then he took up his briefcase and walked out the door. I was mortified. Mortified and relieved."

"When did you first have sex with a guy? Have you ever had sex with a woman?"

"Freshman year at Prep with a boy named Hugh. His family moved to San Francisco after Christmas. I moped for about a month. It was easy in a way, you know, Orla, to seek each other out, to find one another. For God's sake, it was an all-boys school. Every day a tease and a torture. Certainly some of the instructors were like me, even some of the Jesuits. Each of us knew." He patted both my ankles with his hands. "Nope, I've never made love to a woman, Orla."

I straightened the pillow behind my back. "Well, at least I've got that," I said. Tad took my hands in his and kissed both of them.

"What about you? Who was your first?"

I felt hot. "Well, though I wish it had been you"—I swatted both his hands—"it was Harry Bentley. We did it in the arched passageway between the school and the convent at Ursuline. It was at the Senior Snow Ball. Just after the Snow King and Queen were crowned and there was a rush to congratulate them. 'Come on,' Harry said, and we ran back of the throne set and into the passageway. The sisters had already left for their cells right after dessert was served. All I can say is it was as quick as the wick on a candle goes out. Quick." Tad laughed. "Okay, back to you. I'm the questioner tonight."

"Ready," he said, and looked at me, waiting.

"How did you and your Secrets meet?"

Tad laughed at that one. "The irony. The very institution that rails, officially at least, against this kind of love brought us together. We met at a Prep reunion. Luke was Class of '48; me, as you know, Class of '68." He scratched his nose. "But I'll let Luke tell you the story, that is if you're still willing to meet him tonight. He does love to spin a yarn."

I ran my hands down my dress, smoothing it. "Yes, I want to meet him, Tad. If only to sate my curiosity. To fuel my jealousy. And, if for nothing else, as Diego, who is, by the way, more than a fuck but less than a love, always says, 'Everything is material, Orla. Everything is a potential work of art.' So thanks, Tad, for providing so much material today. I'm sure my paintbrushes will demonstrate my gratitude."

Tad lifted his eyebrows in mock (I think) dismay. "I will await your interpretation with great anticipation," he said.

"One more question."

"Okay, shoot."

"Does Luke live here?"

Tad sat up straight at that one. "God, no. I couldn't risk it, though he might. He has a place in the Garden District, another in the Adirondacks, and a flat on the Grand Canal. If the firm got wind of us as a dedicated couple, they'd fire me. Look, everyone at the office knows who's straight, who's not, who's having affairs, who isn't. Where to get our drugs if we want them. But there is a code of silence, a strict, unwritten code. You know that folder you opened in the bedroom? Most of the guys incinerated in the UpStairs Lounge fire were never officially ID'd. They didn't, couldn't, carry legitimate identifications. If they had papers on them, they would have certainly been fake. One fellow, a teacher, who eventually died from his burns, actually got fired right in his hospital bed. Even though the Lounge was in the Quarter, Orla, even though we all say 'Laissez les bons temps rouler,' we'd better all act straight come Monday morning. That's just the way it is."

Outside, a car screeched to a stop. I couldn't believe we'd fallen asleep.

"Up." I pushed his legs with both my feet. He stirred. "Shouldn't we get ready?" I asked.

"I'm sorry, I never meant to drift off."

147

"I'm glad we both did," I said. "These revelations have been nothing short of exhausting."

He laughed and stood up. "I'm going to get dressed."

"Me, too." I stood and struck my sexiest pose. "Shall I wear widow's weeds or a third-wheel's hot pants?"

Tad tried to look stern.

"Whichever you prefer, my lady," he said, and disappeared into the bedroom.

I chose a black linen mini with coral beads and matching drop earrings. The earrings would sway with me when I finally got drunk. Alcohol, I decided, would be my date.

Chapter Sixteen
Meeting Luke Segreti

"Finally we meet."

Luke Segreti stood, walked toward us, and put out both hands. He was old enough to be Tad's father, tan enough to seem a beach bum, and charming enough to make me notice the blue glint of his eyes and not hate him at once.

It was five minutes after eight and the Quarter was working itself up to a Saturday evening lather. Tad and I had taken a leisurely walk from his place, and I was glad I had chosen a pair of bronze leather flats to wear on the cobblestones instead of my sexiest heels (which served no purpose here now). Tad was in his standard rugby shirt, this one pale blue, khakis belted in leather that matched his loafers, and, of course, sockless. Maspero's was already crowded. A waiter was removing a "Reserved" card from a table and saying to Luke, "Good to see you again, Mr. Segreti."

149

"To be sure, Peter," Luke replied, as he turned away from us. "We'll start with champagne to celebrate my meeting this very important woman. She's an acclaimed painter, you know."

Luke turned back to me and pointed.

"Pleased to meet you, miss."

I smiled and nodded at waiter Peter, then raised my eyebrows at Luke.

"Are you trying to win me over, Mr. Segreti?" I asked. I was failing at sounding pert.

"*Mr.* Segreti!" Luke responded. "I'm not that old."

I softened a bit.

"Okay, then, 'Luke.'"

"Much better," he said. "And, as to your initial question, yes, of course. I've been wanting to try for months."

I glared at Tad. Luke joined me. Tad crossed his arms against his chest, sentry-like. Then, with what I can only describe as genuine jollity, Luke took both my hands in his. His nails were manicured. Clear lacquer made each one shine.

"Well, you are important, Orla. All Tad does is speak of you. It is enough to make a man jealous."

I twitched some, but Tad, releasing himself from his pose and taking my arm, steadied me.

"I am ready to dine," he said to Luke. "Lunch seems to have evaded us."

"Oh," said Luke, "and why is that?"

It was a casual question, but I felt myself stiffen.

Tad looked at me the way he always did whenever I needed calming down. I looked back, my eyes steadying themselves, their way of confirming I was okay. I'd try, I had told myself while changing into my meeting-the-other-man clothes. I'd try to love Tad the way he needed me to. Damn it, though, I wished I didn't have to.

Luke and Tad shook hands then, as if they were meeting to close a business deal. Broad smiles both, but no eye contact that would reveal anything but good cheer. As for me, Luke kissed me on both cheeks as he and Tad escorted me to my seat.

"I'm just back from Italy," Luke said, I guessed by way of explanation.

He pulled out my chair. They would face each other, and I would sit between them. Their choreography appeared rehearsed. And I admit it was smooth. Clearly, this was not their first dance.

I wasn't yet ready to like Luke, though I could see that he and Tad were easy together, chatting as close friends do, and at the same time making sure that I was taken care of.

No sooner had Peter popped the cork and poured the champagne than food showed up as well. Two waiters who could barely be out of high school carried family-sized trays of pastrami sandwiches, hamburgers oozing with melted cheese and bacon, fries, and breaded shrimp with Tabasco-laced dipping sauce. No courses, just everything piled on at once. An objective correlative if I ever knew one.

"I like a bountiful table," Luke said.

"Which necessitates my running six miles a day," Tad countered.

He smiled broadly at Luke as he spoke.

Luke waved his arms over the food.

"And that is why walks were invented, my dear."

God, "dear."

I swallowed the contents of my glass.

Luke turned to me, saw, and poured me another.

"You must educate Tad, given your experience with the Contessa from Fiesole he has told me about. We Italians, and I consider myself one, if only by ancestry, favor the *passeggiata*, the walk after dinner. It's the only way I can control my weight, even in the States."

"I'm glad we walked here in anticipation, then," Tad said. "One perambulation prepared us for the next one."

He unfolded his napkin, placed it on his lap, and waited. Again, I saw that he and Luke had habituated themselves to a protocol for dining.

Luke commanded the table, taking the serving utensils from each tray and filling my plate completely with a piled-high pastrami on rye, a burger, fries, and coleslaw all at once. I couldn't help but notice that his plating of the food was as orderly and as pleasing as his dress. He wore a beige linen sportcoat, a lime-green bowtie, and a brown-and-white-striped dress shirt. A yellow cotton square with tiny lime-green dots rose from his breast pocket like a just-bloomed flower. No color strayed into another. Everything was somehow crisp, even in the humidity. His only concession to the day's fashion, such as it was, was his hair cut, which included substantial sideburns. But even they had been expertly trimmed and tamed. He was clean-shaven, and I had known instantly when he bent to kiss me that his aftershave matched the scent of Tad's candles. A realization that both pleased and pained.

"Now, Tad," he said, when he finished with me.

"Thank you, sir," said Tad, and handed him his plate.

Luke grinned across the table. He had a dimple on his left cheek.

When Tad's plate could hold no more, and before Luke took any food for himself, he lifted his glass, smiled, and said, "To friendship, the three of us."

His teeth were as sparkly as his nails.

I drank too eagerly, emptying the champagne flute a second time in two swallows. Luke poured me a third glass without comment. I felt Tad trying to catch my eye. But I fastened my gaze on Luke instead.

"Tell Orla how we met, Luke," Tad said. "Notice my timing, Orla." He forced my gaze back to him. "Now I shall be able to eat without interruption."

"Ha! As always, you mock my verbal proclivity," Luke said.

Tad nodded and chewed his food, lifting his knife in what appeared to be an appreciative gesture.

Holding his own knife and fork in the European way, Luke went after some shrimp. But he merely speared them, holding the utensils prone while he spoke.

"Just after the New Year last January," he said, "the venerable Father Leonard Jaspers, S. J., who happened to have taught both of us Latin at Prep, announced that at long last he was retiring, and we alum arranged a send-off. We had to pretend the gala was simply a routine scholarship fundraiser." Here he cleared his throat. "Jaspers never would have agreed to a party solely for himself." Luke put his napkin on the table and let go the utensils. He ran his right hand over his hair. "Tad and I happened to be in the receiving line next to each other." He spoke across the table to Tad. "You were just ahead of me, right?"

Tad nodded, enjoying the pastrami, his napkin protecting his shirt like a bib.

"As soon as Tad reached Father Jaspers and had paid his respects, the fellow, seeing me and always trying to seal some sort of deal, said, 'Luke Segreti, my boy. Class of '48, I believe. Please take no offense. You will all and always be my boys. It's good to see you. Let me introduce you to Tad Charbonneau. Class of '68. Of that I'm certain. The year I narrowly escaped a transfer to the heinous north, Buffalo and LeMoyne, to be precise. At any rate, Tad here is just the fellow to solve your worker visa problems." Tad nodded between bites of bacon he slid from beneath a hamburger bun. "'He's an immigration law specialist.'"

Tad laughed and stopped eating long enough to interject, "Mind you, Orla, I had been with the firm only for a few months. My total experience consisted of translating for a French-born nun whose family in Nice had left her a small sum, which she, of course, was obliged to turn over to her superior."

Luke put his napkin back on his lap, picked up a forkful of fried shrimp, popped them into his mouth, chewed, and swallowed, then put his fork down again. This time his napkin stayed on his lap.

"Little did Jaspers realize how the introduction would evolve."

"Au contraire, my friend, I think he did," Tad said. "Jaspers is a sly one. A jesuitical Jesuit."

"Perhaps," said Luke. He surveyed his plate, deciding where to use his fork next. "He always knew who stole the answer keys from his desk drawer when I was in Latin IV."

He decided on more shrimp. Then, patting his lips with his napkin, he said, "It was usually me, Orla. But never fear, Tad has been trying and succeeding, I'm sad to report, to turn me into a man of honor."

"To be sure," Tad said between bites of hamburger. He had opened the roll and was using the fork and knife to eat the burger.

Luke chuckled. "Now that he represents me he insists I obey every legality when bringing over tile workers and stone masons from Italy to indulge my clients' wildest and, I must add, lucrative wishes."

I listened to the two of them banter while I drank and ate with intention and energy. It had been more than twelve hours since breakfast in St. Suplice.

Done with the meat, his uneaten bread and roll a column-like structure on his plate, Tad moved on to the greenery. Before digging in he said, "Oh, I meant to tell you, Luke, I've seen Jaspers recently. I met with him just last Thursday, and he asked after you. He knows we see each other."

"Does he, now?" Luke said. "And how is that?" He grinned across the table.

"Never you mind," Tad answered, grinning back.

I speared a stray piece of bacon as if with a harpoon. There it was, the secret language of lovers.

I waved to waiter Peter.

"Yes, miss?'

"Vodka, please. Straight up."

Tad raised his eyebrows, then went on.

"He brought in his sister and her husband to revise their will. They intend to let a summer place in Cornwall, where Jaspers was born."

Tad paused as Peter returned with my drink.

I swallowed a hefty portion of it.

"She's thirsty." Luke smiled, then winked at me. "Understandable."

He looked at me straight on, kindly. My eyes filled.

Tad sighed.

"You're encouraging her."

Luke winked again, and Tad redirected.

"By the way, when you were his student, Luke, did Jaspers tell you about Cornwall and Morgan le Fey or King Arthur's castle?"

I swallowed again. The vodka burned nicely. Preferable to Listerine, at any rate.

Luke stopped and thought.

"Not that I can remember. He was always talking about what a bad deal the Roman soldiers had when they were sent to Britannia."

"Oh," Tad said.

"Too much rain."

I felt light, as if I were floating in a hot air balloon and at the same time watching *The Dick Van Dyke Show* on television. Tad and Luke were Rob and Laura Petrie, and I was their guest. A welcome one, but a guest nonetheless.

"Let's go back to my place," Tad suggested when we were done.

"Let's," Luke said. "We'll make a *passeggiata* home."

I blanched. Home? Good Lord. Would he stay the night? Did Tad expect me to listen in from the front room? I starting planning my leave-taking. The Monteleone or Katie's, if she were home. Better the hotel. No one to phone, nothing to explain. Blessed quiet. Nice being Mrs. Castleberry's heiress. It gave me options.

"Excuse me a moment," Luke said, and stood. He smoothed his jacket and walked back toward the bar, its drinks and service generally considered Maspero's best feature.

"You're drinking too much," Tad tried to whisper.

"Fuck you," I said, and emptied my glass of vodka.

"Okay, okay, I'm sorry."

I glared at Tad, then watched Segreti navigate the room. Everyone in the place knew him. He stopped at one table long enough for Tad to interrogate me.

"Well?" he asked, taking my hand in his.

I let him.

"Well, what?"

He rolled his eyes.

"Do you like him?"

I rolled my eyes back at him.

"You do, that's for sure."

"Ouch," Tad said. "And you *are* drinking too much."

"Of course I do. What's not to like, Tad? I'm trying to be glad for you. For you both. I hate it. I'm trying to get drunk. Help me get drunk. "

Tad bent over and kissed me on the cheek. His lips were smooth. I didn't like knowing where else they'd been. All the places they'd been. Funny, we'd been touching all day long.

"Good," Tad said. "About liking Luke, I mean. Not about getting drunk."

"Too bad."

He threw up his hands.

"You can get drunk when we get home."

I smiled.

"Now you're talking sense."

"You have my father to thank. He brings liquor every time he has to appear in court down here."

Luke returned, putting his wallet back into his pants' pocket.

"Thank you for dinner," I said. "Tad suggests I can get as drunk as I want to back at the house. As you might have noticed, I planned on doing so here."

Luke grinned.

"A much better plan," he said. "Let the counselor take the blame for getting you inebriated."

"You're as bad as she is," Tad said.

"We shall have to see," said Luke. "Won't we, Orla?"

He offered his arm.

I took it, nodding in agreement.

"Shall we, then?" Luke asked. "Perambulate back to Shotgun Alley, that is?"

Just as they took me between them—mind you, I still hadn't had enough to sway—a much older man, dressed in a white suit, white bucks, and a vivid purple tie, with a bejeweled cane and a straw hat atop his head, called out from behind us in a gravelly voice, "Not so fast, Segreti!"

Luke turned, saw the man, smiled, let go my arm, and went over to help him.

"Phineas!" he said.

The two walked toward Tad and me, Luke's arm now under Phineas' free one.

"Is this she, me man?" Phineas asked Luke, his Scottish burr clear. "I couldn't help but listen in when I spied you settling up. I was sitting right next to the bar."

Luke laughed. "No flies on you, my friend. I get away with nothing when you're nearby."

He let go the old man, made sure he stood steady, then came over and put his arm around me. "Yes, this is she. The very one."

Luke's arm felt muscular under his jacket, and his hold was as comfortable as it was firm. I tried to stop thinking of what he must look like naked. What he and Tad looked like naked together.

The old gentleman moved closer to my face as if to get a good look at me and, with his free hand, chucked my chin.

"Your Aunt Yvette DuBois and I are great friends," he said. "Over the years she's advised me whose work to purchase. I've amassed quite a nice collection, thanks to her." He stopped to catch his breath. "She's told me so much about you, my dear lass. But I thought it would take a trip to Manhattan to meet you." He let go my chin. "Perhaps you'd let me see your work. To see what I might consider buying, you understand."

I flushed, then tried to act as if this sort of thing happened to me regularly.

"Certainly, sir, I'd be honored."

I was taken aback. I didn't know Tante Yvette had any friends in New Orleans. And I didn't want to be drunk at all with this fellow. I wanted to be brilliant. I smiled my most brilliant smile.

Luke's voice turned formal.

"Mr. Phineas Rossiter, may I introduce Miss Orla Castleberry," he said. "And of course you already know Tad Charbonneau."

"Yes, yes," Mr. Rossiter said. "Good evening, Tad. I understand you're making a name for yourself at the firm assisting the Vietnamese orphans. I do hope this onslaught of refugees proves a positive intrusion into our city."

His hand trembled on his cane. It was difficult for him to stand.

"Don't believe everything you hear about me, Mr. Rossiter," Tad said, eyeing Luke in an exaggerated way, then, in a professorial tone, "As for the refugees I've met thus far, they appear eager to contribute. A number of them worked at the U. S. Embassy in Saigon until the Communists took over."

"I see," Mr. Rossiter said. "They are educated, then."

"Yes," replied Tad. "Or expert shrimpers. And, Lord knows, New Orleans can always tolerate more good shrimpers."

Luke smiled.

"The counselor here is overly modest."

Tad's cheeks reddened, but he didn't speak.

Mr. Rossiter chuckled and coughed.

"A fine quality, modesty," he said. "Would that I had had the temperament to acquire it."

We all laughed.

"No number of whippings at the Dickensian institution where I was imprisoned during childhood were able to inculcate me with it."

We waited for him to continue.

"Well, at last I was able to escape to here, to a clime that was just as damp but much warmer and forgiving."

"We're glad you did," said Luke.

Mr. Rossiter turned his attention to me again.

"I have seen some of your work, my dear," he said to me. "Your aunt walked me through your Civil Rights collection just before it went up at The New-York Historical Society last November. You are quite good. Pointed, very pointed."

His voice had become raspier during the conversation.

"You are very kind," I said.

My hot air balloon was skipping from one cumulus cloud to another.

Tad laughed.

"I encourage Orla to be pointed only when she paints."

Had we been alone, I'd have stuck my tongue out at him. But now I said to Mr. Rossiter, "Tad can be impossible, you understand."

"No doubt," he replied.

I countered.

"I put up with him only because he is my oldest and dearest friend."

Tad took my right hand and squeezed it.

Luke patted me on the back.

"Keep up the flattery and maybe he'll spring for our next dinner," he said.

Mr. Rossiter tapped his cane on the floor, focusing our attention on him again.

"Perhaps you'll consider the Vietnamese mess for your next subject?" He wet his lips with his tongue. "I like work with a political punch," he said, and lifted his cane, thrusting it forward like a spear. He wobbled, then let the cane resume its original position on the floor.

"Yes, sir, I know what you mean. I can't seem to keep politics out of my work. Even when I think I'm painting a purely personal piece. The subject is never separate from a political context, no matter what."

I was trying to feel him out, to see where his interests might intersect with mine. And I wanted to keep floating in the hot air balloon for as long as I could.

Tad bent down toward Mr. Rossiter so he could hear better.

"Orla," Tad said, "I let Mr. Rossiter see the photos I took of your sketches following Denny's death."

"Oh, I see," I said. "I've got the painting finished now."

"Yes, I remember Tad telling me," Mr. Rossiter said. "Perhaps you'll consider doing some others about the unfortunate fellow's experiences?"

He averted his eyes and looked upward, as if in a private reverie. Before I could answer, he continued.

"No one took heed of Wilfred Owen," he said, "or any other of the World War I poets, for that matter." His eyes lowered to focus on mine again. "Maybe you'll have better luck. Maybe a lass like you could succeed."

I nodded and touched my hair.

"I hope so," I said. "You've set me a lofty goal."

He closed his eyes and said, "Let me see if I can recall the lines properly.

'The old Lie: Dulce et decorum est/Pro patria mori.'"

"It is sweet and right to die for one's country," Tad intoned.

Who was this Rossiter fellow?

He grabbed Luke's free arm, instantly agitated.

"Please, Luke, you must see to it that Miss Castleberry and I meet within the next few weeks, before my sister Lavinia arrives from Glasgow." He just as quickly recovered his calm. "That is, presuming you are available, Miss Castleberry. I should not have presumed." He smiled at me and I smiled back. "Once Lavinia gets here, my dear, my time will not be my own, you understand. She will expect guests for high tea every afternoon. She comes from Glasgow from September through February."

"I am available, Mr. Rossiter, and at your disposal."

I reached into my evening bag and took out one of my cards.

"You can reach me at the number printed here or through Luke or Tad, if you prefer."

I snapped my purse shut.

"And thank you for your interest in my work, Mr. Rossiter. I am most grateful."

I held the smile until I felt top and bottom teeth touching.

"Good," he said, and smiled again. "I am in the market, you know. I am always in the market. But at my age, my dear, I can't be too sure the market will remain open much longer."

He looked again to Luke, who wore a bemused look.

"Will you see to it, then, Luke?"

Luke let go of me and put both his hands on Mr. Rossiter's stooped shoulders.

"Count on it, sir," he said. "I shall work it out with the lady and phone you by ten tomorrow, if that suits you." Luke looked to me and I nodded.

"Ten is fine. I'll have been well caffeinated by then and had a chance to stretch my legs around the garden."

He chuckled to himself.

"Until tomorrow, then. And now, I must go. My driver waits outside."

"We'll leave together," Tad suggested.

And the two of them left me alone as they escorted Mr. Rossiter out of the restaurant.

I followed to the doorway and watched them assist the old gentleman onto the sidewalk, now illuminated by the Quarter's wrought-iron and glass street lamps. As soon as his uniformed driver saw him emerge, he crossed the street, from where a black stretch limousine idled, and took over. Mr. Rossiter looked back over his shoulder, lifted his cane, and said, "Until the next time, Miss Castleberry."

I waved.

"It was lovely to meet you." My voice trilled.

Then he was gone.

Tad and Luke watched until the car had disappeared down Decatur Street.

Then, as if electrified, Tad ran in, grabbed my hand, and said, "Come on!"

Luke waited outside smiling.

"The night is young and Orla is about to become a celebrity," he said.

I didn't know which of the two possibilities unnerved me more.

They flung me between them, each stretching an arm across my back. I felt their hands clasp behind me and registered both jealousy and joy. We strode as a trio, annoying any number of other pedestrians who felt that they, too, were entitled to free passage on the cobblestones.

"Musketeers," Luke bellowed, though he was not remotely drunk. "Make way for the Three Musketeers!"

"Act your age, old man," Tad snickered across me.

"Never," Luke retorted, and he clicked the heels of his beautiful shoes together.

I might have smiled. I felt like Dorothy in Oz.

Chapter Seventeen
Riding Shotgun

"When are the blasted fish arriving?" Luke called back to Tad from the front room. He looked at the water bubbling in the aquarium. Aquatic plants of varying heights swayed in the moving water. "A fishless tank is like a school without students."

He shrugged his shoulders at me and smiled.

Luke had gone immediately into the bedroom and returned right away *sans* sport coat and bow tie. He rolled up the sleeves of his starched shirt, walked over to the bar-trunk, lifted the lid, and said, "Single-malt, Orla? To celebrate Phineas Rossiter, Scotsman and collector. Patron of painters. Millionaire. The man who will seal your fame."

"Why not?" I answered. "Who is he, anyway?

"Well," Luke began, taking his time unscrewing the bottle cap, "he is, as the gentility of days gone by preferred to call him, 'a confirmed bachelor' and a patron of the arts. After his

Uncle Angus Rossiter in Scotland died some sixty years ago, Phineas and his sister Lavinia inherited a bundle. They are Angus' nephew and niece by his brother Carruthers and Carruthers' wife Eloise."

He took a sturdy club glass and poured me two fingers.

Tad, who'd gone into the kitchen, said, "I'll be right there," and in short order returned with peanuts, lemons, a peeler, and ice, each in a proper container, all on a teak tray. "The napkins are right on the end table, Orla."

I stood stock still in the doorway, aware of my overnight bag tucked into a corner on the left side of Tad's desk, and trying to figure out my place in the domestic activities transpiring before me.

"Oh, the fish. Next Thursday, between four and six." Tad paused, took stock of the room, then pulled out his desk chair, and sat down. "I hope I don't kill them. I'll never know what happened to the turtle I hovered over during kindergarten." He peeled a few bits of rind off the lemon. "I returned home from school one day and Mother reported that Frederick had taken his leave. She made a show of searching for him under the sofa and wing chairs with me. At dinner Dad offered a prayer, as I recall. 'Godspeed, Frederick.'" He laughed. "Neither of them cracked a smile. No doubt the poor animal had gone shell up."

"Just don't overfeed them," Luke said. "Unlike me, fish, I am told, prefer a moderate diet."

"Come, sit, Orla," he motioned, moving a pillow so I could nestle into one corner of the couch.

I did, and nodded my thanks as he handed me the glass of Laphroaig.

"Some lemon rind around your glass?" he asked, and I reached to take one. I rubbed it inside, on the glass, round and round, then dropped the rind into the scotch.

"Ice?" Tad asked.

"Thanks, no," I answered.

Luke took a seat at the other end of the couch and said to Tad, "A piece of good fortune, eh, meeting up with Phineas?"

Tad nodded.

"It very well could be."

Luke sipped his own scotch while Tad spooned some peanuts into the palm of his hand.

"So, Orla," Luke said, easing his broad shoulders into the couch's leather, "what if I were to suggest to Phineas that we drive down to St. Suplice in two or three weeks, say, on a Saturday or a Sunday? Could you have a display ready for him?"

I wondered if Mamma would let me take over her whole salon, just for a few days.

"I guess so. If Mamma will let me have my way with her bridal salon."

Tad stood, filled a glass with ice, and poured some scotch over the cubes.

"She will, Orla. You know she will."

I sipped from my glass, the liquid's amber color as pleasing as its taste. My hot air balloon had landed and I felt as if I were lolling in a field of tall grasses.

"Luke," I said, lifting myself upright for a moment and leaning toward him, "I hardly know how to thank you for making such an introduction. What is your usual finder's fee?"

Luke crossed one leg over the other at the other end of the couch and put a forefinger to his lips.

"Hmmm, let's just have this be the first of what I hope will be many gestures of friendship between us, Orla. Really."

I couldn't speak, so I simply raised my glass to him.

I glowed when earlier I'd sworn to glower. The night's supply of liquor helped, of course. But even without it, I am certain I still would have glowed.

Tad took up more peanuts.

"Now that's what I call a generous deal, Orla," he said. "I've never heard Luke offer a deal like that before."

He was smirking and smiling at his lover.

"Now that you mention it," Luke said, standing, "maybe it *is* too generous after all."

"Oh, no," Tad said.

Luke winked at me. He certainly was a winker.

"On second thought," he said, making his way to Tad, "if I can get Phineas to come down to St. Suplice with me, I wonder if you can work your magic, too, Orla, and have Tad agree to join us."

Tad stopped popping the peanuts into his mouth and said not a word. The silence hovered like an unplanned gap in television programming.

"It's time, I think," said Luke, "for *Mère et Père* Charbonneau to make my acquaintance."

Tad stood statue-like. He didn't even turn his eyes my way. His lips made a thin, quivering line across his mouth.

"As I've told Tad," Luke continued, now right before him, "I've waited a very long time to be with anyone whose family I wanted to know. To thank them for their son."

My heart skipped a beat. And for a moment I believed it possible that all could be well among the three of us. In fact, that all could be well in the world.

Luke rubbed his broad tan hand over the back of Tad's long neck. Tad took a breath, reached back, took Luke's hand in his, brought it to his lips, and smiled. The two locked eyes the way all lovers do. I was mesmerized. Their pantomime looked fantastical and natural at the same time. Like the afternoon before Christmas vacation in sixth grade when my class watched male seahorses giving birth on a Disney nature film.

"No way," I had called out spontaneously, unable to pry my eyes away from the screen. "True nonetheless," Miss Taylor had said. And so it was.

The phone rang, its shrill two blasts interrupting my momentary wonder.

"Who could that be?" Tad asked, as he made for the kitchen.

Luke waited until Tad was gone, downed the rest of his drink, and asked, "So, will you help me?"

He poured himself another drink, looking away from me while he did.

It's not as if I needed to think about my answer.

"Yes," I said. "Of course. Of course I'll help you."

He raised a glass to me. And in a synchronized movement, we drank.

Chapter Eighteen
Nurse on Call

"It's Katie," Tad said, returning. "She's asking for your help, Orla."

I blanched and got up fast.

"Is she okay? Not her father-in-law bothering her, I hope."

Luke groaned. "A real louse, I understand."

Tad sat down on his leather swivel chair. "No, no, nothing like that."

I breathed in relief.

"It's one of her patients, a little girl," Tad said. "The child is my client, as well."

My look must have been one of surprise.

"One of the Vietnamese children."

"Oh," I said. I looked to Tad. "Shall I call her back?"

Tad pointed toward the kitchen.

"She's still on the line if you'd be willing to talk to her now."

"Of course," I said. I put my glass down on the end table and walked the long hallway to the phone in the kitchen.

"Katie!"

"Sorry to phone so late, Orla, but no one answered earlier. Tad said you went to Maspero's. How do you like his place?"

I took the phone's lengthy cord in my hand and circled the perimeter of the kitchen. I realized I hadn't actually been in it yet. This afternoon already felt a long way gone. I wonder if Katie knew about Tad's secret life. If she knew I had an inkling about hers. Good God.

"It's really a terrific place," I said, putting my thoughts aside. "As you would imagine, well-planned and well-executed." I smiled at the teddy-bear teapot Tad's Granny had given him. It graced a corner shelf above the stove. "I'm sorry to hear you and Keith can't join us for breakfast tomorrow."

I returned to the wall phone. An *Important Phone Numbers* pad was affixed to the wall by the receiver with a list of names in a long column to the left of numbers:

Charbonneau
Home
Dad's office
Segreti
Orla
NYC
St. Suplice

Firm
Katie and Keith
Emergency
Fire
Police

"Right," Katie continued, "I'm sorry, too. I've got to work and Keith's got an early start on the golf course with his dad and Dagin."

I imagined taking a swing at Mr. Clayborne's penis with one of his golf clubs.

"Well, we can save Brennan's for another time."

I strolled over to the wall by the refrigerator where Tad had nailed one of those monthly blackboard calendars a mother with a passel of children might favor. His was color-coded: red chalk for work, blue for Luke, green for social. My name was printed in green from Saturday morning through Sunday evening. A smiling stick figure, also in green, stood beside it.

"So, Orla, I could use your help if you can spare the time. And see you tomorrow in the mix."

"I hope I can help. What's up?"

Someone went into the bathroom. I heard the toilet flush and water run in the sink.

"There's this little girl named Mercy, just five years old. She's one of the Vietnamese. Tad is in charge of her legal file. He said he'd show it to you tomorrow morning if you're willing to have a look."

"Yes, Tad just mentioned her to me."

I walked back to where the receiver was attached to the wall and wrapped the phone cord around my hand.

Katie continued, "She's in our psych ward right now because she won't speak. In fact she has not spoken a word since her arrival at the Ursuline orphanage by way of Arkansas, three weeks ago. Not that a scenario like that is unusual for traumatized kids. According to Sister Ann, who's in charge there, the staff waited to see if she simply needed time to adapt."

"And?"

"No dice. The nun says she is perfectly cooperative, just won't talk."

I peered at the space between two swags of the cottage curtains. The alley separating Tad's place from his neighbor's was illuminated by two yellow spot lights, one affixed to the top corner of Tad's back porch, the other to the same of his neighbor's. An enormous black cat was slinking around the neighbor's metal garbage pail. Three red bricks had been placed over the lid. The cat licked each one.

"Is something wrong with her vocal cords?" I asked.

"No," Katie answered. "That's just it. She checks out physically just fine. She even hums. Religious hymns and nursery tunes the nuns sing to the children."

"Huh."

I looked down at my feet. My flats had not gotten too beat up in the Quarter's detritus. Just a piece of flattened green gum under the right heel. I scraped it off, rolled it into a tiny ball, and threw it into the trash container by the door leading outside. Then I washed my hands with the bar of Ivory in a black ceramic soap dish shaped like a bull.

"Has she been traumatized by something she saw?"

"Maybe. No doubt, actually. My goodness, her mother put her on one of the Tan Son Nhut planes. You've seen the news. It was chaos. Terrifying for anyone. But the doctors don't think that is what's keeping her quiet. She responds to commands and emotes normally with facial gestures. She recognizes the needs of others. Sister Ann says she helps one of the younger children, a little boy, eat."

"Okay."

The cat leapt from the neighbor's garbage pail to Tad's. The bricks on his were painted white.

Katie sneezed.

"God bless you," I said.

"Thanks."

She sighed.

"But, Orla, she's not just silent anymore. For the last two weeks this little girl has been walking about putting her finger to her lips as if to say, 'Be quiet.' She cups her hand to her ears as if to say, 'Listen.' And, most disturbing of all, she makes circles with her thumbs and forefingers, holds them up to her eyes as if they were binoculars, and searches for something or someone, turning herself around in circles until she drops."

"That's odd."

"Yes. And, mind you, she does this all day long except to eat, sleep, and paint."

"Good Lord," I said. "She must get very tired."

Katie laughed, neither humor or derision in her tone.

"I'll say. My goodness, we on staff get tired just watching her."

I rested the phone between my left chin and shoulder and pushed back the cuticles on each finger.

"I heard you say 'paint,' so I'm guessing that's where I come in.

"Yes, I'm hoping so," said Katie.

I looked at my nails. The mauve polish on my right thumb was chipped.

"So how do you think I can be of help?"

Whoever was in the bathroom came out and walked into the bedroom.

It must have been Luke because Tad came into the kitchen to place his glass in the sink.

"Need anything?" he whispered to me.

I shook my head.

"Okay, then."

He went into the bedroom, too, and closed the door.

I put my back to the doorway and tried to focus on Katie's voice."Well, the only thing that distracts her is painting."

"Really?"

The house had gone completely quiet but for our conversation. I heard nothing from the bedroom.

"Yes. She wields a brush with confidence on as many large sheets of paper as we can supply."

"What does she draw?"

178

I walked over to the light switch near the hallway and pressed the lever down. The kitchen went dark. Still dead silence from the bedroom.

Here Katie paused.

"So far, nothing we can identify. She paints only vertical strokes of colors, three strokes every time."

"Interesting."

I heard Luke laugh.

"Yes, one stroke is always much taller than the others and at the left edge of the paper. As if half of it is missing. As if it's bled off the page."

I pulled out one of the bistro chairs from the little round table and sat down. I put my hand over my free ear and tried to listen solely to Katie.

"Are the strokes always the same colors?"

"Funny you should ask," Katie said.

"The two shorter ones are brown, with some yellow painted over the brown. They're not the same size, but both are much shorter than the really long one in red, always red. And always dripping off the paper."

"That must be a clue. She's likely trying to tell you something. Repeating herself."

"Yes, no doubt. But most of the children her age draw stick figures that tell the narrative and then add their own words aloud. This little one's designs are more abstract. And, as I mentioned, she won't tell us anything aloud. Not with verbal language, anyway."

The bedroom door opened and closed. My heart was beating too fast.

"So, I was wondering, Orla, if you might come visit and just paint with her? Maybe she'll show or tell you her story. Maybe you can connect as fellow artists. I'm hoping she'll share with you something we medical folk can't get her to offer."

My right eyelid twitched the way it always did when I couldn't control my nervousness. Only my nervousness wasn't for the little girl.

"Sure, I'd be glad to, Katie. Anything for you."

Katie let out a long "Ohhhh, good. Thanks. Thanks a lot, Orla."

The bedroom door opened again and Tad came back into the kitchen, switching on the light. He was wearing one of the white terrycloth robes. His feet were bare and his hair was mussed.

I hadn't counted on seeing him like this, at least not with someone named Luke in the house.

"I'll let Mercy's psychiatrist know you'll visit," Katie said.

Tad opened the refrigerator door and took out a peach.

"Want one?" he whispered again.

"Thanks, no," I whispered back.

"What's that?" Katie asked.

"Just me telling Tad I don't want any more to eat," I said.

Luke came into the kitchen, as well. He had put his bowtie back on and carried his sport coat over his left arm. Tad offered him the peach. "One bite," he said, and sunk his teeth into the fruit even as Tad held it. Tad grimaced as peach juice dripped down his robe. Luke laughed. Tad placed the half-eaten peach on the table.

"Can you come by tomorrow, or is that asking too much? I'll be here and it'll be quieter than usual unless there's an emergency admit. The translator, Kim Luong, will be here, as well. She's a refugee, too. She used to teach Vietnamese to members of the U.S. Embassy staff. She'll be able to help you."

"Why not?" I said. "What time?"

Tad wet a paper towel and dabbed at the peach juice.

"Hold on." I put my hand over the receiver and looked to Tad. "Might you be willing to drop me at the pediatric psych ward tomorrow?"

Tad nodded.

"As a guest?" he asked.

He fussed with the peach stain even as he teased.

I gave him the finger.

"Such unladylike behavior," whispered Luke. "I'm shocked."

I smiled at him.

"Fine, Katie. Tad will drop me off. When?"

"How about after lunch, around one o'clock?"

I motioned one o'clock to Tad, who mouthed "Fine."

"May I bring along some treats?"

"No need," Katie said.

"I will anyway," I laughed. "Maybe some beignets will get her talking."

"Sounds good," Katie said. "You never know."

Having cleaned the robe as best he could, Tad put the paper towel on the table, too, and cinched the fabric belt tighter around his waist. Meanwhile, Luke got a slip of paper out of his sport coat pocket.

"Alright, then," I said, "I'll be there by one."

"Great," said Katie. "Say goodnight to Tad for me."

I saw that Luke had found a phone number and was waiting for me to hang up.

"I will. Good night, Katie. Big hug to Keith."

She giggled. And I placed the phone on the receiver.

Luke came over to the phone.

"I'm going to call for a car."

"Oh," I said, and handed him the phone.

"Can you help her?" Tad asked.

He had finished the peach and threw the pit into the trash container.

"Maybe painting will. I hope so."

We walked back out to the front room while Luke said, "Five minutes, then."

"Dashing," I pointed to Tad's stained robe.

"I have a spare, and it's clean. Would you like it?" he asked.

Not now I wouldn't. My chest burned.

"Thank you, no. Why would I when I have the best of NYU women's basketball-wear to show off?"

Luke joined us.

"It's been a very satisfying night meeting you, Orla. Thank you."

I curtsied.

"Likewise, Luke."

"Co-conspirators we will be," he said.

"Just so," I answered.

Tad's lips twisted and turned.

"You look like a confused fish," I said.

He shook his head at both of us.

"Time for bed," I told them, having reconsidered my sleeping options now that Luke was leaving for certain. "I'm going to bid you goodnight, gentlemen."

Luke hugged me tight. His breath smelled like scotch, toothpaste, and peach.

"I'll let you know Phineas' plans as soon as he and I talk tomorrow."

"Good," I said. "Thank you."

Tad went around the front room, putting out all the lights but for the green reading lamp on his desk. With a few handle pulls and one bounce test for stability, he turned the sofa into a guest bed. Luke walked over to the closet just right of the hallway and retrieved two pillows already in striped pillow cases, seeing to it that I'd have a soft place to rest my head. It had been a long day.

"Good night, then," I said, took up my overnight bag, and walked the hallway to the bathroom while the two of them stood together waiting for Luke's cab. In a few minutes I heard the front door close. Tad's voice traveled with his feet and carried through the bathroom door. "Call if you need anything, Orla. I'll be here."

When I came out of the bathroom, the bedroom door was shut and no light shone from beneath it. I was tired and let myself fall onto the guest bed. I looked up at the spinning ceiling fan and let it hypnotize me. Lulled by the sounds of sirens in the distance and muted jazz from somewhere across the street, I drifted off. No dreams, I prayed. Please, no dreams tonight.

Chapter Nineteen
A File

I woke to the seductive aroma of fresh-brewed coffee. Before I even padded barefoot into the kitchen, Tad had poured me a substantial mugfull. Fresh beignets rested on parchment where confectionery sugar and just the right amount of grease mingled. He must have gone out for them. His tennis shoes rested on a straw mat by the back door and he had a white cotton sweater draped over his shoulders. He was in his summer weekend uniform of madras bermudas and rugby shirt, today's being the color of lemons. Sunday's paper sat atop the counter, too.

"A breakfast for the gods," I said. "Thank you.

"I thought we'd do Brennan's when Katie and Keith can make it."

"Good idea," I said, conscious of future visits implied in his words.

For a while we fell into the comfortable silence we had always shared. After he had wiped his plate clean and smiled across the table as I finished off a third beignet, Tad said, "I wondered if you'd like to stop off at the firm so I can locate the little girl's file?"

"Sure," I said, getting up to pour us both a second cup of coffee. "Her name is Mercy, Katie told me."

Tad looked across the table.

"It's good of you to do this," he said.

I shrugged my shoulders. "I'm curious, I have to admit." I sipped the coffee. It had a silkiness the New York brews lacked. "And I wonder if just painting itself will lead somewhere helpful."

He nodded. "I bet it will." He smiled. "If anyone can make that happen, you're the one to do it."

I smiled back.

"Are you trying to sweet-talk me?"

"Anything that will keep you by my side, Orla."

He sounded serious.

"Then yes, let's go to your office and see what we can dig up."

He stood.

"Good. Then you'll have a little preparation."

He stood to refill the cream pitcher.

"I'll drop you off at the hospital, then go back to the office for a couple of hours while you paint with Mercy. At three, I'll pick you up so we can head over to Luke's place, grab an early supper he has planned for you, and have you ready for Earl Sharp by—when did you say he'd be arriving? At nine?"

"Sounds good," I said.

"You take your time getting ready," he said. "I'll just have a look at the headlines while I wait."

I stood and started for the shower. But a question made me pause.

"Tad, I have to ask. Do Katie and Keith know about Luke?"

He looked up from the paper.

"Not yet," he said. His eyelids flickered a bit. "I'll be counting on you to make the introduction."

I felt put out and flattered at the same time.

"You're not kidding, are you?"

His expression turned to supplication.

"Would you?"

"Depends."

"On what?"

"If you promise not to hide things from me anymore."

He stood up, put his right hand over his heart, and said, "I promise."

"Okay."

"Thanks." He sat down again. "I mean it, Orla. Thanks."

"Oh, it's nothing," I said, and glared at him as long and as hard as I could.

By the time I returned from showering and dressing, the kitchen had been cleaned and my bed returned to its couch status. I fiddled around in my purse and overnight bag to see if I had any doodads a little girl might like. All I found were some purple ribbon and a clear plastic barrette in the shape of a starfish. Of course I did have the small box of brushes and water colors I was never without.

The firm of Ciampi and Vester was located at 123 Canal Street, not too far from the main shopping district and the trolley line that took you uptown into the Garden District. We needed to take the elevator to the second floor, then enter a locked anteroom decorated with Audubon-like sketches of Louisiana birds. The couches and club chairs were muted grays and greens, arranged into two conversational groupings. Reading matter was limited to news magazines and lawyerly journals. The receptionist's desk, immediately to the left upon entering, loomed like a sentry's post protecting the attorneys' offices from intruding forces in the waiting area.

"Serious business," I said.

The subdued atmosphere of the room cautioned against raised voices.

"Come into my lair," Tad leered, and motioned for me to follow him.

His office was as small as a convent cell, but as elegant as the rest of the place. A mahogany desk and matching high-backed chair in black leather, two arm chairs in a green-and-white linen stripe across from the desk, neat stacks of labeled briefs, and a tall file cabinet with the top drawer labeled "Refugee Children"."Please." He motioned for me to sit on one of the striped chairs and opened the drawer.

He wore the same determined look he had as a child when leafing through Old Doctor Castleberry's World War II papers. The grandfather clock in the hallway just outside his office ticked its way from eleven o'clock on through the hour, and the hum of air conditioning soothed like a soporific.

I looked at him to memorize his face. To hold it in my mind. For paint him now I would. I knew that. My brush more precise than any words I might utter. Tad. As I hadn't previously understood him. Still-and-different Tad.

"Aha." He reached up and held his hair. "Here she is."

He pushed a file, black-and-white photograph attached, across his desk.

"She's beautiful," I said.

"Yes—Mercy. That's her given name. Last name, Cleveland. She's six years old."

I stared at the photograph. Jagged bangs decorated Mercy's forehead, each pointed arrow combed flat to form a splay of black daggers. Straight black hair fell below her face to her shoulders. Her well-defined chin came to a pleasing almost-point. But, what was this? Her nose turned upward and her cheeks were freckled.

"She's half American," I said, "right? I can see it."

Tad took the paper clip off the photo and took it in his hand.

"Yes," he said. "And the notes here read, "Birth father unknown. Mother reports that he was a non-military translator originally from Cleveland, Ohio. First name, Hoyt. Surname unknown or unreported."

I motioned for him to hand me the picture. He did, and I stared at the photograph again. A dark smudge interrupted the child's expanse of right chin. Her forehead was furrowed, though it oughtn't to have been. The war had to have done that. She was standing in the picture, while three other children, one an older boy, sat on the ground behind her. Their clothes were ragged and soiled. Not showing up as clearly as Mercy was depicted, but blurred instead. A young American soldier stood at ease in the background, his machine gun pointed at the ground. He was a Negro. No one was speaking. Jungle foliage filled the photo's background.

I placed the photograph on Tad's desk.

"Is she really an orphan, then? Is the mother, or father, or both, alive? Was Hoyt actually her father's name?"

Tad sat down to read and re-read the typed notes.

"According to this," he looked up at me, "Mercy was handed to one of the flight attendants on a plane leaving Tan Son Nhut on April 19, 1975, by a frantic woman dressed in a nurse's uniform. The child screamed 'Mamma, Mamma,' and clung to the woman, who gave the attendant a sealed envelope. The attendant, a Marcella Kipp, wrested the child from her mother and brought her onto the plane. She pinned the envelope to to the child's blouse. After the plane took off, she opened the envelope. It contained the child's birth certificate and one thousand American dollars. Miss Kipp told the head flight attendant, who re-attached all to the child, and turned the contents over to the officer in charge at Fort Chaffee, Arkansas, where the child eventually arrived."

I listened and tried to imagine the mother's desperation, the child's confusion and terror.

"My God, no wonder she doesn't speak."

"And, would you believe it, Orla, the one thousand dollars made it all the way to the orphanage. Sister Ann opened a bank account in Mercy's name. The bank documents have been forwarded to me."

A couple of other official-looking papers were clipped together in the folder, as well.

"Huh," I said.

"Imagine, a terrible war, massive chaos, and still a chain of individuals who acted honestly as far as I can ascertain in this case."

Tad re-attached the photograph to the papers and slid all back into the folder. He stood up and returned the papers to the file cabinet drawer.

"So much for a carefree childhood," he said.

"Are they ever, I wonder?"

"Beats me."

He turned to look at me.

"Ready to go meet her?" he asked. "You said one o'clock, right? And you want to stop at a bakery."

I stayed seated. Had to ask.

"Tad," I said, "has anyone, have you, maybe, tried to find her father?"

Tad looked a long while at me, played his fingers against one another, then laughed sardonically. He appeared hesitant to speak.

"I'm serious," I said. "Have you tried?"

He sat down.

"You're kidding, right? You do realize there are hundreds of children, hundreds of parents, maybe dead, maybe wounded, and perhaps some American fathers who are not really their fathers at all. The women, many of them, were prostitutes. How could they be sure who the fathers of their children were?"

He looked straight into my eyes as he spoke. His defensive tone surprised me. "No, Orla, I have not tried to find Hoyt Whoever-he-is. My job is just to place the child with people who won't abuse her, who'll offer her a secure home and an education, who'll help her forget her past."

I felt my face reddening. I felt myself mounting a proverbial high horse, this one mine, a horse I had ridden myself.

"Orla, what?" he asked.

I stood up. High and mighty is how I felt.

"Of all people," I said. "Of all people, I'd expect you to understand."

Though I tried to speak calmly, I failed. My hands made fists.

"How dare you?" I said. "How dare you not try!"

"Orla," he said, "be rational. Calm down."

"Don't 'Orla' me," I said. "And don't expect me to be rational," I heard myself yelling. "How many translator Hoyts from Cleveland can there be? How hard can it be to find him?"

His eyes became kind again.

"Okay," he said, "I grant you there is probably only one translator Hoyt from Cleveland. But how can we know for sure he's our man? How can *he* know for sure that Mercy is his child?"

At least he had started to listen. But I was not going to back down.

"Right," I said. "We can't. But what if he is? What if he actually *is* Mercy's father?"

I slapped my palms together. I shook my hair, aiming for the wildness of a Medusa.

He could tell I was being purposeful, not crazed, now— that my gestures were intentional, like my brush strokes, for effect.

I went on, "Would you deny her her father? Would you deny him his child? My God, Tad, I was half an orphan for eleven years. You know that. How can you not know that, Tad? Who are you, anyway?"

My final question was too much. Even I knew that as soon as the words were out of my mouth.

Now he glared across the desk at me and spoke angrily, wagging his right index finger at my face exactly the way he had been taught not to. "I'm just me, Orla, not some magician or knight in shining armor. I'm just Tad Charbonneau, a closeted junior associate at a pricey law firm with fifty-seven children to place as foster children or adoptees. And by December, no less, so they can all be poster children for Catholic Charities and, more important still, for my boss Vester, who is counting on me to do this job,"—he

193

was yelling now—"who told me, 'Get it done, Tad. However you need to.'"

He stood. He was livid. "I'll be right back. I need to use the restroom. You stay right here, and don't go hatching any inane plans."

I ignored him. He was talking to me like some dean of students after I had smoked a joint in the girls' room. I felt him brush the back of my chair as he strode out of the office.

As soon as I heard what I guessed to be the men's room door open and close, I got up, went to the file cabinet, opened it, found the "Cleveland, Mercy" folder. I opened it and wrote down all the information I could on a sheet of paper from the notepad by Tad's phone. I folded the paper and put it in my purse just as the men's room door opened again and Tad walked back to the office. This time his tread was slow.

"I'm sorry," he said, standing behind me. His voice had returned to its normal, measured state. "It's just that there are so many children to place and competing families that want them. The would-be adoptive parents and foster parents phone constantly and want their cases completed pronto. They don't comprehend that it takes time and personnel for social services to investigate each and every family. To eliminate predators, abusers, alcoholics, and the like."

I stood up, facing him.

He was calmer, but he was still annoyed at me.

"Part of me thinks they believe the children are better off with them even if they *do* have one or both birth parents living. These folks are not interested in finding the birth parents. They just want children themselves. Sometimes they haven't been able to conceive. Sometimes they've lost a biological child to illness. Sometimes, I have to say, I think they're expressing a type of chauvinism, or at least American do-gooderism."

I kept quiet as he continued.

"Also, when a father, or a man who at least suspects he may be the father of a particular child, presents himself, he must submit to a blood test and be vetted, as well. Accepting paternity does not always equal ability to raise a child."

He ran his right hand through his hair.

"Nonetheless," he said, turning off the lights, "I should have realized how close this is to you."

"Damn right," I said. Then, quickly, "Sorry."

His second sigh was audible and sustained.

"Let's go."

"Yes, let's."

He dropped me at the main entrance of the hospital after we stopped at Josephine's Bakery to pick up beignets and macaroons. He wouldn't let me pay.

"You two have a lovely afternoon," the sugar-dotted clerk in a pink smock said.

I guess we looked like the perfect couple.

It was a silent ride until he pulled into the hospital's demi-lune drop-off zone.

"I'll meet you out here at three," I said.

He nodded, but looked straight ahead rather than at me.

195

"If anything changes, just phone me at the office. You have the number, right?"

"Yes."

I got out of the car, walked around the front of it and onto the raised sidewalk. Then I stopped, turned back, and put my left hand on the hood of the Volvo. I looked at him and spoke through the windshield.

"Please forgive me. I was being completely egocentric."

Really, it was a plea.

Tad scratched his nose.

"Forgive you for what?" he said. Then, "Do you plan on removing your hand from the hood of this vehicle, or shall I take it with me?"

"Oh!"

He smiled then.

"You," he said. "You."

I grinned.

"Paint well. Be merciful to Mercy."

And he drove away with a wave.

Chapter Twenty
Signs and Wonders

Of course the ward was a locked one. Each room was private. Nine rooms surrounded the nurse's station in a square. Every room housed one child. Two toddler-aged girls, one pig-tailed, were sleeping in beds that were screened even on top. One square-bodied boy in plaid shorts and a tee-shirt that read "Frogs" screamed inconsolably and pounded his face with white-gloved hands that looked like squishy boxing gloves. Five others, four boys and one girl, all primary school-aged, it appeared, played on their beds, kneeling with soft toys, or paging through fabric books. And one more, couldn't tell whether boy or girl, completely covered with mask and bandage turban, had a solemn-faced adult standing at the bedside soothing him or her with cooing sounds I could hear in the hallway.

Carrying my gaily ribboned box of pastries and cookies, I met Katie at the nurses' station. "Come on to the observation room," she said. So I followed her down a bright yellow hall decorated with painted Disney characters to a long, narrow room half-shadowed by Venetian blinds across an entire wall. An oval oak conference table and heavy matching chairs commanded the center of the room, and too many boxes of tissues topped all the flat surfaces I could see. The room smelled of cleaning products and old cigarette smoke. The ashtrays on the conference table and on the small ebony tables at either end of a sofa upholstered in bold coral and yellow stripes had indentations in them for cigars. That puzzled me. It was as if the observation room shared the attributes of a lounge bar. As if men in cheap suits came here to wait for racing results. Or practiced, red-lipped women, arms draped over the couch, waited unconcerned until the men's attentions turned to them. "Here, look," Katie said, and raised the blinds, revealing an observation window the full length of the room. Mercy and her translator peopled a playroom that, in other circumstances, would have made most visitors smile.

"Kim's wonderful," Katie said, pointing at the translator. "Twenty-six, Sorbonne-trained, and fluent in English, French, and Vietnamese."

Kim Luong sat on one of the six soft fabric cubes on wheels that offered movable seating. Her jet-black hair was cropped so that it framed her fresh face, and she wore a simple shirtwaist dress of pale blue. Her loafers were so new they still shone against the florescent lights that ran in lines for most of the ceiling. She held a closed book on her lap. I couldn't make out its title. Round and square child-sized tables scattered about the room held quilted boxes filled with malleable puzzle boards and large puzzle pieces. Rag dolls and rag farm animals were arranged on built-in shelves. What looked like a round plastic wading pool was filled with soft multi-colored balls a child could fall onto and bounce on in safety.

None of the items attracted Mercy, though. Instead they might have been part of a jungle or a maze she was trying to get through. She cupped her ears by the rag dolls on the shelves. She crawled under the tables and encircled her eyes with her thumb-and-finger binoculars. She stood and shaded her forehead with her right hand, searching the room, smiling a little whenever she saw Kim Luong, then proceeding with her search mission.

"Mind you, Orla," said Katie, "she's been at it for about thirty minutes in here already. She sits and finishes her meals only because we give her a crayon and let her draw while she eats."

"Now what?" I asked.

Katie went over to a wall-length closet in the conference room and opened the louvered doors. There were coat racks at one end and easels and record players at the other.

"Help me?" she asked.

Together we took two easels out of the closet. One was child-sized, the other standard adult.

"Here, new water colors and brushes," she said, and handed me a sturdy cardboard box with the materials I'd need. The children's brushes were sized to fit a child's hands.

"I've got my travel set," I told her, and patted the canvas bag I routinely carried along with my purse.

"Kim knows the plan. We don't know how much English Mercy understands, so Kim will repeat everything you say in Vietnamese. Just keep talking normally and you'll get used to Kim's echo. I'll introduce you. We'll set up the easels and see what happens."

"I'd like to start by painting Mercy, if you think that's alright."

Katie paused, then smiled.

"You're in charge now," she said. "And, Orla, thank you. Thank you very much."

I gave her a quick hug, took a last look into the playroom, and saw that, indeed, Mercy never stopped searching.

"Ready?" Katie asked.

"Here goes," I answered, and we lugged the two easels into the playroom.

The moment we set the two easels in place, right next to each other, Mercy uncupped her eyes and walked toward the smaller. Katie affixed a pad of at least ten papers in place, and set the water and the paints with brushes on the easel's ledge. Mercy herself rolled one of the cubes, a red one, up close to her post. Katie waved goodbye to us and let herself out the door. It locked, and a red light shone over it. I imagine one did so on the other side of the door, as well.

"Hello, Mercy, hello, Kim," I said, while I arranged my own paints in a row on a movable blue cube that had a gadget on one side allowing me to lock it in place. "I'm Orla." Kim translated while I pulled up a pink cube on which to sit, though I often stood and leaned into canvases while I worked.

Smiling, I sat down and put out my hand.

Mercy took it and shook it, as did Kim, who had risen from her chair. She took a place on the floor behind us and sat cross-legged, listening.

"I am told you are a painter, like me."

Kim's voice lilted and sang like a hummingbird.

"I started painting as a little girl, just like you."

The hummingbird made my words sound musical.

"Let's paint together," I continued.

But Mercy didn't need any encouragement from the hummingbird or me.

I watched as she found brown and swept her brush upward from the bottom of the paper. She held the thick brush handle in a grab. Wielding the brush from her fisted hand, she painted two brown vertical swaths, one about three inches shorter than the left one. Then, she dipped her brush into the water and let the brown disappear. She found red and, at the leftmost edge of her paper, painted a long vertical pole of red that ended only an inch or so from the paper's top. She looked only at her work. Blowing on the brown poles, she cleaned her brush once more, then found yellow. She added yellow to the two brown poles about two-thirds of the way up each one. While she placed her brush into the water again, she sought the red pole, blowing above its center, as well. Then she found white and added it close the the top of the red pole. She stood to do so.

After she put her brush into the water, she folded her arms across her chest, and stared at her work. She appeared to be done.

"Strong colors," I said.

The hummingbird concurred.

"I wonder what they are telling me."

Mercy did not respond to the hummingbird's version of my words. But she brought her right hand to the shortest pole and, placing her forefinger in its center, took some of its color and rubbed it on the top of the similarly-colored pole to the left of it. Her rub was a caress. Then she dabbed at her eyes with the topsides of her palms. She might have dabbed away a few tears.

I started to paint her.

"Mercy," I scrolled black letters at the top of my paper.

She watched, but didn't emote in any way I could tell. She simply folded her hands on her lap and crossed her legs. She swung them forward and back, forward and back, as though my brush were accompanied by some music whose melody only she could hear.

I took in her white sneakers, laced over bare feet. Her knees, though clean like the rest of her, wore the remnants of old scrapes. Her jumper, the same blue and white stripe of pillow ticking, was brightened by a shocking pink cotton tee-shirt underneath. The daggers of her bangs remained as they had in the photograph I had seen in Tad's office. But a barber's scissors had evened the length of her hair so that now it skimmed her narrow shoulders evenly. Her neck was long, and she'd be a swan by adolescence. Her eyes were wide open and bright. Hazel-colored. Her freckles and upturned nose told of a foreign incursion into her mother's womb. And her uneven teeth were likely one of the unfortunate results of impoverishment and a war that didn't allow for regular dental visits or consistent nutrition.

I moved my brush quickly, looking back and forth from child to canvas, from Mercy to my iteration of her as she was here, wordless yet exquisitely alive.

When I got to her cheeks, she became more energized and pointed repeatedly to the yellow on her painting's shortest pole. She poked the yellow. Then she repeated the gesture on her own cheeks.

"You," I said. "That's you, right?"

I felt myself getting excited.

"Your face. You."

The hummingbird trilled.

Mercy moved her head up and down. Yes, it was nodding. Yes.

I kept painting until her image had become a complete person on my easel.

"You," I said again. "Mercy."

She looked at me, then pointed to herself.

"Right," I said, "you," and pointed to her as well.

The hummingbird did not sing, but only watched, smiling.

Mercy touched the second, taller pole.

She stroked it from top to bottom so that her fingers took on its brown and yellow dampness. Then she slapped it. Hard.

"Who is this? Someone like you?"

The hummingbird's voice rose, too.

Mercy put her right arm under her left and rocked an invisible infant. She hummed a soft tune and her lips quivered.

"Is this your mother?" I asked.

I rubbed her right arm as I spoke. She stared at my hand, but did not push it away.

The hummingbird's voice was as soft as dawn rising.

Mercy nodded, then let the infant drop. She stood, kicked the cube away with her right foot, and zoomed around the playroom, arms outstretched. Her humming had turned to a strident "Eeeeeeeeeeeeeeee."

"A plane," I urged. "Your mamma sent you away on the plane."

Mercy ran and ran and screamed and screamed.

I ran and flew and screamed with her. Somewhere after our third flight around the playroom together, she stopped. She stared at me. I knelt to her.

She took my hand and led me back to her easel.

I tried to compose myself so I could hear her as she communicated without words.

She pointed to the tall red pole and shrugged her shoulders. She hit herself on her forehead again and again.

"You don't know where he is," I said. "Right? You are looking for your father and you don't know where he is."

The hummingbird sounded louder than it should have been able to.

Mercy took my hands into hers and shook them mightily up and down. Affirmation. Yes. Yes.

I tried to figure out the next question. I stared and stared at Mercy's painting. She watched me with the patience of one who's had to practice patience too soon.

"Let the painting tell you, let the colors and shapes school you." That was what my mentor Rachel Consalvo had taught me: "Don't impose meaning on the painting. Find the meaning the painting expresses."

I rested my right elbow on my knee, my chin on my hand, and stared at Mercy's painting.

The child watched me. Then she nudged my arm off my knee and motioned to sit on my lap instead. I could barely restrain myself from blubbering. She leaned back into me as if I were an easy chair, and together, holding hands, we stared at her work.

I don't know how much time passed or if I even realized she had drifted off to sleep, but all of a sudden, I knew. The painting told me. Rachel had been right.

"Mercy," I exclaimed, and she jolted awake. "Mercy, your mother told you your father was a tall white man, a Caucasian man with red hair or maybe ruddy skin, who went away. You showed me. He has left your painting. He has fallen off the edge of your painting."

The hummingbird's sounds came fast, fast.

The child sat up straight, rubbed her eyes, turned round on my lap, and looked up at my face.

The playroom felt as still as a concert hall in which a tuxedoed conductor has just raised his baton before the full orchestra. All was in abeyance. All was anticipation. Then Mercy moved her lips.

"Yes," she said in English. "Where is he?"

And the hummingbird's wings fluttered.

Chapter Twenty-One
Transported

Katie burst into the playroom. The red light above the door went out. She was ecstatic, pulling at the ribbons on the bakery box she carried, then placing the open box on the table nearest Mercy, who dug in, ignoring the beignets and selecting two macaroons instead. She made short work of them, chewing energetically as she did.

I was the speechless one now, standing in front of Mercy's easel and marveling as I often did at the power of paint. Kim got up from the floor, stretching her arms and shaking her legs. She came to stand by me. "Good, good," she said, patting me on the arm. "Mercy will be alright now."

"Yes," was all I could muster.

Only then did I see Tad. Katie waved at him and spoke to me.

"Oh," she said, "he got worried that something had gone wrong by the time three o'clock became three-thirty." She was breathless. "So he parked his car, came into the hospital, and announced himself as Mercy Cleveland's lawyer." She giggled like a little girl. "A security officer allowed him access to the ward where he found me in the observation room." She clapped her hands. "He saw." She paused and shook her head. "He saw when you figured it out, Orla."

Katie was glowing.

Tad stood the other side of the playroom's door, framed by the oak wood that supported the protective glass. His hands were in his pockets and his gaze was one I would hope to capture on canvas in the still-summer days to come. He tipped his head to me, then raised his right hand as if he were doffing a cap. I pursed my lips to hold emotion back and instead put my hands together in the gesture of prayer. Then I raised my hands to him.

Katie waved at him. "Come in. You can come in."

And again in the same weekend Tad stepped over a threshold.

Mercy, who had finished eating the macaroons and was making a tunnel out of pillows, heard the door open and close. She looked up from the floor and saw Tad. Standing up, she walked over to me, took my hand, and pointed to him.

"My father?" she asked.

She knew the words. The hummingbird had only to observe.

Tad's skin was ruddy enough, though his hair was not quite red.

"No," I said. "He is not your father. He is the one who will find him."

At least Tad's stare was not a glare this time.

He came over to us, lowered himself and sat on his haunches. He offered both his hands to the child. She hid hers behind her back.

"A tough customer, I'm afraid, Tad," said Katie.

Tad sat on the floor looking up at Mercy, then folded his legs in criss-cross fashion. He placed his arms behind himself, like Mercy had.

"I am Tad," he said. "I am Orla's friend. I will try to find your father."

The hummingbird echoed him.

Mercy nodded solemnly. And with a sigh that seemed not sad but instead long-suffering, she reached out her paint- and sugar-covered hands and placed both palms atop Tad's head.

A benediction, I tell you. That's what it was. Holiest thing I ever saw.

Chapter Twenty-Two
Another Surprise

As if it had been a plan all along, in the instant I decided to become Mercy's teacher. No worrying about whether I should or shouldn't. No wondering if I could. No rationalizing. No talking myself out of it. It would be easy enough to work out. The nuns couldn't help but agree. They'd get someone with credentials for whom salary was irrelevant. What could be better? But I'm getting ahead of myself. First, the New Orleans weekend that changed everything had to come to an end. And it did at the first of Luke's three homes, the one I visited Sunday afternoon.

The grand Victorian house stood at the corner of Coliseum and Fourth Streets in the Garden District. A black wrought-iron fence made a decorative and protective perimeter around the property. Inside the fence, a tall hedgerow of expertly trimmed rhododendra blocked the view of the interior yard and what Tad called the guest cottage just feet from the main house's kitchen and vegetable garden.

The long narrow windows that comprised much of the facade of the house were completely covered in white from the inside, and the half-room windows on the second and third floors allowed no view inward, either. Plantation shutters ensured relief from the sun and prying eyes.

"It's really a gallery," Tad said, opening the car door for me and pointing to the big house. "Luke keeps only a bedroom, a sitting room, and bath for himself on the top floor. Though an entire apartment takes up the second floor. He's never rented it as far as I know."

I started for the main gate, the only open space between the tall hedgerows. White wicker rocking chairs and settees, softened by plump pillows in fabric of deep purple, detailed with blood-orange day lilies, filled the veranda.

"No, this way," Tad directed me, away from the front gate and instead around to the Fourth Street side of the house. There, a small gate interrupting the otherwise complete perimeter of hedgerow opened for us with a sweep of Tad's right arm.

"My goodness," I said.

Before me stood the guesthouse and a kitchen garden that took up at least a third of the spacious yard. To my left, at the far end of the property, a rectangular pool was surrounded by teak furniture. A grape arbor long enough to hold a refectory table that accommodated twenty iron bistro chairs (like the ones in Tad's kitchen, I saw, except that these were turquoise blue) stood in its welcome shade. And, lastly, a square-shaped blue-and-white striped canvas tent, underneath which sat, in matching folding chairs, an older man and woman in bathing suits. They wore wide, straw-brimmed hats and were playing cards on a small table between them. A large pitcher of water, filled with mint and lemons, was as fragrant as a vase of flowers. A tall glass, partially emptied, sat beside each card player.

"Ah," the woman said, taking a long drink from her glass, "you have arrived. Good, good. Welcome."

She lifted herself off her chair and came toward us. As she did, she called into the main house, "Luca, your friends have arrived." He couldn't possibly have heard her, as the entire main house was closed up tight. The sound of central air hummed from within.

She was a small, compact woman. I guessed she might have been seventy. Nonetheless, her strong, vein-decorated calves suggested a physically active life. Her bathing suit was a riot of flora in turquoise, celadon, and coral. Nails, both finger- and toe-, were coral, and she wore lipstick to match. She emanated a feeling of the tropics. She seemed festooned with color and life. She rose and walked barefoot with ease.

Tad bent to kiss her on both cheeks.

"Mamma Beatrice," he said, and she pinched his cheeks with both hands.

"*Ragazzo avvocato*"—"boy lawyer"—she called him, and she waved him on, to her husband, I imagined, who was wiping the heat off his reddened face with a monogrammed towel that contradicted his simplicity of manner.

"Tad," he said, "good to see you again. And you brought the artist. Luke has told us about her."

He walked toward me. He had a limp and a scar the length of his left leg, but seemed not to be in any pain.

"You honor us," he said, and kissed my hand. He was charming. And he looked straight into my eyes, holding his gaze as if I were the only person in the world he wanted to see.

"I am so pleased to meet you," I said. And I meant it.

I had no idea who they were.

"*Signor e Signora Segreti,* may I present Orla Castleberry," Tad said.

"So you are Luke's parents," I countered. I'd had no idea they lived with him.

"Of course," Mrs. Segreti said. "We have been waiting all day to meet you. Come."

We followed her into the guest house, which felt cool compared to the yard.

"Sit." She motioned for us to take our places at her kitchen table, which was replete with screen-topped domes that covered platters of antipasti. Prosciutto, salami, cheeses soft and hard, crusty bread, olives, pickled eggplant, red and green roasted peppers, stuffed artichokes, a pasta salad with lentils and basil. Rosemary and olive oil potato salad, fried breaded veal cutlets with wedges of lemon between each piece. And chilled in a rowboat-shaped brass container, bottles of Prosecco, beer, soda, and seltzer water.

"We must eat," she said, lifting the screen domes two at a time. "You have had a busy afternoon Luke told me, after his attorney here called."

She chucked Tad on the cheek, standing on tiptoe to do so.

Luke must have seen the car, for he came into the cottage with his arm around his father. He, too, was in bathing trunks, only he wore a front-buttoned linen weave shirt over his. Curly tufts of dark brown hair poked up above the shirt's loosened collar. Father and son shared the same piercing eyes.

"We wondered when you'd arrive," he said, and sat down beside me.

"Miracle worker," he whispered in my ear. "Your friend here called me while you were finishing up at the hospital."

"A mercy," I said. "Pun intended."

"I'll say," he answered. Then, with a nod to Tad, "How about we start with Prosecco?"

I smiled at him.

"You do know what to serve a girl."

We clinked our glasses together.

"Oh, and all is well with Phineas. He has come up with quite a proposal."

"Oh?"

Luke poured.

"May I phone you tomorrow at home so you can check the availability of gallery space with your mother?"

"Of course," I said. "What's a good time?"

"How about noon?"

"Fine," I said.

Things were happening faster than I could process them.

"Salute," Luke's father said.

"*Salute,*" we answered.

The chilled Prosecco tingled in my throat and I struggled against both outright giddiness and tearful self-pity. My weekend lotto bonanza included a child who talked again and a lucrative artistic future. All the winning ticket had cost me was Tad.

The tumultuous events of the last two days had sated my consciousness the way the food and drink were filling my stomach now. I let my bodily urges trump my brain's workings. Everyone was talking at once, but not of matters of any import. We were just five of us taking in sustenance the way the soil takes in rain. Salt of the earth is what I heard in my head. Salt of the earth. And the thing was, I felt completely at home. As if we had all known one another a very long time. Perhaps it was the wine, which did not stop flowing. But maybe there was something else I couldn't identify or name.

When the platters of food and wine glasses were just about empty, Tad said, "Oh, I meant to tell you, I spoke with Earl Sharp, just to confirm. He'll meet you here since we've already packed your belongings in my car."

"Thanks for doing that," I said.

I sat back in my chair.

"Thank you," I said to Luke's parents. "That was delicious."

"Ah, just Sunday," Mamma Beatrice said. "It is what we do every Sunday. And when we are lucky, Luke invites his friend."

She waved both hands at Tad.

"How do you like that? The lawyer is the friend," she said. Tad raised a glass to her.

"But now, come with me," Mamma Beatrice said, and she took me by the hand. "The men will put away. This is how my husband and I do it. We leave them now. Then we can all talk about each other."

I must have looked surprised at her candor, because Luke laughed. Nonetheless, I got up from my chair and, sated, followed Mamma Beatrice as she went out the guest cottage door.

She led me into the main house, "So you can use the restroom we save for our guests." She added, "For some privacy. I'll be right outside watering the garden. Take your time."

Lucky thing, too. We had barely left the cottage when wetness warmed my panties. Ugh. My period, though I wasn't expecting it. Good thing I was wearing a dress. As soon as I closed the bathroom door in the big house, I rummaged through the cabinet under the sink and was able to find a still-wrapped box of tissues. I opened it, threw the cellophane wrapper into the wastebasket, and fashioned a make-do pad from as big a wad of tissues as I could arrange. It would have to do for now.

"Don't need you now," I spoke to my blood. "I might as well dry up. Don't want to get pregnant by Diego, won't get pregnant by Tad. Maybe I'll never get pregnant at all."

I imagined painting a great big canvas of ovaries, fallopian tubes, and a birth canal, each filled with tiny pictures instead of tiny babies. Make a narrative of the female reproductive system like Dante did of hell, purgatory, and heaven. A journey somewhere, but where? A painting close up and in your face like Georgia O'Keeffe's. I cleaned up and talked to myself some more.

"Nature. You are some bitch. Generous with the material you're giving me. But a real bitch."

I heard water from a hose outside the bathroom window screen. The window was open at the top, with the bottom blocked by folding wooden shutters painted white.

I was so tuckered out, full, and now annoyed that even my natural curiosity was subdued. I didn't snoop through the main house, but decided to wait and see if Mamma Beatrice offered me a tour. When I went back outside, she was rewinding the garden hose and surveying the tomato plants. She made no mention or suggestion of going inside.

"Listen," she whispered like a conspirator, "I wanted to talk to you alone."

She stooped to pull some weeds out of the tomato patch.

"I want you to know my husband and I know the real story between those two. We know you are not Tad's girlfriend."

She pointed to the guest house.

"But we pretend. We pretend we are too simple to understand. It works better for everyone."

I didn't know how to respond, so I just stared dumb as a cow into Signora Segreti's eyes.

Finally, I said, "I see."

"Good," she said, and continued. "So now you understand and can be comfortable among us. That is why I tell you. I want you to be comfortable."

"Thank you," I said.

Were all families the same? Are secrets a prerequisite for survival in groups? Does every parent lie? Oh, I wish I could suppress my questions just for a little while.

Mamma Beatrice picked three tomatoes off a vine almost as tall as she and handed them to me. I steadied them in the crook of my left elbow. Wished I knew how to juggle. They were still firm enough to survive it.

"I cooked three decades for the Jesuits so Luca could go to Loyola eight years for free," she said. "High school and college. And one of the priests, the oldest one, Father Jaspers, told me, 'God made him like that. Just love him.' So that's what I did. That's what we both did."

She flicked a buzzing bee away from her nose.

"Although my husband misses the grandchildren. I, too. But in this life we are lucky to have even some of what we desire."

I looked at her happy, tan and wrinkled face.

"You make it sound easy," I said.

She looked hard up at my face. Then she shrugged. "And you know what?"

"What?" I asked.

"He loves us back. He includes us. He pays for everything we need. Even when we will be too old to care for ourselves, he has made sure we will have people to care for us right here. No nursing home. His home."

I looked at Mamma Beatrice. And if you can believe it, I saw radiance in her eyes.

She rubbed her nose with the back of her hand.

"I will ask you. But you don't tell me if you not want."

I waited as she surveyed the other tomato plants.

"Did you know about them before you visited Tad's new house?"

I looked down at the three tomatoes as if they held some special meaning.

"No," I told her. "I thought I would marry Tad. That we would be married."

The words were an almost-sob.

"Ah, *bella*, I am sorry."

She patted my arms with her beautiful, work-worn hands. "You will find your husband. You must be patient and wait for the plan."

I raised my eyebrows.

"What plan?" I asked her.

She smiled at her plants.

"The world has many mysteries, Orla," she said. "Many."

She motioned with her head for us to stroll about the yard.

"Who thought that when my husband and I came on the boat from Campania with our families, as children, little children, we would find each other? That we would retire to the Garden District in New Orleans with a son reknowned in his field, who would make so much money? He makes so much money. We could not have imagined it."

She knelt to pick some shiny black beetles off the zucchini flowers.

"Who would have believed my husband could retire to this—it's like a resort—from the Vaccaro fruit and vegetable business after the crates fell on his legs?"

She stopped in her tracks. "No one, that's who."

She spoke with certainty and tested authority.

Then she stood, cradling the beetles in her left hand. Though they might be anathema to her plants, they seemed but another of God's interesting creatures in her friendly, capable hands.

"Tad told me already on the phone that you want to come to the city to teach the child, the Mercy."

I nodded.

"Yes," I said, "I'd like to."

She walked away from me to let the beetles loose at the edge of the yard, where the hedgerow and the fence stood, then came back, bent, and pulled up more weeds as we walked the length of the garden. We were by lettuce plants now.

"And you will come and visit. Come every week. We will cook together. Perhaps the nuns will let you bring the child. This Mercy, she has suffered much?"

"Yes," I answered. "She has no family here."

Mamma Beatrice shook her head.

"Terrible," she said. "No family. It is terrible not to have a loving family. Even mixed up ones. As long as they are loving."

We walked on, to the asparagus.

"She can be calm and enjoy herself here. She will swim. We will be like a family to her."

I felt myself a human cornucopia being filled with a bounty I didn't deserve. Bereft and blessed, befuddled and beholden, all in two days.

"Thank you, Signora Segreti," I said. "I'd love to come back."

"Good," she said, and linked her arm in mine.

The tomatoes didn't even wobble.

"Let's hope the men are finished. My husband always leaves puddles by the sink."

She laughed as she told me, seemingly unperturbed by his foible.

"Ah, *caffe*," she said, as we returned to the cottage, where *espresso* and a *torta* awaited us.

"*Salute*," Signor Segreti said, and poured generous helpings of sambuca all around.

When Earl Sharp arrived right at nine, everyone hugged and kissed me goodbye. I felt as if I were embarking on a great adventure sanctioned by people who wanted me to discover my heart's desire and come back to tell them all about it.

"Soon," I said.

"Yes," they answered, and every one of them hugged me again.

Together and alone was how I felt. Both at the same time.

Chapter Twenty-Three

At Last

"Miss Orla, you're home. Wake up. Wake up, Miss Orla."

Earl Sharp had already opened the door behind the driver's seat of the town car, and I opened my eyes, disoriented and confused. He stood by me, hat in hand, while I adjusted my eyes to the glimmer of light inside the car.

"You must have enjoyed quite a time in the Quarter," he teased, "to fall asleep not five minutes after we got started back."

I sat up and saw that it was dark outside.

"What time is it?" I asked. "Yes, it was quite the time."

Earl checked the watch on his left wrist.

"Ten o'clock," he said, motioning to the watch with his other hand. "Right on the nose."

And at that the bells at St. Marguerite's rang.

"Even the Lord agrees," he chuckled. "Thank you, Lord,"

He gave me his hand as I eased out of the back seat.

"I got your luggage out here already, Miss Orla."

I felt as old as a great-grandmother. So much life packed into one weekend.

"Doesn't appear anyone's waiting up for you," Earl said.

"Hmm," I answered, and saw that no lights shone from inside the house. Only the veranda lights either side of the front door and the lantern light by the kitchen entrance were lit. No sound of television or hi-fi wafted out the screened windows either. Only the crickets and night birds interrupted the quiet. Even the palm leaves were still.

"I guess all is calm, Earl."

"Looks that way," he said.

I reached into my purse.

"It's all taken care of, Miss Orla. Your daddy already paid me."

"Oh," I said. "I'll have to thank him."

Earl carried my overnight bag and canvas bag up the three stone steps to the kitchen door. "I'll just wait until you're safely in."

I fiddled for my key. It was an old-fashioned iron one original to the 1847 house. Grandmother Castleberry had given it to me after I took first place in the French poetry recitation competition St. Marguerite's hosted on alternate years, taking turns with St. Emile's down in Convent. I had competed against three other fifth-graders. "You won because you knew how to articulate the 'e' properly," she had said. I hadn't known then that she was my grandmother. She had made me rehearse many times over. "Make your mouth in the shape of an 'o', then vocalize a long 'e'." I don't rightly know if I won for that reason. I do know for sure, though, that my winning softened Mrs. Castleberry some. She had patted my head with her afternoon-length white leather gloves as we made our way to the punch bowl. "*Bien*," she had said, loud enough even for Mamma to hear.

"In," I called, as I pushed the door open and went inside.

"Night, then," Earl said. "I'll see you soon."

"Good night."

I listened to Earl's car crunch over the gravel and flipped on the light over the stove. Got some lemon water out of the refrigerator and let it quench the thirst that came from all the salty food I had eaten earlier. Then, after shutting the stove light and walking from empty room to empty room on the main floor, I tiptoed up the stairs. Sure enough, the door to Mamma and Daddy's bedroom was already closed, and no glimmer of light streamed from under the bottom. They must have made it an early night. It was just as well. I wouldn't have to tell them anything or edit the busy narrative streaming through my consciousness. I hadn't even decided what to tell them. Maybe about Phineas Rossiter's offer and Mercy Cleveland's tumultuous journey. Those two stories would prove ample texts. More than ample, that's for sure.

No sooner had I let myself into my own room—the bedroom that used to be Grandmother Castleberry's—than I heard the reassuring sound of the grain train making its steady chug-chug past Hester's Ridge in the distance. I listened for the owl that generally made itself known, hoot-hooting before midnight most evenings. I waited to see if a breeze would make the palm leaves on our squat trees scrape against each other, like sandpaper across big brown bark bellies, or if some waterlogged Volkswagen of a beetle would crawl up one of the window screens and latch on until the morning sun baked it into place so it would have to struggle to get free.

Everything felt the same here. Yet much of my life had changed for a second time. Maybe that's just what happens to folks every now and again. Don't know with any certainty, of course. But anecdotal experience tells me there's no way to retrieve and replicate the past, no matter what that dreamer Gatsby claimed. No matter how hard a body wants to and tries.

I looked around my periwinkle room, its soft white fabrics cumulus clouds in which to lose myself, where I could enter the white puffs and disappear.

I'd just have to treat the present, this present, like another blank canvas and look again to my paints for counsel and solace. Splash some form around the more pressing and inscrutable subjects. Tame what felt like chaos, or at least an earthquake. Delineate some structure with very fine lines. Compare and contrast. Parallel. Refute. Adapt. All so I wouldn't feel as if I were lost at sea, but safe in a harbor instead. If not safe, at least treading water, at least staying afloat in a boat slip I'd crafted myself.

Habit compelled me to wash my face and brush and floss my teeth, take care of my feminine needs. Habit, too, sent me to the dresser drawer that held the cotton nightgowns the Contessa sent me every birthday. Six of them each and every year without fail. They fell below the knee, and showed delicate cutwork of daisies or snowflakes above the breast. They smelled of lavender from the scented pouches I kept scattered in my drawers, and comforted my skin against the humid heat. I slipped out of my day clothes, the clothes that had accompanied me to Ciampi and Vester with its disturbing find, to Mercy in her locked playroom, and to *Signor e Signora Segreti's* contented cottage. The clothes that had taken me places I never expected to go. Now I craved familiarity. I wanted the birthright long hidden from me to wrap its metaphorical arms around my tired self and rock me to sleep in my inherited Castleberry bed. To calm and soothe me. To sing me a lullaby. To croon my name.

BOOK THREE—NAISSANCES

The ground of mercy is love, and the working of mercy is our keeping in love.
—*Julian of Norwich*

Chapter Twenty-Four
Mail

I woke to the sound of an electric saw somewhere in the distance, got up, stretched, and spied the little pile of must-have-been-Saturday's mail on the dresser. Mamma would have left it for me. I lifted each piece one at a time (a catalog of art materials, the NYU alumni rag, and an invitation to apply for an American Express credit card). Another, return address Diego's. He had written using potted ink on parchment stationery the color of wheat. The envelope was sealed with persimmon wax.

Orla Bella,

I hope you are having some fun in that small town town your family calls home. Without my grandmother, who smokes a cigar with me after dinner every evening (she says we must hide from my mother, so we stroll past the pool to the horse pasture), the farm would be dull. It is all work and no play for my parents, who manage the servants strictly. But regardless. I write to tell you that Reva Stone has offered me to house-sit her co-op for the academic year coming. It is a one-bedroom in the West Village. She will be teaching in Barcelona. Do you want to join me? We can split food and utility costs and not have to plan dates and keep going from one apartment to the other. Too much work, hahaha. I must let Reva know soon, so I will phone you next week for your decision. Move-in date would be 15 September.

Hoping you will agree,
Diego

"Hoping you will agree"—What a romantic.

Less work, maybe. Then again, maybe not. Like string on a cardboard spool that unwinds easily at first, then use by use, eventually knots. Harder to untangle.

I flung the note on my unmade bed, showered, dressed, and went downstairs.

Chapter Twenty-Five
The Morning News

"Where's Mamma?" I asked Daddy.

He was already back from his morning rounds in town by the time I came into the kitchen. Had a bow tie on, which meant he had already had or would later have some messy suturing to do. He was whistling a sea shanty whose title I couldn't place. I had not bothered to dry my hair, but had instead pinned it up and dressed in a loose shift and white sneakers, preparing for a full day of painting in the garden. Even before Daddy answered me, I settled on *La Traviata* as background music for my brushes. I had lots to do before Phineas Rossiter showed up, whenever that would be. All I knew was that it would be soon. Too soon to make for easy preparation. And I made a mental note to be inside for Luke's promised noontime phone call.

The radio crackled some in the background, a counterpoint to Daddy's whistling. The Captain and Tennille were promising that love would keep us together. I wasn't sure who comprised the "us" anymore. And I wondered if the two of them believed the lyrics. Who knows? Maybe love would. I hoped it would.

At any rate, Daddy took four slices of toast out of the family-sized Sears Catalog toaster he was inexplicably proud of, and, with a lift of his ginger eyebrows, offered two of them to me. I nodded yes and got the sweet butter and raspberry jam out of the refrigerator. I heard the coffee percolating, so I grabbed the two heavy mugs Mamma had purchased from a potter at the church fair, and filled them both, leaving just enough room for the light cream Daddy and I insisted on every morning. We sat down on opposite sides of the kitchen table.

"She's resting upstairs. She'll be spending a good part of every day resting for awhile."

I stopped short, my mug just about to reach my mouth.

"Why? Is she sick? What's the matter?"

I was worried, actually a bit scared.

"No," Daddy said, so I drank. "Just tired."

He held his toast with his left hand while he wrote notes on a steno pad with his right. All I could read upside down was, "GI series warranted".

"Is she going through the change of life, like she told me you thought?"

He looked up from the pad and held his pen aloft.

"She's going through a change, alright."

Daddy chuckled to himself and started writing on the steno pad again. When he was done, he flipped the pad's cover over his notes and ate his second piece of toast. Crumbs settled near his left bottom lip, where a dimple functioned like a tiny take-out carton.

"Crumbs," I pointed, and he wiped his napkin across his lips, catching his breakfast's detritus in the palm of his left hand.

"We'll go up and see her right after breakfast. She wants to hear all about your weekend."

I ate one slice of my buttered and jellied toast, pressing my forefinger onto the plate to see how many toasted crumbs would adhere to it. It all depended on how damp the butter was. Daddy was being cryptic. Of course I was curious as to why. But look what my curiosity had cost me on Saturday. I decided to stop asking questions and sighed instead. I stared at the second slice of toast and paid attention to the way the jelly oozed into the butter, the way the butter found its way into air holes and crevices. Then I ate, enjoying the crunch, the fat, and the sweet.

On the radio, Van McCoy was doing the hustle now and Daddy stood up and did the same. His plate and mug were dance partners he held onto with each hand. I laughed at him as he hustled his way to the sink.

"You mock me?" he asked, incredulous.

"I do."

"Suit yourself," he answered.

I stood up, imitating him on my way to the sink. He smirked and, once he had loaded the tableware into the dishwasher, we finished out the dance together.

"Well, I do thank you, Orla. That bit of hoo-ha has gotten me properly revved up to see patients," Daddy said. "I wonder if I'll be able to get any of them to dance this morning."

I wondered if "GI warranted" would be willing.

Something clanged and clattered outdoors, so I looked outside the window over the sink. A raccoon had just jumped off the top of one of the three aluminum garbage pails we made sure to keep locked and was now lumbering into the brushy woods back of the yard proper. Almost waddled. Left, right, left, right, disappearing, gone.

I turned round to Daddy. Couldn't help myself.

"Why is Mamma tired?"

He didn't say, just motioned for me to precede him.

"Ready?"

I walked into the foyer and up the stairs with him. Their bedroom door was ajar now and all the plantation shutters had been opened. I had to blink against the streaming-in sun.

"Morning, Mamma," I said, and she smiled and stretched out her arms.

She looked normal. Her hair was plastered down on the right side of her head like it had been every morning of our lives together. She always slept on her right side. Rarely moved during the night.

"Did you have a good time? Was Tad the impeccable host? What's his house like?"

"Yes," I answered. "His house is beautiful. And I had quite the time."

Little did she know.

"Maybe we can go to Sam's for lunch after you've rested enough. I promise you won't be disappointed with the stories I have to tell. You'll be able to write a book or, in your case, maybe a screenplay."

She smiled again. The ever-present stack of her beloved movie magazines took up half her night table.

"It's a date. If not today, tomorrow."

I fiddled with the taupe cotton coverlet that had come loose at the bottom of the bed.

"Now, Minerva, what kind of rest would that be?" asked Daddy.

He sounded bossy, or at least clinical.

"Here," she said, and patted Daddy's side of the bed so I would hop on and sit next to her.

I got serious.

"Why are you so tired? What's the matter? Don't you feel well? Are those dizzy spells still making you woozy?"

"They certainly are," Mamma said.

She looked up at Daddy, who stood by the door, his arms crossed against his chest, with a big smile on his face.

She adjusted herself against the two plump pillows behind her.

"Only now we know why." She was smiling too, but at Daddy, not me.

"Why?"

I couldn't imagine what she'd say that would make her smile.

"I'm pregnant, Orla. Can you believe it? Your change-of-life Mamma is expecting a baby at the end of December."

Boom.

Fireworks exploded inside me. Bursts of light and smoke, flashes and cracks, screaming trains of falling sparks, sooty residue of burnt-out Roman candles. All happening at once.

I wanted the fireworks to end. For the spectators' approving "Ahhhs" to stop and their appreciative applause to begin, rise to a brief crescendo, then fade away once and for all. For the hoopla to be done. But none of that came to pass. Nor would it. My brain now thinking as fast as my body had quickened in revolt, I realized that Mamma's announcement and Daddy's swaggering smile was only the start of bombastic celebration. I would be expected to participate, to enjoy the show, perhaps to shower the mother-to-be—to knit some booties, for God's sake. My feet felt nailed to the floor. The sun shone on me, a prisoner under nature's interrogating spotlight. I had been fed my cue. But how to respond? What to say?

Suddenly, like a cloudburst, my voice rose in spite of itself.

"Mamma!" I yelled at her on the bed. "Daddy!" I hollered, spinning around to fix my eyes on his in the doorway.

Then I turned halfway between so that I was angled perpendicular to each of them. I spread both arms and pointed. My forefingers wagged in recognition and (could they tell?) censure. I might have been flagging a just-landed jet into its gate. Or preparing duelists to aim and fire. Or fingering two perps for the cops in Times Square. As hyped and as hot as Manhattan, I was pumped, ready to have it out with anyone who crossed me. Bob and weave was what I wanted to do. Throw the first punch. Because, Lord help me, though I didn't choose to view this spectacle, I imagined them naked and sweating, banging each other on the bed before me. As if they had a right to. As if they were still young. As if they didn't think. As if they had forgotten—here it is, the God's honest, selfish, despicable, irrational truth— THEY HAD FORGOTTEN ME.

Daddy came over and pushed me gently to the bed and into its center. Then he sat down next to me so I was sandwiched between them. Mom in her pink-striped cotton pajamas, me in my painting clothes with sneakers still on, and Daddy sporting a flashy bow tie on the collar of his short-sleeved Brooks Brothers shirt. The only problem was, I was twenty-four, Mamma's forty-three, and Daddy's almost forty-four. This family portrait should have been photographed when I was two. When they ought to have been living together. When they ought to have been married. When my name should have been Orla Gwen Castleberry instead of Orla Gwen Gleason. This shouldn't be the photograph of us now. How was this happening now? We were all posing in the wrong picture.

I had to move, had to let loose, so I stood up on the bed and I bounced. Mamma got silly, and laughed like a girl. Daddy looked up quizzically and said, "What if we break the box spring?" I got angrier and angrier. I bounced and bounced as if to trample the trampoline they shared. On who knows what bounce I lost my footing and—Gah!—landed on my behind between them again, laughing like a hyena and crying dollops of tears into as much of the scalloped top sheet as I could grab.

"Tears of joy," Mamma would later say. "Enthusiastic," Daddy's version.

"Orla!" they echoed each other in a simultaneous orgasm of naming and wrapped their arms around me. Felt like an octopus had taken hold.

Dutifully, I kissed them both on their cheeks, first Mamma, then Daddy. I kissed them twice, the way Luke had kissed me at Maspero's. That bought me time. Gave me the chance to talk to myself, to edit the monologue in my mind.

"Well," Mamma said, wiping her palm across my wet eyes, "what do you think? Huh, Orla, what do you think?"

What did I think? My God, I thought it was ridiculous. Awful. Stupid. Embarrassing. Unfair.

I sat up straight on the bed, pulled my knees up to my chest and hugged them tight with both arms. The soles of my sneakers had streaked the coverlet with garden soil.

"I'm so happy," I lied. "So glad."

"We are, too," Mamma said. "Surprised, mind you, but happy."

Soon as the words were out of my mouth, I understood that I was just like them. A lover lying. A lying lover. My childhood had come to an end.

Chapter Twenty-Six
Preparing for Phineas Rossiter

Only moments after I heard the news about the imminent arrival of a flesh-and-blood sibling, I knew I needed to channel Grandmother Castleberry once again. I had not the time (as she might have put it) to wallow in self-serving pity. I had a life to live, conditions to create. Two obligations to meet immediately: 1) to prepare my show for Phineas Rossiter, a substantial step toward my goal of becoming a NOTED AMERICAN ARTIST, and 2) to figure out how to teach Mercy Cleveland to paint for real so she'd be protected, too, from losing her mind, no matter what else happened to her.

I now had full confidence that Tad would indeed seek out Hoyt "Cleveland", so my certainly illegal and definitely unethical filching of Mercy's file information and identifying photograph could fall into the all-for-nought category. And Mamma's pregnancy, with its concomitant medical requirements of immediate and sustained bed rest, had, poof, just like that, effectively edited *Easels and Lace* to *Easels*. The bridal salon, it appeared, would be closed until the Spring of 1976. Until then, brides already contracted with Mamma would be fitted and dressed by Mrs. Makepeace, Reverend Makepeace's wife, along with his church ladies who'd been working with Mamma some ten years now. The brides would appear for their fittings in the Makepeace parsonage front room. (Grandmother Castleberry had to be smiling down from her heavenly *grande dame* sitting chair at this turn of events. Integration had now extended its reach in St. Suplice to encompass both the marriage sacrament and the solemn genitive act of her son's marital bed.)

My discipline properly restored by the spiritual steel and ironic attitude of my late, great, departed Grandmother Castleberry, I could proceed.

With Mamma upstairs in bed rifling through articles about Liz Taylor, Natalie Wood, and Jackie O, with an occasional *Time* or *Newsweek* thrown into the mix to keep up with the news, and Daddy gone down to his Main Street office to hustle with patients, I was free to paint. I turned on Grandmother Castleberry's old record player in the front foyer, opened all the windows as well as the front double doors, and let the seductive power of opera free up and transfer the images in my mind onto the canvas my brushes stroked. I'd do a Vietnam bundle, a group of paintings pointed enough for Phineas Rossiter to take notice. And I'd remember to phone Tante Yvette tonight, to fill her in on my prospects and invite her down for the show. She might come. In fact, she'd be sure to now. She wouldn't be able to stop herself. If not to see me, at least to opine vociferously on her nephew's grand, middle-aged undertaking.

The garden rioted flowers. Butterflies flitted from petal to petal. Lizards scurried with a speed and fluidity I have always envied. I slathered sunscreen anywhere my skin showed and tilted the tall white umbrella Daddy had set up for me so that there was no glare on the easel. Wide-brimmed straw hat atop my head, I arranged my paints on the glass-topped lawn table to my right.

It was Mercy I would paint now, not the Mercy of the psychiatric ward, but the Mercy of Vietnam. From the photograph I'd stolen. I'd be merciless in my rendering of the scene. The whole thing would be a study in blacks and grays and not-quite-whites. Some shadow and the tiniest bit of light.

Maria Callas' voice as Violetta dove and soared as I dipped my brush. Its timbre helped me feel the depth of character I was after. How I was attempting to show sustained and blatant suffering on the forehead of a six-year-old girl whose wrinkled visage was not in the least softened by the glint of sun that lit it in the photograph.

When the baritone joined Callas/Violetta to forge an antiphony of contrasting voices, I turned my brush to the Negro soldier, his machine gun aimed downward rather than at the children. But so close, so dangerously close to the children. His slumped shoulders showed passion gone from him, if he'd ever owned it. Was it someone's freedom he was supposed to be guarding? Fighting for, killing for? Had he been ordered to keep his machine gun in hand? Perhaps the children would become a threat. Children, for God's sake! If he was afraid or righteous, his expression didn't tell. Maybe he was just stoned. Or tired. There he stood, body tilted like a human Pisa, left knee forward, hands by his sides, helmet covering his forehead and eyebrows. He might have been a model for hurry-up-and-wait. And why, anyway, is Mercy in the forefront of the picture? What are her eyes fixed on? Is she witnessing something she is seeing for the first time? Or has she observed the something, or something like it, four, forty, one hundred-forty times? Where is her mother? Off with a client, a Translator Hoyt from Cleveland? Or is she making an honest living in a hospital while she lives with a man she cares for, a Translator Hoyt from Cleveland? Or can she she tell a third, and many more stories? I know no answers to my questions. I can only paint what I see. And what I see is agency vanished. Neither the soldier nor the children act. They watch and wait. Their stilled gestures tell me they are not in charge. The soldier's gun ignores its function. The children's dirty clothes and smudged faces, their anxious expressions, tell me they are without immediate access to what we Americans call the basic necessities of life. Food, clothing, shelter, love.

Oh, Mercy! I cry and paint. Lord have mercy.

"Orla. Orla."

I hear Mamma and I run.

"Are you okay?" I yell up the stairs.

She laughs. "I'm fine."

I pause a moment.

"Do you want something?"

242

I'm annoyed at being interrupted.

Mamma laughs again.

"Yes, I want you to pick up the phone so I can hang up. Someone named Luke wants to speak with you."

I hadn't even heard the phone ring.

"Okay," I call up again, and, wiping my hands on one of the cotton dishcloths I keep around my neck when I paint, I turn and lift the receiver on the front foyer phone. I hear Mamma hang up upstairs.

"*Cara,*" Luke says, "I'm already missing you."

I laugh.

"Keep it up, wise guy," I tease him.

"Are you sitting down?" he asks.

I lower myself onto the needlepoint-covered bench by the phone table. The foyer offers cool comfort.

"I am now."

"Here it is. Phineas can come either Saturday, August ninth, or Sunday, August tenth, then not until next March. 'By Fall I'll have my sister and it will become a production. Frankly, August is better.'"

He did a spot-on imitation of the come-to-NOLA Scotsman.

I was elated and terrified both. Phineas was coming and I was not in the least ready for him.

"Holy cow," I said.

I fiddled with the pencils and pens standing upright in the maroon leather cylinder decorated with gold *fleurs de lis*. A notepad with sage green paper to the right of the phone was at the ready. I selected a ball point pen and pushed its lever down and up, down and up on the paper, making inky blue dots. I realized before I said so out loud that, of course, I'd be delighted to welcome Phineas on Sunday in two weeks' time.

"Well?" Luke said.

"Sunday," I answered. "Sunday the tenth."

Booming, generous voice. "Good, Orla. Very good. I'll let Phineas know."

I paused.

"How about one o'clock? Then I can entertain him, all of you, after."

"Hmm," said Luke.

"Yes, I insist," I said.

Pause again.

"Orla, listen, I'll take care of a spread. Tad's already given me your address. I'll send a caterer up there Sunday morning."

"Oh, Luke, there's no need..." I began.

"But there is, *cara*. You see, I'm sending out invitations to the event. And one of them is going to *Mère et Père* Charbonneau."

I gasped.

"Does Tad know?"

"Not yet."

"Oh, Luke, I don't know if he'll go for that."

"Now, don't you worry a bit. I'll handle the *ragazzo avvocato*. You just keep painting, and be sure to arrange your gallery gorgeously. Tad tells me there are three ceiling fans in the studio. Phineas loves ceiling fans. 'If I am ever bored,' he says, 'I look up at a ceiling fan and become hypnotized. A capital invention, the ceiling fan.'"

"Are you implying my paintings will bore him?"

"No, *cara*, certainly not. But they might bore some of St. Suplice's notables. Tad's been giving me a rundown."

"Hmm, I wonder who Tad's been gossiping about?"

"My lips are sealed."

I wait.

"And, anyway, *cara,* it would be a terrible *faux pas* for me to invite my own guests to your party and expect you to pay for it, now, wouldn't it?"

I stop playing with the pen.

"Luke, you are as generous as you are impossible."

"Nonsense, I want only that you will be my friend and not hate me."

I sigh.

"I will be your *cara*. You can count on it."

Pause.

"Now, as for Tad. I mean it. Don't worry, Orla."

Pause.

"I'm sending a messenger this afternoon so you can approve or edit the invitation. He should be there by three. Then you can send him back with any revisions you might have."

I shake my head.

"You already have the mock up, don't you, Luke?

Luke chuckles.

"Of course I do."

"You're a sly one, Luke Segreti."

"Foxy, that's me."

"I'll call you back tonight, then, after I see the invitation. I'm sure it's wonderful."

"Yes, call me. After ten, is that alright? I'll be home by then. I have dinner with clients prior."

I print in bold letters on the notepad: CALL LUKE AT TEN TONIGHT.

"Okay, bye for now, then."

"Yes, *cara,* for now."

Chapter Twenty-Seven
Long Distance

"Tell him I'm not here," I whispered.

Daddy was holding the foyer phone in his hand when, from the veranda, I heard him say, "Yes, this is the Castleberry residence. Diego, you say?"

We had finished dinner and gone outside. It was just before nine. Mamma reclined on one of the chaise lounges while I tried to ignore her unforgivable state. I thought reading Greene's novel would accomplish that. But its title (You remember, from the train, *The End of the Affair)* was deceptive. It promised sex, but delivered faith instead. I had already edited Luke's invitation, simply deleting *"...and Lace"* from the name of the gallery and reminded myself to phone him at ten. I planned to stare up at the porch's ceiling fans until then.

But at Diego's name I leapt up, ran inside, and pantomimed "Safe" over and over again while Daddy and Diego conversed.

Daddy tried to stifle a laugh.

"Let me go see if she's on the veranda, Diego," he said.

His voice sounded as kind and as soothing as a voice can be.

"Thank you, thank you," I whispered again and bowed from the waist.

Daddy covered the phone with his hand and waited a reasonable amount of time.

"Who's Diego?" Mamma called in.

"Shh," I said, leaning out the door with a finger to my lips.

"Be that way," she pouted, and closed her eyes.

Daddy spoke into the receiver again.

"I say, Diego, she must have strolled over to the Haldecott place for a swim. She's nowhere to be found here."

I heard chatter but no distinct words from Diego's end of the line.

"Yes, I will. I certainly will, Diego."

Daddy was taking down a number on the notepad by the phone.

"Good to speak with you, as well. I'll be sure Orla phones you."

He raised his eyebrows at me. I had covered my mouth with my hands.

"Good night, then. *Adios.*"

Mamma opened her eyes.

"Tell me who Diego is," she said.

"Aren't you the curious one?" I teased.

Daddy sat down on the porch swing affixed by chains to the ceiling. He had changed into bermuda shorts when he came home and his knees moved in and out as he swung.

"Yes, Orla, do tell," he said. "But first let me fill a glass with scotch and some rocks."

He stood up to go inside to the bar.

"Make that two," I told him.

"A little lemon rind okay?"

"Sure."

He looked to Mamma.

"Soda or juice?"

"No, thanks," she said.

He came back, drinks in hand. He whistled in little bursts, like a truck's warning when backing up. I took one glass.

"Thanks," I said.

"Welcome," he answered.

Then the two of us eased ourselves onto the swing, clicked glasses, and rocked. I popped the rind into my mouth and rolled it around.

"I thought Tad was your one and only," Daddy said.

I took the rind out of my mouth, dropped it into my glass, watched it settle, then swallowed rather than sipped.

"Does he know about Diego?" Mamma asked.

"The question is, do you know about Tad?"

Mamma sat up on the chaise lounge.

"What about him?"

At last the three of us had something new to discuss. And, this time, I got to control the narrative.

Chapter Twenty-Eight
The Pleasure of Your Company Requested

Here's what the invitation looked like in the end. I selected almost-honey parchment with black script, and Luke approved.

Mssrs. Luke Segreti and Thaddeus Charbonneau
request the pleasure of your company at
EASELS, THE ART GALLERY OF ST. SUPLICE,
Sunday, the tenth of August,
one o'clock in the afternoon.
Paintings by Miss Orla Castleberry
will be on display for purchase.

Reception to follow on the premises

RSVP
Luke Segreti, Art Dealer
Thaddeus Charbonneau, Esq.

Precisely at ten that night, I rang Luke.

"Did the return messenger get you my one edit?" I asked. "And did Tad approve?"

"Not only did he approve, *cara*, he opined that maybe one day the two of us might be able to ensconce ourselves in a getaway shack by the Chartres River."

Pause.

"Seriously?"

"Yes."

"Oh, my."

I twisted my hair with my fingers.

"Should I quiver at the thought? That river ain't no Grand Canal, or so I've been told."

I laughed.

"The old LaFrance place, I'm guessing."

"Yes, that's the place Tad mentioned."

I imagined it instantly. It was alternately thrilling and horrifying to think how St. Suplice would absorb such a shock.

"It's St. Suplice that will have to do the quivering," I said. "No one here is used to the life force that is you, Luke Segreti. You'd no doubt go for the glamorous. Maybe little blue lights along the perimeter of the dock. Or something like that."

"Hmm," he murmured. "That's a good idea, *cara*. I like that."

I could just imagine Luke stopping for groceries in a blazer and gold cufflinks, chatting about his cruise on the Nile with our aging Klansman meat-cutter.

"You never know," I said. "A body never knows."

251

Chapter Twenty-Nine
Registered Letter

The Thursday evening just three days before Phineas was to descend from his limousine onto St. Suplice's damp soil and grace *Easels*, Daddy had taken Mamma on what had become their evening ritual, a car ride for ice cream at Sam's Fish Shack, followed by a leisurely tour of the houses banked on the Chartres River. I was lying prone on the veranda, plumb painted out. Done. Finito. Tomorrow I'd set up the gallery. Mamma had gotten stir crazy just two weeks into her imposed bed rest, and both Daddy and a few neighbors had taken on the task of entertaining her while I painted. The entire population had received an invitation to the art show via personal messenger, thanks to Luke, and it was as if they felt compelled as fellow citizens to see to it that one of their own showed to best advantage.

Even Father Higgins said, "You just paint," when I saw him at Sunday Mass. (Yes, I admit I was bargaining with the Deity.) And he had taken to dropping by about four in the afternoon most days. Always accepted lemon water. "Nothing stronger until after five o'clock." He'd make the Sign of the Cross on Mamma's forehead before he left.

Mrs. Charbonneau had been the next to let me know of the "Let Orla Paint" community initiative when I returned a stack of books to the library the very morning her invitation arrived. A couple of westerns Daddy liked, romances for Mamma, and a coffee table book on Georgia O'Keeffe for me. Mrs. Charbonneau had spent the better part of her mornings in the library ever since Tad learned to read when he was three. A fixture there every morning since, she checks books out and back in for folks. Never one to socialize after her "slow" sister, Tad's aunt, was raped by the Hardisty boy and two of his fellow hooligans, back when Tad was just a baby, Mrs. Charbonneau has walked to the library every day at nine, and from the library every day at noon. A body knew where to find her. When Tad went off to college she started editing cookbooks. Every couple of months, a thick package holding a cookbook manuscript arrived from one New York publisher or another. Tante Yvette had given one of her City contacts Mrs. Charbonneau's name. And like every other name Tante Yvette ever dropped, Mrs. Charbonneau's had found its proper home as editor of *Bayou Cookery*, *Stews for Every-night Suppers*, and *Root Vegetables for the Holiday Season*, among a host of others.

"I majored in chemistry, Orla," she had told me when I was first allowed to walk to the library by myself and found a book about cupcakes. "That must be why I like to bake so much." I had nodded, but didn't understand until she added,

"You see, baking is chemistry. You have to follow the directions exactly." "Oh," I said. "And I like that," Mrs. Charbonneau told me. "I like following directions, knowing that whatever I bake will turn out right."

So now that Mamma was "confined," as the St. Marguerite octogenarians liked to say at Mass, Mrs. Charbonneau altered her noon path five days a week and walked to our place, always with some freshly baked confection. Just before her arrival, the grocer's delivery boy, pimply-faced Jude Brock, dropped a fresh supply of cold cuts, or pre-made tuna or egg salad, fruits already cut up and arranged inside a half cut-out watermelon, and plenty of raw vegetables for dipping in ranch dressing. I'd arrange the feast and leave it on the kitchen counter. Then the two ladies would fix themselves trays and eat lunch on the veranda. At about two, Mrs. Charbonneau would leave, and Mamma would go inside and lie on the couch in the den. I have to say she was getting a little plump, and not just where Baby Castleberry was developing. Her cheeks bulged like Georgia peaches on her formerly oval face.

But the footsteps I heard crunching on the path now did not make the same pock-pock-pock-pock as Father Higgins', nor the high-heels-catching-on-stones sounds of Mrs. Charbonneau's. It was dark, and the veranda lights had been attracting too many bugs, so I couldn't make out who it was. Whoever was walking whistled, too. Sounded like "I'll Take You Home Again, Kathleen." That was the song Tad told me his mother had sung to him every night as a lullaby after his Granny Siobhan left them.

"Anybody home?"

"Tad!"

He felt his way up the veranda steps. I got off the chaise lounge and reached up to hug him. This was a surprise I could enjoy.

"Come on in," I said. "Or at least let me light a few candles out here."

"Out here is good," he said. "Might you spare a nice cold brew?

"Here, sit down," I said, and lit one of the long matches on the table nearest me. "The citronella will keep the bugs at bay."

Tad sat down while I went inside to get two beers.

"I'm glad to see you," I said. "But I thought you'd be coming on Sunday with Luke."

"Me, too," Tad said, and took a long swig from the bottle. "I've just had dinner with my folks. I'll stay with them overnight."

"What happened? Are they okay?"

He stretched out his legs and took another drink. He was half dressed in his lawyer's clothing. No jacket and tie, but wingtips, rolled sleeves on a starched white shirt, and belted linen slacks.

"Well, two things."

I waited, taking a seat at the edge of the chaise nearest him.

"First, the response to our invitation has been outstanding. You'll be receiving over one hundred guests come Sunday. Even Ciampi of Ciampi and Vester is coming. I was able to arrange my schedule to meet with a client not too far from here early tomorrow morning. After that, if you'll accept my offer, I'd like to help you set everything up the way you want it in the gallery."

"Oh, Tad! Thanks, yes, of course."

I reached over to hug him.

"Now for the second reason I'm here. I'm afraid it isn't good news."

He took an envelope that stood upright in his shirt's breast pocket.

"What?"

He finished his beer, then placed the empty bottle on the table between us.

"It's about Mercy."

"What does it say? Who's it from?"

Tad stood now and went over to the largest of the citronella candles so he could read the letter to me. Before he did, though, he said, "The State Department was most helpful. And as you rightly surmised, it didn't take them long to find a translator Hoyt from Cleveland. It took me only one phone call and the kindness of one Louis Fogg."

Tad scratched his chin with the corner of the envelope.

"You've found Mercy's father, then?"

"It turns out this Hoyt, as Mercy's birth certificate indicated, was a civilian from the States, not a military man."

Tad crooked his left elbow, hand to his waist.

"And we can't with any finality determine if he is or he isn't her father. Only that his given name is Hoyt Demirs Delaney, he is a graduate of Middlebury College, and a foreign language expert with State."

I rose from the chaise lounge and came and stood by Tad.

"Why can't you be sure if he's her father or not?"

Tad crouched by the candlelight.

"Listen."

"*Dear Attorney Charbonneau:*

It was with a degree of shock that I read your recent letter regarding the paternity of "Mercy Cleveland." I will try to offer some clarity to your query as best as I can.

During the time I worked as a translator in the American Embassy in Saigon (January, 1969-March 1973), I met Therese Luong, a nurse. Our initial meeting occurred in the home of a fellow translator, Karl Shrove, whose wife was suffering from stomach cancer. Miss Luong was Elaine Shrove's private-duty nurse. A common interest in French language and literature brought Therese Luong and me together numerous times in the Shrove apartment. After a month or so, we shared an intimate relationship until soon after Elaine Shrove died in April, 1969. At that time, Therese broke off with me, suggesting that she planned to move in with her widowed mother in a village some thirty-five miles away from the city. I never saw her after that. Nor did she ever contact me regarding a child that she deemed mine. She had the means and the wherewithal to do so. I have no explanation as to why she would not have.

At present I serve in Washington D. C., translating for the government in matters of international trade. I have married, and my wife and I expect a child in three months' time.

I do hope that "Mercy Cleveland" will be adopted into a loving family. It is not, however, in my own family's best interests that she join ours."

We were both quiet for a time, in my case out of respect for what seemed like a death of some sort. Then, I sighed.

"So," I said. "We can't know for sure that he's her father?"

"No," said Tad. "But listen, there's more."

He continued reading:

"I trust that communications between us will cease with this letter.

Thank you for your efforts to place the youngest victims of a war that continues to impact many long after its ceasefire has been declared.

Sincerely,
Hoyt Demirs Delaney"

"Oh, boy," I said. "So now what happens?"

Just then, headlights shone into the driveway. Mamma and Daddy had returned.

Daddy came round the rear end of the car to open Mamma's door on the passenger side. He helped her out. She looked up at the candles on the porch and said, "Why, here's Tad!"

We both came down into the drive to greet them. Then the four of us went inside where Tad explained the two options open to Mercy—foster care or permanent adoption.

"Unless," he said, "the Ursulines turn their temporary orphanage into a permanent one where children can live until their majority."

"Do you expect they will?" I asked.

"I don't know," Tad replied. "It would take the sisters some time to get approval from the diocese and the city if they proposed to do so."

He folded Hoyt's letter into its envelope and returned the envelope to his breast pocket.

"But should they decide to, Mercy could well age out there."

Mamma shook her head.

"This sounds horrible. Stuck in an orphanage."

"Better than war, though, I'll wager," said Tad.

Sometimes the cut-and-dried lawyerliness of him grated.

"I suppose," Mamma said. She looked tired.

Daddy took her arm and said, "Let's go to bed."

As they left the kitchen and headed toward the stairs, Tad and I ventured back out onto the veranda. I lifted my arms and placed my hands on his shoulders. He rested his chin atop by head. We stayed still for a time. Then I slipped out from under him.

"What are we going to tell Mercy?" I asked.

"The truth," he said.

I stared up at his face.

"What is truth, though?" I asked.

"*Touché*, Orla. What is it indeed?"

Chapter Thirty
Art Show

Precisely at one o'clock on Sunday, August tenth, Phineas Rossiter alighted from his black limousine, aided by Luke Segreti, who had preceded him from New Orleans in his own Mercedes that was already parked by *Easels*. As was his summer custom, Phineas had attired himself completely in white with the exception of a decidedly festive pink and purple diagonally striped tie. His straw hat was banded in purple, and the socks that moved in and out of view as he walked in his spats offered a fabulous pantomime of two kissing pigs. I kid you not.

Tad and I stepped out of *Easels* to greet them. Then, as if the town understood that the principals had arrived, a stream of St. Suplice's citizens began arriving, too, strolling to the gallery from either side of the road, dressed as if for Easter Sunday or a high school commencement. I couldn't help but be reminded of Grandmother Castleberry's annual

Easter party, and wished for a fleeting moment that she were still alive and able to be here.

On Friday and Saturday Tad and I had toiled to turn Mamma's bridal salon into a bona fide art gallery. I think we succeeded. We had dragged all the white-painted spindle-backed chairs out of the storage barn where Grandmother Castleberry kept them when she still hosted garden parties to raise funds for St. Marguerite's or *Alliance Française*. A good dusting was all they had required. While Tad lifted and placed, I made a feather duster fly. We had set the chairs in small groupings in the gallery proper, as well as outdoors surrounding the entrance.

Champagne would be served continuously both inside and out, Luke had informed us, by two waiters he had hired for that purpose. And sure enough, the caterer and her staff had arrived at nine o'clock. The waiters were in white jackets, black slacks, and pink bow ties. Segolene, the caterer herself, was dressed in the chef's gear one associated with men, except that her toque sported small embroidered pink bows every inch or so.

She commandeered the kitchen, where she sliced the crusts off bread for tea sandwiches. There were cucumber, crab, caponata, and chicken salad sandwiches. Tiny bowls of strawberries and cream were arranged on tiered china presentation platters. Baskets filled with crudités for dipping in any of three dressings, each labeled—mayonnaise with pimento and sauerkraut, hot mustard and sour cream with basil, sweet corn dip with dill. They began setting up just after Mamma and Daddy returned from Mass. *Mea culpa*, I hadn't gone. Too busy deciding whether to look outrageous or sleek.

"Sleek," Tad said.

"So it was a gray linen A-line dress to the knee, gun-metal sandals with kitten heels, and nails and toes painted "Hardly Pink." Hair in a chignon.

"Pearls," Tad said. "One strand. And button earrings."

"So staid," I had answered.

"Not so," he had countered. "Classic. They must think you have already arrived."

When I came down the stairs, he looked at me and said, "Yes. Just so," then asked, "May I?" I nodded, and he released several strands of hair from the hairspray that imprisoned them, letting them fall as if in apparent disarray. "Softer. Good."

Tad. Couldn't keep his hands off me. Ha!

Unlike the propriety of my dress, the shock of social commentary was the goal of the exhibit. Phineas Rossiter liked pointed? Well, he had better be ready for some jabs.

Children and War, Mercy's painting, was visible front and center as one entered the gallery. To its left, *Searching*, the piece I had done in honor of Denny. To its right, *The Sporting Life*, based on the photograph that Mrs. Cowles had brought to Daddy. I was delighted that Phineas actually cringed when he saw what the soldier's boot had accomplished.

Further into the gallery's left side, *Flora*, the type of painting Katie's mother-in-law favored. Lush, Southern flowers. Feminine. Safe. It seemed most of the older women from town settled themselves there. Over on the right interior, *Portraits*. Most were recognizable to the locals. Earl Sharp, before and after his tragedy. Grandmother Castleberry as I hold her now in memory. A self-portrait at age two, myself in a ruffled bathing suit, taken from a photograph Mamma keeps in her wallet. And the most recent, just barely dry on Friday morning, *Tad*. I hoped I had achieved it, the way he'd looked at me after Mercy spoke. Maybe I had, for as he walked through the gallery just before noon (I snuck the painting in only after he had left on Saturday), he stopped short and put his right hand over his mouth.

"Orla," was all he said.

"I hope it's okay," I told him.

"You," he said, and hugged me tight.

We held hands and walked from one area of the gallery to another, both of us thanking folks for coming.

"Well done," Luke said, after he had led Mr. Rossiter through and deposited him on a chair where Mamma and Daddy had been assigned to entertain him. He kissed me on both cheeks. "He's already told me he wants the Vietnam pictures. Come on with me," he said, and he walked me outside.

We were in the doorway of *Easels*.

"Now Tad will greet everyone. I'll inform the group about how they may purchase your work, and, if you wouldn't mind,"—here he kissed my hand—"you will speak."

"Of course," I said.

But my hands shook a bit. Painting how I felt was one matter. Saying how was another matter entirely.

Just after Tad joined us at the gallery entrance, Luke took a silver dessert spoon from his sport coat pocket and tapped it against his champagne flute. Lively conversations ceased and general quiet ensued.

"Ladies and Gentlemen," Tad said.

He buttoned his sports jacket as he spoke.

"It gives me the greatest pleasure, as it does Luke Segreti, art dealer and aficionado of all that is beautiful, to host this reception in honor of my best and most talented friend, St. Suplice's own Orla Castleberry."

Everyone applauded.

Tad continued, "As you know, today is the official launch of Orla's career as a painter of note. Collector Phineas Rossiter, who has joined us," Tad pointed to Mr. Rossiter, who tipped his hat and earned several murmurs from the crowd (probably for his colorful attire), "has already purchased the lot of Orla's Vietnam paintings."

"Ahhh," from the gathered, followed by enthusiastic applause.

Luke stepped up, Tad motioning that he was yielding the floor.

"And should others be equally enthusiastic about making a purchase or two," Luke interjected, "just see me and I will arrange all."

Just then, from over by the house, in strolled Tante Yvette. She was with a man I could have sworn—from the photograph by her dresser in New York—was the elusive John. She waved at me, as sleek as ever in simple lilac linen and a matching straw picture hat, and I smiled back as the two of them came closer.

"And now, before you all avail yourselves of the culinary delights provided by Segolene and her staff, let's offer a toast to our guest of honor, Orla Castleberry."

Everyone stood.

"To Orla," Luke said.

"To Orla."

Luke motioned for me to take center stage. As I did, a town car appeared, stopping just short of the gathering of guests. Everyone turned to look. And, to my amazement and surprise, out stepped Father Higgins. He was accompanied by Father Carriere, using a cane now. Then a nun in an Ursuline habit, and, holding her hand, Mercy Cleveland.

The nun stooped down and said something to the child.

"It is!" she said, and, seemingly oblivious to the crowd of people gathered, Mercy ran up the gallery steps and into my arms.

"Mercy!"

I held her close. She wore what looked like a First Communion dress. Somebody else's dress, I realized. I let go of her, keeping her next to me, and spoke to the crowd.

"Thank you all for coming. This is my friend Mercy, a painter herself. She and I would like to express our thanks to Tad and Luke for hosting this lovely reception. Thank you, Mr. Rossiter, for your interest in and advocacy for my work.

And thank you, family, for putting up with all the paint." Here, Mamma laughed out loud. "I hope I will not disappoint you. I hope St. Suplice will add to its many charms by becoming a haven for artists and the arts. Now, please, enjoy the party."

Everyone clapped again.

"I think she's the girl in the painting," I heard someone say, as she pointed to Mercy.

"She is," said another.

And I brought Mercy to meet Mamma and Daddy.

By the time the buffet table was emptied of all but a few stray carrots and a soggy tea sandwich or two and folks had gone home, a core group of family and might-as-well-be-family were on the veranda. Mamma and Daddy, Mr. and Mrs. Charbonneau, Mrs. Cowles, Tante Yvette and, yes, it was John, John Barclay, to be precise. ("His wife passed away in May," Tante Yvette whispered to me by way of explanation when we went inside to freshen up.) Fathers Higgins and Carriere, Sister Ann, and Mercy. Where Tad and Luke had disappeared to, I didn't know.

Unbeknownst to me, Daddy had foreseen such a post-reception grouping, and had prearranged coolers of drinks and more food (po' boys and the like) to stead us as the sun moved from afternoon brightness to dusky gray.

For the time being, I felt nothing but peace. Nobody spoke of orphans or war, bodies not supposed to love one another, other people's husbands, dementia, or sadness of any kind. We just got to enjoy each other a little bit more than usual. Mamma in her new plumpness, Daddy hosting like his mother used to, Mrs. Charbonneau enjoying herself ("I don't know when I've had a better time that didn't involve a book or my own little family."), Earl Sharp not working for a change, Mr. Charbonneau making sure to take care of Mrs. Cowles, Father Higgins pleased as punch about surprising me the way he had, Father Carriere somewhere he partly recognized and felt at home. And Sister Ann, who was up to something, I couldn't tell exactly what, smiling and smiling when Mercy plopped herself on my lap the way she had just before she fell asleep in the psych ward playroom.

While the bells of St. Marguerite's were chiming eight and dusk was making itself at home, too, we turned to hear Tad's voice. He spoke loudly, as if from a podium whose microphone wasn't working.

"His flight was delayed and he had to be rerouted from Dallas to Atlanta, but he's here now."

I stood up and stared into the almost-dark to see what, and whom, he was talking about. A taxi was pulling out of the drive by the gallery.

I couldn't believe my eyes.

"Diego?" I said.

"The fellow from Argentina?" Daddy asked.

Now Daddy stood up, too. He took my hand and we walked down from the veranda.

"Well, I'll be a monkey's uncle," Daddy said.

Luke and Tad stood either side of the just-arrived guest. Diego had a large bouquet of drooping sunflowers in his hand.

"We wanted to surprise you," Luke said.

My legs wobbled a bit.

"Well, you certainly have."

My voice had taken on a higher register than usual. I wasn't sure how I felt.

"Congratulations, Orla *bella*," Diego said, and kissed me on both cheeks. "I am sorry to be so late. The flowers have suffered from the delay, I'm afraid."

"No doubt," I said, and reached for the bouquet. My hands shook. Diego was so very handsome.

"Thank you. I can't believe you traveled all this way."

I sounded as if I were the one who had traversed two continents.

"Believe it."

Diego's smile broadened, and he kissed me on both cheeks. Though a modest and public gesture, it sparked sensations in my lower regions that had lain dormant the past few weeks. I felt like jelly. Everyone on the veranda applauded.

"Never too late," Daddy said. "Welcome. I am Orla's father. We spoke on the phone a few weeks ago. You must be tired and hungry. Come on, let's get you some food and drink."

Diego bowed and made to follow my father. But not before he offered me his arm.

"Thank you," he said to Daddy. "It is good to meet you in person. Orla has your hair."

Daddy smiled at him. Even in his travel-worn wrinkle of a suit, he was charming my father.

I linked my arm in his, then turned back to look at Luke and Tad.

They shrugged their shoulders. I couldn't decide whether to spit or grin.

Chapter Thirty-One
Life Meets Art

It was past eleven when Mr. and Mrs. Charbonneau, the last remaining guests, decided it was time to leave. Mamma had already retired for the night, and Daddy started taking the liquor bottles off the makeshift bar and bringing them inside as soon as Tad's parents rose.

"I'll drive you," Luke said, waving Tad off.

Luke's plan, I could see that.

"Why not?" said Mr. Charbonneau, looking to his son, who did not offer any opposition. "Thanks."

Tad was going along with it.

"How nice of you," Mrs. Charbonneau said.

"And leave me to clean up," Tad joked. "Much appreciated, Segreti. Much appreciated."

"Exactly," Luke said.

"Good-bye, dear." Tad's mamma stood on tiptoe and kissed him on the cheek. "We'll talk tomorrow evening."

I walked over to Tad's parents.

"Thank you for coming," I said to the two of them. "I'm really glad you were able to."

"May the gallery be empty by week's end," said Mr. Charbonneau.

"May your words come true," I agreed.

We all three hugged at once, then Luke offered Mrs. Charbonneau his arm and they walked to his sedan, where he held the door open for her, and she slid gracefully in.

Mr. Charbonneau waved back at us. "Good evening," he said. "It has been a terrific day."

Luke held his door open, as well, as Mr. Charbonneau ducked to protect his head.

Short as the ride would be, I wondered what their conversation would entail. To an unsuspecting observer, no underlying suspicions or troubling emotions had emerged between Tad's parents and the fellow they had to know was their son's lover. Time would tell.

Diego designated himself the trash man. He walked all around the front of the house and grounds, and scoured the veranda, filling a plastic lawn bag with the remnants of a good time.

"Make Diego comfortable in the guest room," Mamma had said before she headed up the stairs.

"Thank you, Mrs. Castleberry," Diego had replied. "I am grateful you are willing to take in an unexpected visitor."

She liked him, I could tell. She had filled a plate for him herself, despite Daddy's admonition to sit down and stay off her feet, saying, "We have plenty of room. No trouble at all. And you've come so far for Orla."

By midnight, Luke had returned (the five-minute ride having lasted almost an hour). Tad hurried down to meet him. They stood by Luke's car talking. When they came back up to the porch, they were holding hands.

"They've invited us to dinner next Sunday," Luke said. "My parents, too."

"Bingo," I said, aiming for pert rather than sarcastic. I was jealous.

Tad put his arm around Luke's waist.

"Your father did have one proviso, though."

Tad looked puzzled, but he didn't let go of Luke.

"And what is that?" he asked.

"I must hang the portrait of you that Orla painted. He just bought it."

Tad smiled. He and Luke hugged.

"Oh!" I blurted, "I'll carry it over to them tomorrow."

"Splendid," Luke said. Then suddenly, as if he had just remembered, he broke away from Tad and announced, "Champagne, the bottle I've saved for now."

Three of us collapsed on the porch while Luke set to his purpose. We were an unlikely quartet, that's for sure. The rest of us by now were almost as bedraggled as Diego.

Luke went down to his car, opened the trunk, lifted out a cooler, and carried it to the veranda. Tad opened the lid. The cooler was filled with ice, crystal champagne flutes protected by rolled bubble wrap, and a bottle of Dom Perignon. Luke popped the cork. Tad unwrapped the flutes and poured.

"To Orla," Luke said. Then, "Actually, to the lot of us."And we drank.

It was all but silent for a spell. Except for the reading lamp on the phone desk in the foyer, the house had gone dark. The citronella candle flames bobbed and waved in their clay pots along the veranda railing. The soothing buzz and whirr of insects surrounded and calmed us. I'd not expected the four of us to be sharing the same space now, or perhaps ever. But paint (and Luke, my goodness, none of this without Luke) had made it happen.

I broke the silence.

"So how did you get him here?" I asked, pointing to Diego.

Tad laughed.

"It was easy to find him," Tad said.

"Yes, I spoke to your landlords," Luke added, "who seemed to know all."

"They do, I assure you," I said.

"I fear they listen in, holding glasses to the ceiling whenever I visit," said Diego. "I have tried to befriend them with the steaks from my parents' ranch."

"True," I said.

Diego leaned toward the both of them, as if he were about to reveal a secret.

"They are polite, correct, you see, always thanking me with handwritten notes."

He chuckled.

"The notes always end with, 'Now you take good care of our Orla.'"

Luke couldn't seem to help himself as he raised his glass again.

"It must be nice to have two fairy godmothers, *cara.*"

I had to admit he was funny.

"Perhaps more than two," I suggested.

"Don't be fresh," Tad said.

But he was smiling.

"Just so," Diego said, and raised his glass again.

"By the way," Luke continued, "they regret not being able to come. They told me they have closed the shop and are vacationing on Fire Island for the better part of the month. They'll reopen in September."

I looked to Diego.

"You've come a long way. Were you planning to return to New York already? You haven't made an additional trip, I hope."

Diego put down his champagne flute and reached for my hand.

"If you had phoned me, Orla..."

I hung my head in mock shame.

"...as you were supposed to, you would have known that Reva's co-op became available a month earlier than expected. Her brother has taken the entire Stone family to Sicily to celebrate his fiftieth birthday."

Luke poured Diego another glass of champagne.

"I apologize," I said. "I have been remiss."

I didn't want to accept Diego's invitation. Nor did I want to tell him my decision.

Luke downed his second flute of champagne in one swallow.

"So," Diego said, "I decided to stop here on my way to Manhattan, even though I still do not know if you will live with me."

"Well, now," Tad said.

I said nothing. Diego waited.

"Perhaps you have found a replacement for me?"

He was serious. And I did feel a little bit guilty.

"Perhaps we should be going," Tad said, motioning to Luke.

"But the conversation is just getting interesting," Luke countered.

Both Diego and I laughed, and Luke stretched out in his chair.

"Why, yes, Diego, I have, I certainly have." I let go his hand and stretched out my arms, then turned them in to embrace my own torso. "Two replacements, in fact. One very old man, the one and only Phineas Rossiter, collector and advocate of artists. Luke introduced me to him, and he is changing my life. Thank you, Luke." I bowed in Luke's direction and he winked back. "The other is a six-year-old Vietnamese child, abandoned by both mother and father. Mercy, another girl who paints. She was here with Sister Ann, the nun from the orphanage."

Diego nodded his head with solemnity.

"Well, in that case, I forgive you. All for art you have ignored me. And that is acceptable, at least for a little while."

"Whew," Tad muttered.

"What a disappointment. We might have witnessed a veritable scene. In fact, I was looking forward to one," Luke said.

Tad finished off the bottle.

"Do you think we should get going anyway?" he said to Luke. "I have court at nine tomorrow."

Luke made no move to leave.

"Frankly, I'd rather have a nice nap over at the gallery and leave early. Then you won't incur the ire of either Ciampi or Vester."

"Stay here," I said, and stood. "Take the guest room."

Diego started, but didn't speak.

"I mean it," I said.

Diego stood.

"Do," he said.

Then he made short work of his drink.

"We can't do that," Tad said. "It's your room, Diego. Plus it would provoke a scandal."

He couldn't have sounded more serious.

I held my half-full flute aloft.

"Alright, Tad. Really. You're being ridiculous. My Grandfather Castleberry, *paterfamilias* of this place, kept secret in Fiesole his contessa lover by whom he fathered their daughter Gabriella. My mother conceived me, probably in a bedroom right upstairs, by one man, but married another she pretended was my father. My grandmother, for God's sake, integrated the place. Now that's something worth talking about. And you're telling me that you and Luke will scandalize?"

Both Luke and Diego chuckled.

"I like how she thinks," Luke said.

"Good night to you both," I said, pointing to the front door and taking Diego's arm. "Up the stairs, first door on the left, Luke."

"Thanks," he said. "Come on, Tad."

He held out his hand. Tad grasped it.

"But what about you two?" Tad asked.

Now Diego didn't miss a beat.

"We've got paintings to look at," he said. "Correct, Orla *bella*?"

I nodded.

"We do."

"Good night, then," said Luke.

"There's a clock so you can set the alarm," I said to Tad.

"Shh," he motioned to Luke. "No talking. I mean it."

"Of course," Luke whispered, winked at me, and went in.

I left the citronella candles burning so Diego and I could see our way to *Easels*.

Chapter Thirty-Two
Missing Painting

Only the night-light by the exit sign shone in the main gallery.

"Come on." I pulled Diego's arm and rushed him past the paintings and back to a dressing room. He flipped on the light switch and lifted my dress. No words. Long time after, we sprawled on the floor and slept.

I woke before dawn when Monty's garbage truck rumbled by. Tiptoed over to the clothes rack and put on one of the pink silk robes Mamma gave brides to wear between gowns they were considering. I doused the light had been burning all night, washed up a bit in the restroom, then put a pot of coffee on in the galley kitchen. I heard Diego moving.

He had put his shirt and slacks back on and rubbed his eyes.

"Show me your paintings," he said, just like that.

All of a sudden, I felt shy, as if we hadn't known each other this way before—or yet, even. As if a year and some months in New York had never even happened.

I turned on the gallery lights and we walked from room to room, display to display. He paid attention. Said nothing. He studied the larger paintings from farther off, the smaller ones close up. He stood a long time at Denny's. Stared awhile at my self-portrait as a child. Smiled a bit. Walked right past the flowers and miniature landscapes. Ended by Tad's portrait. Blinked at it.

I was nervous, anxious to hear what he thought. He is a respected sculptor. He loves to sculpt hands. His own hands are worthy of sculpting, both as makers and as their own objets d'art.

"Beautiful, Orla," he said. "You are an artist, anyone can tell. I am glad to see all your work displayed. I am glad I came."

He looked into my eyes.

"Thank you, Diego," I said. "It was very generous of you to come all this way for me. Very, very generous."

He looked to the gallery.

"Yes. I agree. It was. I wanted to."

He went to find his shoes.

"Coffee?" he said when he returned.

"Of course," I answered, and turned toward the galley kitchen.

"Good," he said. "And then I will go. I can ride with Luke and Tad to New Orleans. Then I will catch a plane to New York."

I paused to look back at him.

"But you can stay a few days at least, no? I am sure my parents would like you to stay."

He sat down on one of Grandmother Castleberry's spindle-backed party chairs and rested his hands on his knees.

"No doubt they would, Orla. They are most gracious."

I poured him a cup of coffee.

"Milk or cream? Sugar?" I asked, before adding the cream to my own cup.

He looked at me as if puzzled.

"What?" I asked.

"Nothing," he said, and drank his coffee black.

I put down my mug, then went over to him and wrapped my arms around his shoulders. We smelled of each other. He placed his mug down on the floor, then took my arms, one in his right hand, the other in his left.

"It's a wonderful display," he said. "It demonstrates your talent."

He paused, then continued.

"I have two questions for you, however."

"Yes?" I said, squeezing his hands in mine.

"Where are we, Orla?"

I blanched.

"Where am I?"

281

He knew

He patted me on the cheek, gently enough.

"Good-bye, Orla."

He kissed both my hands, got the rest of his belongings from the dressing room, then walked back up to the veranda to wait for Luke and Tad. The three of them left even before Daddy got up for his rounds.

I felt bad, I really did. But I ought to have felt ashamed instead.

Chapter Thirty-Three
Halloween

Mid-July, when Tad and I had first encountered Mercy, felt like a long time ago. In August, her showing up with Sister Ann and the priests at the gallery show was a welcome surprise. And since the Monday after Labor Day, when the Ursuline sisters officially opened a school within their orphanage, I met with her weekly for one full hour to paint. She was an avid student, one whose little hands were both deft and willing, and whose powers of observation and attention to detail promised a painter's life should she choose it. She was becoming as important to me as my art. I couldn't seem to look at colors anymore without thinking of her. She had drawn a human question mark in my brain. The why of my existence. Why Mercy and me?

At exactly ten o'clock every Monday morning she appeared in her plaid jumper and white blouse in the solarium on the top floor of the orphanage. There was plenty of light and a spaciousness guaranteed by high ceilings and the absence of ostentatious decorative objects. Tall potted plants anchored the long room's corners and cushioned rattan chairs and couches that would have done as well on an outdoor patio softened the straight lines of the wrap-around paned windows that looked out onto the manicured courtyard of the old convent. Both Mercy and I had easels there—hers a miniature version of mine—with wooden stools before them both. A low cabinet held all our paints and brushes, and paper enough for the semester was stacked on a glass-topped table by the interior wall.

She never arrived alone. Always, she was accompanied by Father Carriere leaning on his cane. With each passing week, he depended more and more on her to help him walk, to lead him to the chair or couch he preferred, to hand him the breviary the sisters kept for him on top of one of the end tables at either end of the solarium.

"Great Father," she called him, and he always smiled and gestured a cross of benediction toward her as she did.

"He doesn't remember my name anymore," she told me on Halloween, just before four in the afternoon. It was a Friday, not our usual meeting time, and Father Carriere was in his room, napping before supper. I had come by to pick up Mercy and take her to Tad's, where he and Luke had planned a little party for her.

The past few weeks, we had been painting sea stars, Mercy's latest interest after a trip to Grand Isle sponsored by Ciampi and Vester. The children had been guests of Attorney Vester and his wife at their cottage. They'd enjoyed a day-long cruise in the Gulf and an overnight in outbuildings near the shore. To spur the children's interest and increase their English-language skills, the sisters had them reading stories about fish and oceans and rivers. I could tell that Mercy was less interested in the science of the aquatic world than in its bountiful swirl of life forms. Her work revealed her passion for the sea's colors and its myriad shapes. More abstract than realistic, more swimming, crawling, floating movement than specific genus of fish. She was, however, most enthusiastic about both the variety of sea stars and any sea star's capacity to regrow its arms.

"Then she must see the fish tank," Luke had said.

"Bring her on Halloween if you can," Tad suggested.

And so we rolled three paintings in orange yarn to take to Tad's.

"Let's go," Mercy said. She was wearing a bracelet of plastic beads that looked like the kernel corn candy that appeared every October and disappeared once the costumed children finished their trick-or-treating and moved on to drawing turkeys and Pilgrims.

"Oh, wait," I said, "I almost forgot."

I went over to my bag and pulled from it a cereal-bowl-sized pumpkin I had painted to surprise her. Her black dagger bangs curved down from the pumpkin's cut vine and her eyes were lit the way they shone when she smiled. I had shaped her mouth like an "Aha," the way it opened when she came upon a sight she liked, just before she pointed to it so I could "Aha," too. Freckles dotted her pumpkin cheeks and her nose pointed upward. She was the cutest pumpkin I had ever seen.

"Happy Halloween," I said, and held out my arms with her gift.

She screamed as she struck the pumpkin from my hands. It fell to the floor and smashed. Then she fell to the floor, as well. Face down, kicking her feet. She held her hands over her eyes. She sobbed and shook.

"Mercy!" I exclaimed, but she didn't respond.

All I could think to do was to sit down beside her and rub her back, say her name over and over again, tell her, "I'm sorry, so sorry." It took until the call-to-chapel bells at four-thirty for her to settle down, to turn her head sideways from the floor and look at me again.

"I'm sorry," I said, and ran my hands over her teary face. "I didn't mean to upset you."

She nodded at me, sniffling a bit.

"I know. It was a present. I know."

She looked away from the splattered mess on the floor and cried some more. I held her close.

"Can you show me why you are upset? Can you paint how you feel?"

She sat up and nodded once more. Then she stood and went to her easel. She prepared the paper and paints as if she had been born to. I kept my place on the floor. She turned the easel away from me and set to work.

As soon as she was completely focused on her painting, I got up and went out into the hallway where I knew a janitor's closet to be. I found paper towels, a mop, and some cleaning fluid. Soon the pumpkin was no more.

The five o'clock supper bell sounded and I heard laughter echo up the stairs. I went to the phone by the reading chair at the north end of the solarium and dialed Tad.

"We'll be a little late." I cupped my mouth with my right hand. "Hide any pumpkins you have."

"What?" he laughed. "It's Halloween, for goodness sake."

"Trust me," I said.

"Will do," and he hung up.

I walked back into the solarium where Mercy had turned the easel around.

It took all I had not to gasp and run.

Three heads minus bodies lay on a ground of high grasses, some water in the background. Red streamed from their necks. One mouth formed a black O, the second clenched its two rows of teeth, and the third lost its definition, both mouth and nose merging instead with slashed neck. Six eyes, wide open, stared at me.

"Oh, Mercy," I said, running to her.

She fell into my arms.

"I want to forget, like Great Father. But I cannot forget."

She wailed and pulled her hair.

"Yes," I said. "I see. I'm sorry I made you remember. I'm so sorry."

She sighed and tried to smile. Still, her paint-spattered hands tugged at the black strands either side of her face.

"Sorry," I whispered again.

"I know," she whispered back.

She let go her hair and touched her own mouth, tracing her fingers along her lips. Felt for her nose. Blinked four times with both eyes.

"Shall we go to Tad's now? Do you still want to go?"

"Yes," she said. And she held herself tall as she gripped the rolled sea-star paintings in her telling hands.

Chapter Thirty-Four
Go Fish

Luke opened the door.

"Happy Halloween," he said, and handed Mercy a Hershey bar.

"Thank you," she said, and took off her candy corn bracelet and gave it to him.

He put it on immediately, right beneath his Rolex. Good thing it was elastic. Nothing else needed breaking, that's for sure.

The house had been rendered pumpkin-less.

"Thank you," I mouthed to Tad.

"They're all in the bedroom," he mouthed back.

Mercy got a little shy. She handed her roll of paintings to Tad. We were all four of us in the front room. The coffee table was filled with treats: peanut butter and jelly sandwiches, brownies, apple crisp, and cider.

"For me?" he asked.

She nodded.

He knelt to her, slid the orange yarn off the paper cylinders. Now Luke and I knelt, too, as Tad spread the three paintings out on the floor.

"So beautiful," he said. "Sea stars."

Mercy smiled now.

"May I frame and hang them?" he asked. "So your work and Orla's both will be on display here?"

Mercy nodded. Her teeth showed now, and her eyes were lit again.

Tad stood and brought the paintings to his desk. Mercy pointed to the fish tank.

"May I go there?" she asked.

"Of course," Tad said.

She tiptoed around the trunk, her right hand reaching toward the fish tank, as if she were coming upon something amazing. She went to the left side of the tank, then took one crossover step at a time until she reached its far right. She moved her torso in time to the swaying plants. She put her face onto the glass and moved her eyes up and down with the smallest fish. She turned herself into a laughing horse and half-neighed, half-chortled—really chortled—at the two seahorses that bobbed and rode the whirring water. She placed her two hands onto the glass, spreading her fingers apart. She sighed a big sigh, then let loose a hearty giggle. We three were mesmerized by her—dare I say?—joy.

At last she turned around. She was radiant. Glowing.

"What do you think?" Tad asked.

She walked over to him and took his hand. He knelt again. She pursed her lips and looked right into his eyes.

"Are there any bad fish in there that kill each other?"

Luke sat down on the couch and pulled one of the big pillows over his chest. I waited to hear what Tad would say.

"No," Tad said. "These fish are all friendly with one another. Like us here."

He swept the room with his arm in a gesture that encompassed the four of us.

Mercy looked to me. I nodded, as did Luke, fingering his bracelet.

"The big ones do not eat the little ones?"

"No."

"Or bite off their heads?"

I took in a breath, wanted to show Tad and Luke Mercy's latest painting. Tad shook his head no.

"Good," she said, and she folded her hands together.

She looked at the food on the trunk.

"Are you hungry?" Tad asked.

Mercy nodded.

"Then let's eat," Luke said, and patted the couch so Mercy could sit by him.

Tad made her a plate.

"Peanut butter sandwich first?" he asked.

"Okay," she said.

But before she took the plate from him, she pointed to the tank.

"I will be a fish," she decided. "I will live there."

And in a flash, Tad's and Luke's eyes locked.

If I didn't know better, I'd have said the planets realigned.

Chapter Thirty-Five
A Proposition

"My place," Tad said. "Six o'clock. Luke and I have a proposition for you."

"Oh, boy," I breathed into the phone. I had been reading on the veranda, anticipating a night at home. Instead I drove Mamma's Oldsmobile to Tad's.

"Here you are, then, right on time."

It was Luke who opened the door.

"The drinks are poured and dinner's coming, courtesy of Logan's Take-out."

"Good," I said. "I'm starving."

In I went and Tad emerged from the bedroom in jeans and a sweatshirt that read "Loyola." He was barefoot.

"Heads up," he said, and we all lifted hefty glasses of single-malt scotch.

"*Slainte*," I answered. "In honor of your Granny."

We settled ourselves in what had become a somewhat routine pattern. Luke and I at either end of the couch, Tad on his swivel chair, moving about the room as if he were riding some Disneyland teacup.

"I'm all ears," I said.

I took off my sneakers and curled my feet under me on the couch.

"Now, then," Tad said.

They were ready to tell me their plan. But three knocks on the door made them pause to receive our supper and pay the Logan's Take-out delivery man. Tad took care of him and carried the bags of food to the kitchen.

"Let's eat," Luke said.

We took up our glasses and followed Tad into the kitchen, lined up the containers of shrimp and grits, gumbo, and breaded catfish, and dug in. I sat at the head of the table, Tad on my left side, Luke on the right, so that they faced one another.

"Shall we keep to scotch or move to beer?" Tad asked.

"Beer, please," I said, and downed the contents of my pre-dinner drink. Luke did the same.

Tad got up and opened the refrigerator. He took out six bottles, placing two at each of our places.

"What are you planning to tell me?" I said, eyeing all the beer. "Shall I get drunk?"

"Listen up," Tad said, and got a bottle opener out of a drawer. He sat down again and looked to Luke.

Luke said, "Here are the rules: We talk, you listen."

"Doesn't seem equitable," I said between spoonfuls of gumbo.

"Nonetheless," he said.

"Only because I owe you for Phineas Rossiter, though."

"Good enough."

Now Tad set down both fork and knife and cleared his throat.

"Here's where the *ragazzo avvocato* speaks," Luke said. "Now, pay close attention."

I was about to say something when Luke motioned "Shhh" with his right forefinger.

"I think you and I should adopt Mercy Cleveland," Tad said.

I stopped eating entirely. My stomach flip-flopped. Then, without premeditation, the words popped right out of my mouth.

"You mean like a virgin birth?" I said.

"Shh," Luke whispered this time, though his eyes were merry.

Tad continued.

"I have already named you the beneficiary of this house."

I dropped my utensils and put both hands over my mouth.

"Good," said Luke, "you're getting the hang of the no talking rule."

"That way, if, or I should say when, I die, you and Mercy will have a home for yourselves in the city."

295

I nodded. Calmly, I pretended. But my heart was pounding against my chest.

"But, wait," said Luke, "there's more."

I looked back at Tad.

"Your turn," he pointed to Luke.

"But..." I began.

"Stop," Tad said. He sounded like a school teacher.

"Ah, yes. My turn," Luke said.

Luke pushed himself away from the table and put both hands behind his head. He looked cheerful. A man with a plan.

"As you know, Orla, I generally sleep and wake only on the top floor of my home. The first floor, with the exception of the kitchen and guest bathroom, is devoted to my art collection. And the second floor, though entirely outfitted for human habitation—six rooms worth of it, to be exact—has not experienced the presence of human beings since its last resident, a widowed friend of my mother, passed away some time ago."

I nodded at him now.

"I propose that you and the child, should you agree, make that space your city home, since Tad here is indeed alive. That way you will be instantly affiliated with an already-noted gallery, if I may say so, and Mercy may attend a proper private school that will prepare her for the life she deserves."

I pushed my plate away and put my head down onto the table. What they proposed was dizzying.

"My parents are aware of our proposal. They love it. It's a way I can give them the grandchild they have always wanted. And they will be there for Mercy when your art requires you elsewhere. They have said so."

"So you've already told them about this?"

"Yes," said Luke. "We had to know if they would accept it before we proposed it to you."

I lifted my head. It was too much to consider all at once.

"Oh, yes" said Tad. "One more thing. A rather consequential one. In fact, the most consequential one."

I sat up straight now and held my breath.

"How do you feel about this? Are you in?"

I stared at the clock on the kitchen wall and watched the second hand move. I thought of what was possible and what wasn't in this world. A body never really knew completely. She could never know for sure.

"The talking rule is now suspended," said Luke.

He pushed himself back toward the table and folded his hands on it, waiting.

I took two swigs of beer. Gave me time to gather my thoughts. I looked to each of them in succession.

"What if the judge refuses?"

Tad poked the remnants of food on his plate with his fork.

"I've considered that," he said. "And I am most certain he would."

He shifted in his seat.

"Our not being married and the rest."

"Two pretty significant facts," I said. "No?"

"Certainly. They are. Significant. Most significant."

His lawyerly voice.

Then he sipped from his bottle.

"So, Orla, I've consulted a fellow lawyer, Justine Carrington. She's handled hundreds of adoptions. Recently, three of the Vietnamese cases."

I felt myself getting obstreperous.

"You consulted her even before you knew what I'd think?"

Tad looked at Luke.

"See, I knew she would be angry."

"I stand corrected," Luke said.

I sighed.

"Not too angry," I said. "Mercy should have parents, I agree. Her parents just can't be us. So why are we even talking?"

Tad's eyes brightened, though I couldn't fathom why.

"Does that mean you'll consider it?" he asked.

I paused.

"Just what did Justine Carrington say?"

Tad put down the beer bottle, reached over, and took my hands in his.

"She said that any Louisiana judge would deny an unmarried couple adoption rights."

"And..." I said.

"And," Tad continued, "she went on to say that the judge would certainly deny a single male, let alone a homosexual, adoption rights."

"She knows about you?" I said.

Tad and Luke laughed.

"She's one of us," Tad said.

I sighed again. "Good Lord."

Being homosexual is as dangerous as being Negro, except in this case without the color showing.

I played my hands, one against the other.

"Then we can't do it," I said. "It's impossible."

"Perhaps not impossible," Luke said. "We think there's another way."

I listened to the soft whirr of the fan above us. Thought of Mercy trying to hold onto her mother, screaming for her mother through the din of helicopter blades spinning, spinning.

"Tell me, then."

I stopped moving my hands, held my forefingers and thumbs together in a diamond shape.

Now Tad spoke.

"You petition to adopt her alone. As a single woman. A judge would likely see you as a reasonable and fit option, according to Justine. And, oh, yes, I'd have Justine represent you. She's agreed to it. Professional courtesy."

He took my hands and held them to his chest. I let him keep them there.

"But I vow to you, Orla. Legally decided or not, I promise to share Mercy's upbringing with you. She will be our child."

"Yes," said Luke. "It's the best way we can think of."

He drummed the table with his fingers.

"She'll get six grandparents in the bargain—my parents, Tad's parents, and yours."

"And an uncle or aunt soon to boot, too," Tad said.

He let go my hands. The three of us sat at the table while the second hand ticked. I said nothing, but stood up and cleared the table while the two of them watched. I threw all the paper products into the pop-up garbage pail. I motioned for Tad and Luke to hand me the utensils, and I slipped them into the dishwasher slots one fork, knife, and spoon at a time. I stacked the three soup bowls on top of the three dinner plates and scraped the leavings into the garbage disposal. I flipped the switch above the sink and the disposal growled, chewing its way through shrimp bits and grits, soupy vegetables, and catfish crumbs. The two of them followed my every move. When I had finished wiping my hands on the red-and-white striped dishtowel and sat down again, it looked like the three of us were at a prayer service, all our hands folded in respectful contemplation.

Finally Tad spoke.

"Well, then," he said, shrugging his shoulders at Luke. "Do you have anything to say, Orla?"

Luke pushed his fingers through his hair, then considered his nails. He looked back across the table at Tad. Their eyes read quizzical.

I pushed my chair as far away from the table as I could and stood up. I felt very tall. It wasn't as if I were listening to opera, like when I painted. No, it was more as if I had become an opera myself. As if I were the music, both played and sung. As if I were emanating an exquisite sensation of joy born of a primal and necessary pain. Too much to sustain for long.

I breathed in through my nose and out from my mouth. Again. A third time. The air expanded my lungs. I was conscious of being alive, tensile.

I was ready. A gymnast on a springboard. Surer than I had ever been.

"Tad," I said.

I had expected my voice to sound wavy. All soft and sinuous with wet emotion. But it rang out like iron instead. Not the iron of weapons or unforgiving will. No, not like that. Rather, the iron of the curved filigreed balconies in the Quarter. Of gorgeously crafted iron braids that connected without and within. The public and the domestic. Away and home.

Home. Tad was proposing a new and different Home. But Home nonetheless.

"Tad," again.

"Orla," he said.

"It appears you and I are trying to have a baby."

Luke laughed until he cried. A body just can't make this up.

Chapter Thirty-Six

A Letter and a Court Decision

Dear Charley and Evan,

I hope this morning finds you both well and happy. It was wonderful to speak with both of you last evening. I have missed the sound of your voices these past six months. Thank you for keeping open the possibility of my return to your wonderful space. You have housed me so well the past two years.

As I know Tante Yvette has confirmed with you both, a combined artistic and personal opportunity is keeping me in New Orleans and St. Suplice. So, as difficult as it is to think of not seeing you both every day after work, I must tell you that I shall not be returning to Manhattan to live in the foreseeable future.

Thank you both for your many kindnesses. I promise to visit whenever Manhattan beckons.

With Gratitude and Love,
Orla

The adoption hearing for Mercy Cleveland was scheduled for eleven o'clock, Tuesday, December sixteenth, Judge John Cashen Donohoe presiding. I was as nervous as I'd ever been.

"Even though you have a good chance," Attorney Carrington had told me, "be prepared for a denial. Though neither her mother nor a father has responded to the legal notices, we can never tell what might transpire, even up to the moment we stand before the court."

She and Tad had coached me.

"Speak only when the judge addresses you. Show no extremity of attitude. And, most important, do not become combative if he offends."

"Sounds like prison, or at least grade school," I had said.

"Seriously, Orla," Tad said.

I had become used to Mercy in my life, looked forward to seeing her every week, missed her when she contracted strep throat and had to miss a Monday in late November. She had taken to pecking me on the cheek when she arrived and when she left. She had loved seeing Tad's aquarium, and he had framed and hung the painting she had done of it. Surrounded by painted wood in a green worthy of St. Patrick's Day, her work hung right next to the coat closet. It was the first thing one saw upon entering Tad's house. And it was signed in printed letters, "M e r c y". He'd written her a thank-you note, she told me. "And I put it in my prayerbook on the Our Father page."

Judge Donohoe's deep voice interrupted my musings.

"As we have learned during these proceedings, the circumstances of this case are quite unique," Judge Donohoe spoke to the assembled. "Much information about the child remains missing, and is likely unattainable."

The expressionless court stenographer crossed her legs as her fingers tapped the keys.

Tad, representing Mercy, sat across the way from Attorney Carrington and me. Mercy was not with him lest the judge deny my petition. We'd all have to put on and fix in place positive faces if that happened. Instead, she was playing in the corridor, Katie and translator Kim with her. Luke and his parents sat in the gallery, along with Sister Ann, Father Higgins, and Mr. Phineas Rossiter, all of whom had served as character witnesses for me. Judge Donohoe had interviewed Mercy Cleveland earlier in the day in the presence of Sister Ann in his private chambers. I had no idea what she had revealed or what the judge had inferred from those revelations.

Judge Donohoe continued.

"We do not know the whereabouts of the child's biological mother or, in fact, if she remains alive today. Though we have sought the father and may speculate as to Mr. Hoyt Demirs Delaney's paternity, again, we have no certainty of it. Nor does Mr. Delaney have any interest in the child. And no other man has come forward."

He adjusted the long sleeves of his robe, removed his wire spectacles from his face, and looked directly down at me. Attorney Carrington nudged me to stand.

"You, Miss Orla Castleberry, from all the testimonies I have gathered, appear fit to raise this child. Do you want to do so, knowing that she has suffered hardships you will have no way to ascertain and whose consequences may be yet unforeseen?"

I took a deep breath.

"I do," I said.

He took up his spectacles and held them in his hands.

"Do you plan to marry, Miss Castleberry?" he asked.

I felt myself shaking.

"I have no present plans. So I don't know, Your Honor."

I wanted to say "Yes, Goddammit, I planned to marry." Past tense. I was beyond tense now. Very tense.

"Should the right man present himself, you would, you say, marry?"

I wanted to tell him to shut up, shut up.

The stenographer uncrossed her legs. I looked over to Tad. He looked back and held my gaze in his. I remembered what he and Justine Carrington had told me. I thought of everything he and I had been, have been, are to one another.

"Only if he wanted the both of us, Your Honor," I said. "Only if he loved us both. His actions would determine that."

At least I was on sure footing now. I knew who Mercy's father was.

But I couldn't tell which way this was going.

"What I need to know, Miss Castleberry, is if you prefer the company of men. That you are not a lesbian."

I heard an intake of breath from someone in the gallery. I didn't dare turn to look.

I stared up at the judge, resented his barging into territory that didn't, shouldn't, belong to him. It felt like Mr. Clayborne touching me. But I had been able to fight *him* off. Here, though, the state said Judge Donohoe had the authority, so he did. And even though his question did not endanger me, still, I burned. I wanted to ask him: "Your Honor, what do you do in private with your private parts? Does anyone ever ask you, as you dole out justice? Do the scales of your justice never quiver? How can you be so sure of every statute?" I know, I know, Tad has explained to me over and over again. A judge's job is to interpret the law, not to legislate it.

I clenched my fists and felt a marble egg where my tonsils used to be. Swallow it or belch it out?

"Miss Castleberry. I asked you a question. Are you a lesbian?"

I swallowed. The marble dropped hard.

"Are you a lesbian?"

I'd answer for Mercy instead of for myself. It was the only way. No sarcasm. No argument. Nothing but a direct, accurate answer. I wondered how Justine Carrington stood it.

"No, Your Honor, I am not."

The stenographer's hands kept moving. But her face was as still as stone.

"Glad to hear it."

It wasn't relief I felt then. Or even satisfaction. I just felt done. I had nothing more to say.

He neatened the pile of papers he had ruffled earlier and blew his nose into a handkerchief that suddenly emerged from under his robe's right sleeve. A magician. He sneezed.

"God bless you," the stenographer said, but he didn't acknowledge her.

Such power. He had so much power. My fists would not unclench.

He went on.

"I see you have made more than adequate living arrangements for the child. You plan to enroll her in the Ursuline Academy. And, lacking any evidence of the baptismal sacrament in her infancy, you have selected Attorney Thaddeus Charbonneau and Mrs. Beatrice Segreti as her godparents. You plan to raise her in the Roman Catholic faith you practice yourself?"

I wanted to tell him, I practice it imperfectly at best. Sometimes I fly in its face. But you'll not learn that. No, sir, that's not for you to know.

"Yes, Your Honor," I said.

The judge put his spectacles back on.

"Well, then," he said, taking his gavel in hand, "by the power granted me by the State of Louisiana and by my own best lights, I grant you your petition and declare Mercy Cleveland your legal child. Congratulations to you both."

The gavel struck wood.

Luke was first to stand up and applaud. The others followed suit. Judge Donohoe did not call for order then, or even retire to his chambers. Instead he came down from the bench and shook hands with me. I wanted to kick him in the balls.

"Raise her well," he said. "She told me you would. She said she would like it if you did."

Tad came over, and we both thanked Justine Carrington. Then he took my hand in his and squeezed it tight.

"Let's go," he said. "Mercy is waiting."

Chapter Thirty-Seven
Christmas Vigil

Mamma was so heavy with child that she and Daddy almost decided not to come.

"But we'll be only five minutes from the hospital by car," Mamma insisted.

"True," Daddy had to agree.

Because of Mamma's age, they had opted to have the baby at a teaching hospital rather than at little Saints Martha and Mary in Convent. So Mamma's hospital bag was at the ready and in the car even as she and Daddy joined the Charbonneau and Segreti families, Mercy, and me at midnight Mass at St. Louis Cathedral. If she did not deliver by New Year's Eve, Mamma would meet Baby Castleberry by means of a Caesarean the morning of January second.

After Mass our three-car caravan made its way to the Segreti residence. Daddy and Mr. Charbonneau helped

Mamma up the front steps and onto the veranda, where she stopped to catch her breath. The night was damp and misty.

"How lovely," she said, panting just a little.

The rest of us stopped, as well. Mamma was right. Strung across the front double-doors leading to Luke's gallery, tiny blue lights glistened in the shapes of letters that read "Welcome Home, Mercy".

"My husband, he did that," beamed Signora Segreti.

Luke hurried inside, only to return with a camera and a tripod.

"We need some photographs for posterity," he said, and situated first Mercy, then all of us around her, under the greeting.

Though it took him four times to get the timer working properly, he eventually succeeded, and we all trooped in, a bit dazed by multiple flashes.

Luke "and some elves," I don't know who they were, had transformed the gallery into a winter wonderland complete with little mounds of soft paper snow on the floor and silver tinsel glistening from the ceiling. All but one of the paintings on easels had been pushed back along the many windows of the gallery. The windows themselves were festooned with swags of plaid silver and white fabric. The covered painting was draped in heavy white damask. A recessed light shone a soft brightness over it. Gifts of many sizes, also wrapped in white and decorated with silver bows, flanked the painting. Each one was tagged in script I recognized as Luke's.

"What is under the cloth?" Mercy asked, pointing.

The others had already gotten comfortable on the camel-back love seats and Martha Washington chairs that normally dotted the gallery. For tonight, Luke had arranged them in a half circle "so we can distribute presents easily." Mrs. Charbonneau insisted Mamma raise her legs on a fringed footstool she had discovered near the grand piano. Then she took a seat herself.

"I'm glad you asked, Mercy," I said.

I walked from the doorway to the center of the room and stood by the painting.

"It's my Christmas gift to you," I said. "All of you. For making what seemed impossible happen."

Mercy jumped up and down, the green satin bow on her new party dress bouncing like a horse's tail.

"I love presents," she said.

She seemed like any other little girl.

I motioned for her to take the damask in her hand.

"Would you like to uncover it?" I asked.

"Yes, yes!" The horse's tail bounced again.

"Just slide it," I told her.

She bit her bottom lip as she did, carefully, carefully.

"Ta-da!" Daddy sang, as the fabric gave way.

I think I heard Tad sob. I know Luke went over to him and put an arm around his waist.

"Orla," Daddy said.

And Mamma took his hand in hers.

The painting had no edges, an endless pool of gentle, swirling water. In the center, the back of her body extended before us, a little girl—"It's me!" Mercy said. "It's me!"—was swimming upward. Her hands, graceful fins, were waving, pushing the water down. Her black hair streamed over her shoulders. She wore her school uniform, a plaid jumper and a white blouse. But her long legs were stockingless, and she had doffed her shoes, which floated downward, their laces unravelling. Kicking like expert scissors, her legs thrust her forward and up as she swam.

At her left, two seahorses, almost as big as she, appeared to be kissing. Bubbles of air rose from their mouths. One was the color of fresh lemons, the other enameled teal. Upright they floated, their postures regal, majestic. Like stallions. Yes, stallions.

To her right, a shield-sized five-armed sea star. Its center a magenta "O", three of its arms whole, two regenerating. Each arm with raised round swellings of purple and blood-orange to ward off predators.

Around Mercy's head, tiny gold fishes, a halo of swimmers. They seemed to whisper to her, to encourage her upward toward a shining, dappled light.

Mercy clapped her hands.

"May we open the others?"

"Why not?" I said.

Tad knelt before the gifts, handing one at a time to Mercy, who distributed them, saying each person's name aloud as she did so.

Mamma held aloft a crib-sized quilt with painted alphabet squares in primary colors. She had designated the nursery "letter-land".

"When did you ever find the time, Orla?" she asked.

But her face twisted as she spoke.

"Mamma," I said.

"Prout." She grabbed my father's arm. Water was puddling beneath her.

"Does she have to go to the bathroom?" Mercy asked.

Mamma Segreti said, "It means she is ready to have her baby."

Mercy jumped up and down.

"A baby for Christmas, a baby for Christmas," she sing-songed

"I'll get the towels," Mamma Segreti said.

Daddy motioned for me to help. We lifted Mamma up and brought her into the guest bathroom. Daddy went in with her and they closed the door. I heard him calming her, telling her he would phone the hospital, that they were coming.

"Is she having her baby now, in the bathroom?" asked Mercy.

Luke smiled.

"Probably not" he said. "Doctor Prout will get her to the hospital first."

"It usually takes some time to have a baby," said Tad, and he lifted Mercy into his arms while Luke cleared the chairs away to make a path.

I heard the bathroom door open and watched as Mamma walked out with Daddy holding her arm. He motioned to me to take his place, then he said, "Phone?" to Tad, who brought him into the front foyer.

"We'll be there in fifteen minutes," he spoke into the receiver.

Luke retrieved Mamma's coat from the foyer closet and we both helped her into it.

"Sorry to cause such a fuss," Mamma whispered

Her face was flushed and her eyes flashed a combination of excitement and concern.

"They're waiting for us," Daddy announced. His voice was all doctor now.

They prepared to leave, Luke and I helping Mamma walk what looked like an aisle now from the main gallery to the foyer. Daddy was already outside, and he moved the car as close to the curb as he could. Signora Segreti was fingering the crystal rosary beads she always keeps in her pocket.

Luke and I, each gripping one of Mamma's arms, led her to the car. Daddy got out and opened the passenger-side door.

"Oh, my," Mamma said, to no one in particular. "I had forgotten what this feels like." She paused and clenched her teeth.

I wondered who helped her when I was born. I hoped she hadn't been alone. Where had Daddy been then?

The three of us got her into the car.

"I'll phone you," Daddy told me.

"Okay," I said.

I kissed my right hand and put it on the glass by Mamma's face. She blew me a kiss back. The car pulled away. Luke put his arm around my shoulder and we turned back toward the house.

Everyone else was standing on the porch. Tad was holding Mercy and she was waving, waving.

"I'll put the coffee on," said Signor Segreti, and he headed up the winding stairs to my new home.

"I've baked a coffee cake," Mrs. Charbonneau said, and nodded to her husband.

"Oh, yes, of course," he said, and went out to their car to gather the cinnamon confection.

"Come on, Mercy," said Tad, as she squirmed out of his arms, "you and I will put the frittata in the oven."

One by one, each of us with a purpose, we made our way upstairs and into the freshly painted kitchen. The table was already set. The clock said two-thirty. I was afraid for Mamma, sorry that I hadn't wanted her baby. I told myself that I would make amends. That there was love enough to share. I knew that now. Mercy had been teaching me.

"It's ready," Tad said within half an hour.

Then, gloved in oven mitts too large for her little hands, Mercy eased the iron pan out of the oven as he stood by.

"Beautiful," Luke said, as we watched the frittata bubble, then settle.

"Let it cool," said Signora Segreti. "Then we can cut it more easily."

I was distracted, thinking of Mamma and looking for an apron in the drawer beneath the dishtowels.

"Mamma, may I cut it?"

I wondered how long her labor would last, if she and the baby would be alright.

"Mamma."

"I think someone is speaking to you," Mrs. Charbonneau said. She was smiling.

"Mamma?" Mercy asked again, "May I?"

I was taken aback. She had called me Orla until that moment. But I was her mother. That was a fact she understood. A fact I had to confirm. Live up to. Be.

My body quivered. I felt flushed. A little woozy. I heard Grandmother Castleberry's voice in my head. As always, she spoke in the imperative. "Attend to the child," she said. "Instruct her."

I turned to Mercy and knelt down before her.

"Yes," I said, taking her hands in mine. "As long as you're careful."

That was it. I would practice.

"Okay," said Mercy, just like that, and she skipped to the table to wait.

"I am certainly ready for some breakfast," said Mr. Charbonneau, "though quite a bit earlier than usual," and he selected a piece of his wife's coffee cake from its Christmas-tree platter.

Tad poured the steaming coffee. Luke took more photographs before he sat down. His mother crossed herself and Mercy mimicked her. We all followed suit.

"Buon natale," said Signor Segreti.

"Merry Christmas," echoed Luke.

"Will I be able to hold the new baby?" Mercy asked.

"Of course," I said.

Her aunt or uncle. An infant aunt or uncle.

She ate with gusto, her legs swinging under the table. The rest of us drank coffee and waited. We would stay together for dawn or the birth, whichever came first. We knew this without saying. What bound us itself a mercy.

The End

ABOUT THE AUTHOR
MARY DONNARUMMA SHARNICK

Mary Donnarumma Sharnick has been writing ever since the day she printed her long name on her first library card. A native of Connecticut, she graduated magna cum laude from Fairfield University with a degree in English and earned a master's degree with distinction from Trinity College, Hartford. She has been awarded a scholarship from Wesleyan Writers' Conference (2008), two Nigel Taplin Innovative Teaching grants (2008, 2011), and a fellowship from the Hartford Council for the Arts Beatrice Fox Auerbach Foundation (2010). A student of novelists Rachel

Basch and Louis Bayard, Mary has participated in the 2014 Yale Writers' Conference historical fiction workshop and has presented at Auburn University's Writers' Conference (2012), the Association for Writers and Writing Programs conference in Boston (2013), the Italian American Historical Association's conference in Toronto (2014), and annually at Mark Twain Writers' Conference in Hartford, as well as at the University of Connecticut's Osher Lifelong Learning Institute, Waterbury, CT (2015-2017). Her research has taken her to Venice, Italy, the Deep South, and monastic communities in Italy, Vermont, and Connecticut. For the past two years, Mary has been mentoring four aspiring adult novelists in a private workshop.

Mary's first two novels, *Thirst* (Fireship Press, *2012*) and *Plagued* (Fireship Press, *2014*), are set in the Venetian lagoon during the seventeenth and fifteenth centuries, respectively. *Thirst* is being adapted for the operatic stage by composer Gerard Chiusano and librettists Mary Chiusano and Robert Cutrofello.

Orla's Canvas, released in 2015, is Mary's first book with Penmore Press. The novel is a first-person coming-of-age tale about a young artist set against the backdrop of Civil Rights-era New Orleans. The novel took First Place for fiction in the 2016 Connecticut Press Club's annual contest and Third Place in 2016 NFPW (National Federation of Press Women) competition. In addition, it was named a Finalist in the 2017 Kindle Awards.

Mary has reviewed books for the New York Journal of Books, Southern Humanities Review, America, and other journals. Excerpts of her memoir-in-progress have appeared in the American Journal of Alzheimer's Disease and Related Dementias, Italian Americana, and Healing Ministry, among others. Her short story, "The Rule," appeared in Voices in Italian Americana.

Please visit www.marysharnick.com for more information, updates, and to contact Mary.

If You Enjoyed This Book

Please place a review as this helps the author
and visit the website of

All Penmore Press books are available directly
through our website, as well as Amazon.com, Barnes and
Noble and Nook, Sony Reader, Apple iTunes, Kobo
books and via bookshops across the United States,
Canada, the UK, Australia and Europe.

Coming Soon: Books Three and Four of the Orla Paints
series:
The Contessa's Easel
En Plein Air

Orla's Canvas

By
Mary Sharnick

Narrated by eleven-year-old Orla Gwen Gleason, Orla's Canvas opens on Easter Sunday, in St. Suplice, Louisiana, a "misspelled town" north of New Orleans, and traces Orla's dawning realization that all is not as it seems in her personal life or in the life of her community. The death of St. Suplice's doyenne, Mrs. Bellefleur Dubois Castleberry, for whom Orla's mother keeps house, reveals Orla's true paternity, shatters her trust in her beloved mother, and exposes her to the harsh realities of class and race in the Civil Rights-era South. When the Klan learns of Mrs. Castleberry's collaboration with the local Negro minister and Archbishop Rummel to integrate the parochial school, violence fractures St. Suplice's vulnerable stability. The brutality Orla witnesses at summer's end awakens her to life's tenuous fragility. Like the South in which she lives, she suffers the turbulence of changing times. Smart, resilient, and fiercely determined to make sense of her pain, Orla paints chaos into beauty, documenting both horror and grace, discovering herself at last through her art.

PENMORE PRESS
www.penmorepress.com

Mistress Suffragette

by
Diana Forbes

A young woman without prospects at a ball in Gilded Age Newport, Rhode Island is a target for a certain kind of "suitor." At the Memorial Day Ball during the Panic of 1893, impoverished but feisty Penelope Stanton draws the unwanted advances of a villainous millionaire banker who preys on distressed women—the incorrigible Edgar Daggers. Over a series of encounters, he promises Penelope the financial security she craves, but at what cost? Skilled in the art of flirtation, Edgar is not without his charms, and Penelope is attracted to him against her better judgment. Initially, as Penelope grows into her own in the burgeoning early Women's Suffrage Movement, Edgar exerts pressure, promising to use his power and access to help her advance. But can he be trusted, or are his words part of an elaborate mind game played between him and his wife? During a glittering age where a woman's reputation is her most valuable possession, Penelope must decide whether to compromise her principles for love, lust, and the allure of an easier life.

PENMORE PRESS
www.penmorepress.com

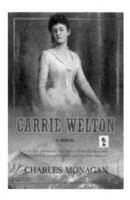

Carrie Welton

by

Charles Monagan

Eighteen-year-old Carrie Welton is restless, unhappy, and ill-suited to the conventions of nineteenth-century New England. Using her charm and a cunning scheme, she escapes the shadow of a cruel father and wanders into a thrilling series of high-wire adventures. Her travels take her all over the country, putting her in the path of Bohemian painters, poets, singers, social crusaders, opium eaters, violent gang members, and a group of female mountain climbers.

But Carrie's demons return to haunt her, bringing her to the edge of sanity and leading to a fateful expedition onto Longs Peak in Colorado. That's not the end, though. Carrie, being Carrie, sends an astonishing letter back from the grave and thus engineers her final escape—forever into your heart.

PENMORE PRESS
www.penmorepress.com

The California Run

by

Mark A. Rimmer

New York, 1850. Two clipper ships depart on a race around Cape Horn to the boomtown of San Francisco, where the first to arrive will gain the largest profits and also win a $50,000 wager for her owner.

Sapphire is a veteran ship with an experienced crew. Achilles is a new-build with a crimped, mostly unwilling crew. Inside Achilles' forecastle space reside an unruly gang of British sailors whose only goal is to reach the gold fields, a group of contrarily reluctant Swedish immigrants whose only desire is to return to New York and the luckless Englishman, Harry Jenkins, who has somehow managed to get himself crimped by the equally as deceitful Sarah Doyle, and must now spend the entire voyage working as a common sailor down in Achilles' forecastle while Sarah enjoys all the rich comforts of the aft passenger saloon.

Despite having such a clear advantage, Sapphire's owner has also placed a saboteur, Gideon, aboard Achilles with instructions to impede her in any way possible. Gideon sets to with enthusiasm and before she even reaches Cape Horn Achilles' chief mate and captain have both been murdered. Her inexperienced 2nd Mate, Nate Cooper, suddenly finds himself in command of Achilles and, with the help of the late captain's niece, Emma, who herself is the only experienced navigator remaining on board, they must somehow regain control over this diverse crew of misfits and encourage them onwards and around the Horn.

PENMORE PRESS
www.penmorepress.com

Penmore Press

Challenging, Intriguing, Adventurous, Historical and Imaginative

www.penmorepress.com